Tripped By You

Chicago Steel
Book 7

Jessica Buss

Cover Design & Interior Formatting by Feed Your Dreams Designs

Cover Photography by Eric Battershell Photography

Cover Model: Shawn Dawson

Ebook ISBN: 979-8-9879801-9-4

Paperback ISBN: 979-8-9879801-8-7

Dedication

This book is for all those who need a change in their life.
May you have the courage and wisdom to do just that.

Chapter 1

Ace

My heart is pounding in my chest and I feel like I'm going to throw up. My ma reaches over the display of multicolored ties at the suit warehouse we're visiting in Minneapolis and squeezes my hand. "It'll be okay, Jethro." Jethro is my given name, but she's the only one allowed to use it. When I was in elementary school, people started calling me Ace, and it stuck. We're here to get me my first suit. It's for the NHL draft. The big day is coming up in a few weeks, and, lucky me, it is being held in my home state of Minnesota. My entire family will make the short drive to St. Paul together. My parents are turning it into a mini vacation and renting a hotel room for a few nights so they can attend the draft with me. Then if I'm selected, we'll celebrate with a special dinner out. Even at the ages of eleven (Graham), fourteen (Levi &

Melissa), and sixteen (Amos), my siblings are stoked. With all the work the farm requires, things like vacations are unheard of. My parents have a few of our employees keeping watch over the fields and our small herd of animals while we're away.

"Here we go, sir. I grabbed a 38R and 38L for you to try in both black and navy," the sales associate says on approach.

Looking at my mom, I notice her gray eyes are misty. "Ma, really?"

She swats at the air. "These are happy tears, Jethro."

Shrugging, I turn back to Allen, or that's what his name tag says.

Once I've been measured, poked, and prodded, the suit is taken and alterations are made while we select a few shirts and ties to match. Shoes and a belt are the final items of the day, and I choose a simple black for both to match the suit. After everything is pressed, Allen presents me with a logoed suit bag and tote. "Here's everything. Good luck with the draft. I'll be watching," he says.

"Thank you for everything, Allen," I say before we leave the store.

Ma elbows me as we walk to the truck. "That wasn't so bad."

I wrap my free arm around her shoulders and laugh. "No, it wasn't. And Allen was pretty cool too. I can't believe he's a hockey fan."

She smirks at me. "We live in Minnesota. It's kind of given."

Later that night, while gathered around the farm-style dining room table we've had for as long as I can remember, Dad runs us through the plan for when we travel to St. Paul. Over the last ten years, I've been all over Minnesota for hockey games and tournaments. Traveling to St. Paul is easy for me. But my siblings, who rarely venture outside of our town, may find it overwhelming.

I live for the hustle and bustle of the city. I crave the energy. That's probably why I love playing hockey so much. Nothing beats the crowd cheering when you light the lamp. And now I might play at the next level. *Is this really happening?*

Since I was five, I've been playing hockey with the dream of one day going pro. Living on a farm in Minnesota meant my mom had to shuffle me to and from town multiple times a week. She was committed to helping me reach my goals. But as we found out, the older I got, the worse the practice times became. By the time I was sixteen and able to get my license, Ma was practically throwing me the keys to an old truck we had.

"When do you think you'll get called?" Graham, my adopted brother, asks while glued to my side.

I scratch my head. "It's anybody's guess. There are a lot of talented players being scouted. I just hope it's in round one."

For the next few weeks, when I'm not doing chores around the farm, I'm focusing my nervous energy on strengthening myself. My siblings have helped me build an obstacle course around the farm that includes hay bale incline pushups, feed bag squats and raises, and the tractor tire pull. We also get on our inline skates for an hour or two before the sun goes down. Everything I'm doing differs from practicing on actual ice, but with the cost of ice time and the fact I'm no longer on a team, I've made some workarounds to keep me sharp and at the top of my game.

When the big day comes, we're already in St. Paul because we traveled down from Minneapolis the night before. I try to stomach breakfast before I dress in my new suit. The drive to the arena is quiet, as no one knows what to say. My stomach churns as we sit in the venue with hundreds of other players bidding for their NHL opportunity. The entire draft is only seven rounds. With thirty-one NHL teams, only two hundred and seventy players are called. We're all hoping to have our name announced.

The first selections are made, and all those players that I judge better than myself have been called. *Not the top ten, then.* I remind myself I could still be called in round one. Pulling my fingers through my hair, my anxiety is at an all-time high. I force out a deep breath and my knees shake. My dad places his hand on my shoulder and squeezes it tightly, reminding me he's there. I smile at him, but I feel how weak it is. He leans over and whispers, "Chin up." My dad is a man of few words, but those two words have remained constant as far back as I can recall, reminding me to not give up, to push forward, strive for what I want. I nod and sit up taller just as the commissioner announces the next pick.

"For the fifteenth pick of the draft, the Chicago Steel have selected Jethro "Ace" Walker from a small town just outside of Minneapolis, Minnesota." *Holy shit.* Hearing my name is surreal. My heart pounds in my chest and I can feel an enormous grin spread across my face. Flexing my fingers, I relax the fist I've been holding since the first announcement. Ecstatically, I turn to my parents, who are clapping and cheering their excitement. I give Ma and Dad hugs before shaking hands with some of the other draftees near me. Then I head to the stage to shake the hand of the commissioner and get my first Chicago Steel jersey and hat. I have never been prouder than I am at this moment.

After being selected, I'm rushed through a gauntlet of media to do ten-minute spots with various networks. I also get the chance to talk to Trey McConnell, who is the owner of the Chicago Steel, and his management team. He's newer to the league, taking over when his father passed away from a heart attack. Rumors are that he runs the club differently from his father, and that isn't necessarily a bad thing.

Before moving on to the second round of picks,

they gather all the first-round selections for a picture. The air buzzes with energy and excitement. Greatness surrounds me as we all stand shoulder to shoulder, posing for a picture that will be discussed ad nauseam over this next season. In a few months, when we show up for training camp, the pressure will be on.

Ma, Dad, and I head back to the hotel to get my siblings so we can celebrate. Wearing my new jersey and hat, I knock on the door. Loud noises of a scuffle on the other side of the door sound out. Ma gasps while Dad chuckles. "Are they fighting to answer the door?" I ask. Again, Dad just laughs.

"This is so exciting!" squeals Melissa as she rips open the door, nearly decapitating Levi, who's six months older than her but over a foot shorter. Looking at her, her mega-watt smile is so bright she could power a whole town.

Recovered from his traumatic near-beheading, Levi scowls next to her. But it doesn't last when he notices my jersey. "Congratulations," he says as he gives me a fist bump.

Melissa pushes him out of the way. "It's my turn," she says before launching herself at me. I catch her with ease. She may be tall, but she's as thin as a twig. "I'm so proud of you."

Hugging her tight, I say thanks while looking for my little man, Graham. When I spot him, my smile falls. At eleven years old, he's not really little anymore, but I notice he's sad, and that tears me up. He's been my best buddy since my parents brought him home when he was only a year old.

"Graham," I call out as I head over to where he's practicing his 3x3 Rubik's cube. Those things confuse the hell out of me. I'm convinced it takes special brain power to not only solve it but to speed solve it. Our parents took him to a competition in Minneapolis once, and he made the podium a few times. Because we've spent so much time together, he's tried to teach me multiple algorithms, but they all get jumbled in my brain. "Working on a new algorithm?" I ask as he turns the cube faster than I can think.

"Yeah," he whispers.

I sit next to him and nudge him. "Did you hear the good news?" This time I just get a nod. "You know that even if I'm in Chicago, I'll always be there for you."

His dark-brown eyes lock up at me. "I'm going to miss you, Ace. You're my best friend."

I wrap my arm around him. He feels so small against me. "I'm going to miss you too. You know you'll always be my best buddy. It doesn't matter how old you get or how far away I am. Only one person will ever fill that spot."

His little voice wavers as he asks, "You promise?"

"I do," I confidently respond. We've always had a connection, and we always will. "Now, are you ready to go eat?"

He shakes his head. "I'm not hungry." But then his stomach growls loudly.

Smirking at him, I feign innocence and ask, "You aren't? Whose stomach do you suppose just made that awful noise?"

Graham's melodic laugh rings out and, once again, I smile. Reaching over, I ruffle his crazy brown curls. "I don't know about you, but I'm starving."

He shrugs his shoulders like the teenager he'll soon be, and says matter-of-factly, "I could eat."

I stand from the hug, tugging at my suit pants. "Great. I'll change and then we can grab dinner wherever you want."

Comically, his eyes go wide in disbelief. "Anywhere I want?" he questions before he looks at our parents. They just smile. "I want a Butterburger, crinkle fries, and a Concrete Mixer," he announces.

"I'm in," I holler before stepping toward the bathroom to change.

Chapter 2

Ace

My rookie year in the league is tough. It feels like every time I turn around, I'm learning some new life lesson. Rocco Romano, who's been playing in the league for a handful of years, immediately took me under his wing, offering unsolicited advice to being successful here. I've already learned so much. For example, he's one of the funniest guys I've ever met. I have to watch my back because he's a giant jokester, and he loves to pull a good prank. In my first home game, he got me good. He roped Josh, our team captain, into it. As we were about to leave the locker room and head out onto the ice, Josh pulled me aside and asked me to lead the group. Wanting to fit in, I didn't question it. There, in front of a deafening crowd, with the spotlights on and the announcers speaking, I led my new team onto the ice. Riding a high I can't describe, I turned around, smiling, to see the rest of the guys, and it was then I realized I was all alone. I skated two awkward laps by myself before they appeared behind the plexiglass, laughing their asses off. Rocco started chanting "Rookie," and before I knew it, the entire arena had joined in. My cheeks heated with embarrassment, but I couldn't be mad. Laughing along, I knew I'd have my revenge.

And he got a taste of his own medicine days later when I beat him into the locker room and stuck tape on his blades. Watching him try to skate across the ice in a start-stop pattern was fucking hilarious. I only wish I had thought to record it or done it during a game, but I didn't want to get in trouble with Coach.

Even though this season has been chock full of learning opportunities, the most valuable one came from another newbie to the team, Lucas Bouchard. He wasn't new to the NHL, just the Steel. Transferring from the New York Chargers, the only team he played for in his seven years in the league. He joined the Steel with an agenda, and he was serious about enforcing it. Because of his experience, he was ready with suggestions. Over the years, he had developed an understanding of what it took to make a team successful. As soon as he arrived in Chicago, he got to work incorporating what he learned into the Steel structure. With his charisma and passion, he easily won over Coach Tristan and our captain, Josh. Even Mika, who always seems broody and quiet, bought in. He even used his defensive tactic of intimidation to get the rest of us involved.

Lucas believed that if we operated as a team on and off the ice, our level of play would increase. So, when he started with team-building activities, many of us questioned him. But just three weeks in, we were already seeing results. On and off the ice, we were communicating better. We were even earning fewer penalties because our frustration was under control due to our ability to execute plays effectively.

By the end of the season, our team easily skates into a playoff spot. The Steel leads the pack, and it's mostly in part to Lucas's approach. After sweeping each round, we arrive at the finals, battered and bruised, but still hungry for the Cup. Facing off against the Montreal Mammoths in the finals is a dream come true. The Steel have never gone this far in the playoffs before, so there's a lot of pressure on us to do well. One truth I knew going into the last round of the playoffs was that the Steel have something that no other NHL team could boast. We have an unshakable, united brotherhood. And it got us to where we are.

We'd worked tirelessly to move our relationships on the ice from coworkers to friends. We now support each other on and off the ice. And it's because of this we're playing stronger and smarter.

Before the season started, the Mammoths drafted an incredible center, Russell Carlson, who is eerily similar to Canadian player Connor McDavid. By the time the playoffs were upon us, he'd amassed forty-seven points in his rookie career. With Russell's impressive speed and puck-handling skills, I knew if he stayed healthy, he'd easily lead the league in points in the coming years.

The first two games of the series are in Montreal and we split them with the Mammoths. The first night, they beat us 3-1, but the second night we pull ahead, winning 3-2 because I score a wrap-around goal during a penalty kill in the final five minutes of the game.

Games three and four are back in Chicago, and it's nice to be on home ice. We have the best fans in the league. Each game, the energy and excitement they bring with them makes the arena electric. We hadn't enjoyed losing the first game of the series to the Mammoth, and we're determined not to allow a loss on our turf.

Both of the next games are hard-fought, but in the end, we win them both. Leading the series 3-1, we head back to Montreal. As soon as I step on the ice that night, something feels off. My skin tingles and goose bumps break out on my skin. The lingering unease leaves my body wound tight.

At the start of the second period, as we're reentering the ice, Rocco suddenly stops. He tugs his hand through his sweaty brown hair before he puts on his helmet, looks at me, and asks, "Do you have the heebie-jeebies?"

Apparently, I'm not the only one who feels something is strange. A shiver travels down my spine as I look around to see if anyone is listening. When I don't see anyone focused on us, I nod. "Yeah, man. I thought it was just me."

That night, something is in the air, and our level of play suffers. Our passes don't connect, our plays are sloppy, and it always seems like we're in the wrong place. It's plain filthy, and I don't mean it in a good way. Since the start of the playoffs, it's the first time we haven't lit the lamp.

Montreal sees we're floundering and manage an easy 2-0 victory. As we leave the arena, the dark, heavy rain cloud above makes me question if the energy I was experiencing was literal karma. Had one of my teammates offended the wrong person? Had I? And if so, how do we fix it before the next game? If we don't and Montreal wins another, we'll be tied 3-3 going into the final game, and whoever wins that will claim the Cup.

Sitting in my hotel room stroking my patchy playoff beard, I question another possibility of why we played so poorly. Superstitions. Had someone forgotten their pregame ritual? I know I hadn't. Will it be weird if before the game tomorrow I ask each of my teammates? Then it hits me. *Talk to Josh.* I reach over and grab my phone off the nightstand. But how do I ask him without seeming weird?

ME

Hey, Cap.

JOSH

What's up, Ace?

ME

You know the game tonight?

JOSH

Yeah.

ME

Did you get the heebie-jeebies every time you got on the ice?

JOSH

It definitely felt weird in the arena tonight. Why?

ME

I'm wondering if that's what caused us to lose. We were all off, and our play was embarrassing.

JOSH

What are you trying to say? Please don't mention voodoo dolls or black magic.

ME

I'm considering everything. But since I don't believe in that stuff, I'm wondering if anyone forgot their pregame rituals.

JOSH

You're asking about the superstitions we all have but don't talk about?

ME

Exactly. What do you think?

JOSH

I mean, it's a possibility, but that
wouldn't alter our game, would it?

ME

I don't know, but you're the captain
and it's your job to find out.

JOSH

My job? So, what, I'm supposed to
go to every guy on the team
tomorrow before our game and find
out if they've completed the
superstition I supposedly know
nothing about?

ME

I knew you'd understand Thanks,
Cap. Night.

After texting with Josh, I feel less anxious. Tomorrow night will be different, and we'll be walking out of the arena as the winners of the Stanley Cup.

Feeling exhausted after having trouble getting to sleep the night before, I'm on autopilot through team breakfast and morning skate. By noon, I've never been so excited about my afternoon pregame nap. Yawning, I consider skipping lunch, but know that will only harm me in the end. So, following a lunch high in protein that I shovel down like I'm a competitive eater going for a record, I sprint to my room, fall face-first on my bed, and sleep hard until it's time to get ready and head to the arena.

The game that night is much the same as the

previous night's, and the Mammoth win. We need to go home and get on our ice.

Back in Chicago, everything feels different. Skating onto the ice for the final game, I notice right away I don't experience the same cringy feeling as those nights in Montreal. As I skate my first lap, I push my fears and worries out of my body, and I center myself. Hockey has become second nature to me. Its routines, nuances, and language speak to me.

The feel of my skates on the freshly Zambonied ice, the cool air I breathe deep in my lungs, the weight of the puck at the end of my stick blade, the excited buzz of the crowd. It's all magical and gives me a high like nothing else can. *This is going to be a night like no other.* Little is said as we do our warm-up laps, stretches, and drills. The locker room is eerily quiet as we sit there waiting for Coach to deliver a motivating speech.

"This is the game. This is the moment. You've worked hard to get here. Let's show these guys who you are. Champions!" Coach smiles before he turns and leaves. We all look around, questioning what just happened. I don't think Coach has ever been that succinct.

Josh stands up and says, "You heard him." We nod and stand to circle him. He smiles like the Cheshire cat. "This is our moment. Let's go take it. Steel. 1-2-3!" Once our cheer is done, we all slap each other's backs as we head toward the ice.

The pace of the game feels like it's going at the speed of light, and before you know it, we're heading into the third period with no goals. Frustrated, I notice Mammoth players are getting chippy and chirpy, and I wonder if they've always been this way or if their behavior is special for this game.

When Rocco leans in to send me a stretch pass, he gets slammed into by Mammoth defensive player, Max Junger, and the puck skitters loose. Switching gears, I swivel and head in the opposite direction. Pushing against the ice, I race for the still-unclaimed puck. I'm just shy of the blue line as I grab it with the curve of my blade. As soon as I see their defender cross the line, I take off like a bullet set on its target. Their goalie, Jovanovic, hunches low, trying to fill his net. He's watching my every move. He knows I'm heading straight for him. His defenders are fast, but I'm faster. And I'm a hungry bastard. I want a goal. I want them to feel the pain of knowing that we are even closer to the Cup. Then I hear the referee's whistle. He's giving Junger some time in the sin bin. And that's all our team needs. During the power play, amazing hockey unfolds. From the bench, I have the best seat in the house to watch as it sails in the air, right above the defending opponents' sticks

Josh cradles it when it drops before him, then he skates toward Jovanovic. He fakes the goalie going right and I see his stance shift. Quickly, he sends the puck to Lucas, who quickly shifts right, aims, and fires.

As if in slow motion, the puck travels through the air, wobbling, and sails right past the goalie's head. Jovanovic notices a second too late. He thrusts his arm up to protect his net. Unfortunately for him, Lucas found his weakness and exploited it. Even from a half a rink away, I hear him curse in a thick Russian accent.

Coach calls a timeout before the next puck drop. With sixteen minutes left on the clock, anything can happen. Both teams do their share of earning penalties, leaving many power play opportunities. But when the clock runs out, we are crowned the Stanley Cup Champions.

It's the first for our franchise and for most of the guys on the team. The arena goes absolutely wild. Matching their energy, I'm thrilled, congratulating my teammates with hugs. Hands down, this is the most exciting time of my life. I drop my helmet, gloves, and stick as I join my teammates as we dog pile our goalie, Simmons. He was a beast, keeping us afloat despite defending shot after shot, never allowing any through. Adrenaline pumps through my veins as I celebrate while the fans throw things on the ice. While we put on our championship caps, rugs are laid across the ice to prepare for the arrival of the cup.

An announcer begins speaking, silencing the arena.

"Ladies and gentlemen. The moment we've all been waiting for... The Stanley Cup."

Two men dressed in suits with white gloves, one being the "keeper of the cup," carry the treasured hockey trophy to a stand in the middle of the rink. As the commissioner speaks, the crowd cheers. As tradition dictates, he invites Josh over and presents the Cup to him. Smiling widely, our captain stands taller before he hoists the Cup high above his head. We each get a turn after he's done. I wish my parents and siblings were here to experience this. I spoke with them this morning, and they promised they'd watch. I'm sure my phone is blowing up in the locker room.

Chapter 3

Ace

In the offseasons, I head home to Minnesota to help on the farm. After a busy season of hockey and the hustle and bustle of Chicago, I crave the slower pace. Don't mistake me, it's hard work, but I love it. There's nothing better than being around my family and working the ground together. The days are long and packed with too much to do, but when the sun goes down, you can't help but feel accomplished.

Summer is the busiest because everything is growing. Harvesting is a must. Then there are the daily farm chores like feeding the animals, collecting eggs from our chickens, and tending the various crops we cultivate. My parents set up a self-serve store a few years ago, and it's nice to lend a hand there when I can. It's great to catch up with locals who have known me for years.

Being home means I can be me. Tugging on my

Wrangler jeans, worn mucking boots, and cowboy hat, I feel like myself. Since moving to Chicago, I've had to alter what I wear to avoid extra roasting from my teammates. I've only made minor changes, but when I first arrived, I hadn't felt one hundred percent comfortable expressing my cowboy side. But at home, I'm just like everyone else.

By the time I arrive, my siblings are all out of school for the summer break.

"Ace," I hear as I climb the well-worn, peeling wooden steps of our farmhouse. Spinning around, my two youngest siblings approach. Melissa is wearing an egg-gathering apron while Graham's holding a wicker basket.

"Hi, you two," I say as I drop my duffel bag. They both rush me, and gently we exchange hugs, seeing that I don't want to destroy their hard work. "Nice apron," I say as I motion to the chicken-covered cotton fabric apron stuffed with eggs.

She smiles. "Mom made this for me last month. It holds eighteen eggs instead of twelve, like my last one."

I smirk. "How are the ladies of the coop?"

Before she can answer, Graham butts in. "They're good. I helped Dad make a sign for their house."

"They have a sign for their house? Why?" I ask, confused.

He shakes his head and points over to where the large multilevel elevated coop sits. Sure enough, there's a sign proudly displaying what looks to be the name of the chicken residence. "What's that sign say, Graham?"

Impressed with it, he smiles, then laughs. "We named it the Hatchery Hotel." I look at Melissa, who just rolls her eyes.

Removing my cowboy hat, I scratch at my head. "That's clever."

"Graham, we need to go put these eggs in cartons for the shop. Mom wanted us to go pick strawberries and raspberries too."

He nods. "We have to go. I'm so glad you're home, Ace."

I reach out and ruffle his hair. "Me too, buddy. I'll come pick berries with you after I say hi to Ma and Dad, okay?" Graham smiles, then shuffles off behind Melissa.

As soon as I step back toward the house, I hear my ma step out through the swinging screen door. Wearing her ever-present smile, she tells me, "He missed you so much."

Placing my hat back on my head, I nod. I missed him too. Truth is, I missed it all; my family, the farm, my hometown. Chicago has definitely been an eye-opener for me. I wish I'd been able to get home sooner, but after our Stanley Cup win, I was committed to so many events. Thankfully, my parents understood. The frenzy around being champions was wild. All the national and local stations interviewed the team. And dressed in our nicest suits, we visited the White

House and met the president. Watching Coach present him with his own Steel jersey was surreal. But as great as that time had been, I was grateful to be standing on the land that had been in my family for generations.

Through the direction of my dad, the farm had expanded. Not only have my parents added a large parcel of land, but they increased planting so that from May through November, something is ready in the fields.

"Hi, Ma," I say as I move up the stairs to hug her. At 5'3", my ma is a tiny thing compared to me. I've been taller than her since I was in eighth grade.

"I'm so glad you're home Jethro." She sighs.

We look toward our little pop-up county store where the kids have disappeared, and I say, "He's a great kid."

"He is. All my kids are amazing," she says with a proud smile on her face.

My summer at home flies by. In between farm chores, spending time with my family, and working out, there isn't much time left to do anything. The first week I'm home, the two eldest of my younger brothers, Amos and Levi, help me rebuild the obstacle course I had around the farm before I was drafted. Instead of dismantling it in a few months, they plan to keep it up so they can work out. At seventeen and fifteen, I wonder if they're trying to catch the eyes of some girls from town. Before I head back to Chicago in August, I plan to find out. As their big brother, I'm never not looking for an opportunity to harass them.

When the middle of August arrives, it brings with it both good and bad emotions. On one hand, I'm ready to get back to hockey. On the other, I'll miss my family. Tossing my extra-large duffel bag over my shoulder, I head down to the kitchen. Familiar sights and sounds envelop me, leaving a warmth in my chest. Stepping down the last step, the sweet scent of homemade strawberry jam swirls around me. I pull a deep breath into my lungs and smile.

"Ma, I sure am going to miss the smells coming out of this kitchen." Standing at the sink, she does a final rinse of her hands before shutting off the water and drying them on the towel she religiously wears thrown over her shoulder. When she turns around, I see her eyes are heavy with emotion. "Ma, don't cry," I beg, my heart flinching.

She forces a smile and shakes her head. "I'm not crying. This is happiness you see on my face."

Dropping my duffel to the ground, I pull her into my arms. "It's okay. I'll be fine. Promise."

Her head of blond hair that's sprinkled with gray nods against my chest. "I know." She sniffles. "I'll just miss you." I place a soft kiss on the top of her head.

"I'll miss you too." We hug for another minute before she pulls away and ushers me to the front door.

"You better get going before you miss your flight.

Did you hug everyone? Is Amos taking you to the airport in Dad's truck?"

Nodding, I answer, "Yes, Ma."

On my way to the truck, Graham catches up and walks next to me. I stop and ask, "Something on your mind?"

He runs his hand through his wild brown hair. "I'm going to miss you, Ace."

I pull him under my arm and further mess up his hair. "I'll miss you too. But just like last year, you can call and text me whenever you want." He nods and I release him. "Love you, Graham."

He straightens up and kicks some rocks, then mumbles, "Love you too."

I laugh at the sullen preteen he's becoming. My poor mother. It wasn't that long ago I was a teenager, and I know I raised some hell, but my four siblings have to run her ragged.

***

The return to preseason is easier than I expected. It must be because I already know what to expect. When I push into the locker room the first day back, I notice the anxiety and uneasiness I'd been drowning in the same time last year is gone. Not the newbie anymore, I stand taller. With a new confidence, I strut into the room in my trusty cowboy boots. I'd abandoned them shortly after arriving at training camp last year because I wanted to avoid all the roasting my teammates were giving out. This year, I elected to leave my Stetson at my apartment, but my boots remained molded to my feet after wearing them religiously for the past few months.

"Nice boots, Ace. Are we headed to the rodeo or practice?" Rocco teases.

Seeing his smirk, I know his comment isn't malicious, so I respond with, "Practice, for sure, but I'll be riding something later." I add a wink just for fun.

He laughs and shakes his head before he mutters, "Dog." I just grin in reply. It isn't true. I'm not a playboy. I won't say I've been celibate since being in the NHL; I'm just selective. I flirt with everyone, but there's only a few I've hooked up with.

It's typical locker room banter as we dress for our first preseason practice. My body surges with energy as I strap on pads, secure socks, and make sure every piece of equipment fits right.

Over the summer, my workouts and chores around the farm contain a lot more upper-body exercises than anything else—lifting feed bags, harvesting and lifting large containers of produce. Between them and the runs I took nightly, I tried my best to balance it all. Honestly, it had been an enjoyable break from the monotony of my trainer's workouts, and I've never felt stronger.

That practice is the first time I've been on ice in weeks, and a rush of endorphins pours through my body, giving me a high. Being at the farm meant I had limited opportunities to skate. Twice during my break, I'd made it over to the nearest town arena for a brief skate. My ma had begged that I take my siblings with me, so I did. We enjoyed skating together before grabbing pizza and heading home. Each time, it was nice to be on the ice, but it wasn't the same as practice or games. I brought a stick and puck with me the first time, but the rink was jammed full and I couldn't use it. To compensate, during the week when we didn't operate our country store, I moved things around in the barn and inline skated on the cement floor. Using an old stick, plastic pucks, and old milk crates, I set up my miniature version of a rink.

The sound of Coach's whistle reminds me of where I am. "Guys, welcome back. I trust you each had an enjoyable break and that you're ready to get to work. The training staff recently reworked many of your diets and exercise plans. Over the rest of this week, you'll need to schedule a time with them to meet. The pressure on our team this year will be magnified. As the most recent winner of the Stanley Cup, everyone will watch us extra closely. We need to stay strong and stay united.

"Lucas and I met last week to plan some team-building activities that we will get on the calendar soon. This week is all about assessing your fitness levels. Be prepared for a lot of drills." His whistle dismisses us, and while he moves to the team box, we all skate to the goal line, ready for his first order.

"Holy shit. Is he trying to kill us?" Rocco pants next to me a little while later as I greedily suck water down. Playing for as long as I have, I should know better, but it's so cool and refreshing, I'm not thinking about the repercussions. "You're going to regret that," he says.

"Ace, leave some for the rest of us," Mika shouts. Tossing him the bottle, I feel an embellished slosh of the water in my empty stomach. My mouth goes dry and I lick my lips despite just forcing down twelve ounces. My stomach churns and I feel nauseous. My body breaks out into a cold sweat. *Danger!* My brain shouts. Quickly, I sidestep my teammates, moving toward the end of the bench. My stomach clenches only a moment before it empties itself into a thirty-gallon-sized trash can just over the wall.

Once I'm sure it's passed, I lift my head and wipe my mouth. Turning back, I feel better until I notice everyone staring at me.

"Dude, I told you." Rocco laughs, and the rest of the guys join him. I shrug my shoulders, knowing we've all been there. At least mine wasn't after a full night of booze. Hangovers and practice never end well. I'd done that once and decided to never repeat it. On that single occasion, I didn't vomit until I finally made it back to the locker room. I learned my lesson in a hard, practical way. Unlike today, my mouth tasted like rotten assholes, and the nausea didn't resolve after I'd emptied my stomach. Our next break I'm smarter, taking sips instead of gulps. By the time practice ends, I'm feeling pretty good other than being tired.

Training camp goes on as scheduled. At the end of it, we're sore and exhausted, but being together again feels amazing. Within weeks, we hit our stride. And that's a fantastic position to be in heading into preseason games. Unfortunately, too many of us rely on that confidence and we suffer a pathetic loss of 5-1 in our first game. *That wasn't good.* I'm sure the media will berate Coach and Josh when it's their turn in front of the cameras.

Our shuffle to the locker room is like shutting yourself in an anechoic chamber. Unnerved, a shiver races down my spine. *At least tonight's humiliation wasn't on home ice.* I sink down onto the bench in front of my cubby and hang my head. Still dressed in my gear, I look like a turtle poking its head out of its shell. Peering up, I notice my teammates look much the same.

Finally, Coach walks in, and all the air in the room is sucked out. Apprehensive, my chest tightens, fearing what's next. I've never seen Coach lose his temper before, but there are rumors it's scary. I try to read his emotions, and what I see only troubles me more. His eyes are dark and stormy, but he wears a slight smile. *Is he happy about our loss? That can't be right.* My gaze pans over to Josh, who came in with him. He's sitting on the bench, looking calm and collected. *What is happening?*

Coach clears his voice, and my head whips in his direction to pay attention. "That was quite a game tonight. Our first after winning the Stanley Cup. The pressure on us is intense and it won't let up. So we need to take a step back, make some adjustments and improvements, and get back to work. In anything that you've worked hard to achieve, maintenance is the key. If you rest on your laurels, you will inevitably fail.

"When we get back to town, our first practice is going to be watching this game. I have big expectations for you. I know what you're capable of, and I'm holding you accountable to it. Do I think we can win the Cup again this year? I do. But it'll depend on how you work for it."

Stunned, I bend over, beginning to unlace my skates. He didn't yell once. He didn't criticize either. The locker room remains quiet as we all strip out of our gear, shower, and dress for the ride back to the hotel. Our flight leaving Quebec City departs early in the morning tomorrow. I don't know about the rest of my teammates, but I'm ready for this day to be over.

After reviewing the film of our first preseason game, Coach reminds us we have another seven preseason games to play. We make necessary adjustments, and when all is said and done, our record stands at 6-2. Coach is happy with that as we prepare for the official start of the season.

Our first home game is exhilarating. We're informed that management has decided it wants more entertainment before, during, and after the game. So, they hire someone to choreograph a production that involves flashing lights, loud music, steam, and a show they broadcast on the Jumbotron.

Last year, toward the end of the season, I noticed some of the other teams leaning toward making the game more theatrical. As I stood there, a visitor, at the blue line, it was easy to be sucked into the show they were putting on for their fans. I'd been watching hockey since I was a kid, and never had it been so loud, colorful, and artistic. Hockey on its own could be dramatic, but this took it to a whole new level. By the time our team began participating, it was its own monster, taking on a life of its own.

At each home game, our gravelly-voiced announcer summons us to the ice. My body buzzes with anticipation as I stand waiting for our cue. My eyes are drawn to the perfectly timed explosions of our team colors—navy blue and yellow—as they bathe the entire arena. Skating through a smoky arch, sparks from the theatrical welders who sit above rain down on us as we take the ice. A spirited crowd cheers, bringing a smile to my face. Even though I haven't been with the team long, it took no time for me to realize how incredible our fans are. Since adding the pre-show, their excitement has been on a whole new level. Skating a few laps, it feels like the arena is alive, living and breathing. As solid as it is, you can feel the bass thump from the music being blasted. From the first time I saw the show, I was amazed.

Even now, at the end of our season, I still remember that first time. Feeling my skin prickle under my gear. With each new visual surprise, my breath caught in my throat. The air was electric. Each game started with a literal bang. The end of the pre-show always concludes with a scene at center ice.

Under the spotlight, a steel worker dressed in a torn, stained jumpsuit uses a hammer to strike a piece of steel he's working on. The reverberation from his strike resembles that of a gong. Its noise carries through the supercharged air, sailing smoothly and registering deep in my bones.

Much like the pregame show, our season is full of excitement. Our stats heading into the playoffs are impressive. We lead our division with one hundred and eleven points—that's fifty-one wins and twenty-two losses. We easily sweep the first series against the Seattle Sharks. The next series is a nail-biter as we face off against the Montreal Mammoths. The games are tough, but in the end, we win the series in five games.

After we won the Cup against them last year, they were forced to do some major rebuilding when three of their players retired. They drafted two hot-shot rookies from top-notch colleges. From what I could see, those guys hadn't yet gelled with the team's style of play. They needed more time and then they'd once again be leading their division.

The road to the Cup hasn't been an easy one, but we count ourselves lucky to have made it to the finals again. This year we're playing against the Sacramento Sabers. Their rookie, Sean Robinson, won the Calder Memorial Trophy the previous season, and this year he continued to impress the hockey community with a notable fifty-seven points.

He and I entered the draft the same year, and he'd been selected before me. We've faced off against each other many times, and there is no denying he's an amazing player, but there is one major thing he hasn't learned: how to share. He's still selfish with the puck. He doesn't pass when he thinks he might get a chance at a breakaway. And because of that, his team suffers many missed opportunities. Although, I can't fault him entirely. I know if I hadn't been drafted by the Steel, and my teammates hadn't expected more of me, I would have done the same thing as Sean.

Every time we face off, we glare at each other as we wait for the puck to drop. I want to say something, but with his ego, I know he won't listen. Instead, I just lower my eyes, returning to my focus. He'll figure it out, or maybe he won't. Either way, I'm grateful to play on the team I'm on with the teammates I have.

July sets in, and after the barbeque at Samantha and Lucas's, I'm ready for some fun, and a quick trip to Vegas is exactly what I need.

"This is amazing," I say as my gaze travels around the spacious black and white interior of the private jet we're flying to Vegas in. For the duration of the four-hour flight, Mika tries to teach us how to play Blackjack. Of those on the trip, Lucas and Rocco catch on quickly, while Jace and I are more interested in the slots. After about the third time of them telling us to stop interrupting with questions, Jace and I move to the back of the plane.

"What's on the agenda for the next few days?" I ask Jace, since this trip was his idea. He looks at me and shrugs.

"I don't know. I've never been to Vegas for anything but hockey. Anything you're desperate to do?"

"From what I know, there's something for everyone. I'm down with most things other than being arrested," I admit.

Jace laughs. "Mika said the same thing. I'm down with fun, but I'm not about to get in trouble with the team. I thought maybe we'd hit the casinos, catch a show or concert, hang out by the pool, see if any games are in town, and, of course, eat."

"That sounds great. I bet the hotel can help us out with some of that."

"The weather has been incredible this entire time," I say to Mika, who's lounging in the cabana we've rented every day at lunchtime. Our only mistake is securing the same one every day because by day two we were already drawing a crowd. Ladies of all shapes and sizes saunter by us the entire time we're there. Many of them approach, asking for pictures and autographs. It's tough to refuse them, but by the late afternoon, it starts wearing on my nerves. I guess if I were Jace, I'd be happy. I think he's collected at least fifty phone numbers. I'm sure he's taking full advantage of what's being offered. Me? I may have collected a few numbers that were thrust at me, but no one catches my eye. Only two years into the league, and I'm already tired of the one-night stands and quick hookups. They've lost their appeal. Unlike some of my more senior teammates, I have no idea what I'm looking for. But I do know that isn't it.

Chapter 4

Ace

"Have you guys seen this?" Rocco shouts as he enters the banquet room of our hotel. It's set up for our meals while we're in New York for a series of games. Normally, the league doesn't schedule back-to-back games between the same two teams, but a conflict earlier in our season caused us to cancel the previous Chargers game. The makeup game is scheduled for tomorrow night. Reaching the table where Lucas, Josh, and I are eating breakfast, he thrusts a New York newspaper forward while mumbling, "I can't believe this shit."

In big bold letters, it says *New York's former golden boy has returned. Let's give him hell.* It's a smear campaign against Lucas. Upset on his behalf, I look at him. Sitting calmly next to me, he rolls his shoulders and smirks. *How is he not pissed off?*

As if he's reading my thoughts, he counters with,

"It's just one of many." And he's right. New Yorkers have not forgotten he left them, and they share their displeasure with anyone who'll listen.

The morning skate goes well. Following that is lunch and then my favorite part of the day, the pregame nap. During it, I'm able to recharge my batteries and reset for the game ahead.

My skin prickles as I board the bus. There's an energy surrounding us. I give out fist bumps as I find my seat. Slipping on my noise-canceling headphones, I'm able to visualize and focus on the game during the ride to the arena.

About halfway through the game, I realize that all the visualizing I did to prepare for tonight was pointless. The Chargers are playing dirty.

"This game is a complete clusterfuck," Mika growls while heading into the locker room after the first period. *I couldn't agree more.* We've been lucky that with the way they've been playing, no one's gotten hurt.

Skating onto the ice before the second period, I see the Charger's center, Jeremy Kane, shove Lucas. I can't hear what he says, but his snarl is undeniable. A shiver racks my body as I skate over to our bench.

On my second shift, I win the puck in our corner. Turning quickly, I dig my toes in and tear off toward the Charger's goal. I've barely crossed the center line when I'm checked hard from behind. Within seconds, I slam into the board headfirst with such force that I see stars. Lying on my stomach, I lift my head. The slight movement makes me instantly dizzy. *Am I going to throw up?* I've been hit many times in hockey, but until now, I never reacted like this. Sliding my arm forward, I push myself over. The arena lights are blinding, almost as if I'm staring straight into a flashlight beam. Fuzzy gray spots float in my vision, and I squeeze my eyes shut. With the darkness, the nausea seems to lessen, but I find I'm sleepy. *Would now be a good time for a nap?* I can't remember what I was doing, so why not?

"Ace. Ace. Can you hear me? Open your eyes." Panicked voices surround me, and I try to focus on them, but they seem so muddled. *Are they far away?*

I feel pressure on both sides of my head before it's slowly lifted. The sound of Velcro ripping startles me, and my eyes fly open to bright light. *Shit, that hurts.* A shadow passes over my face and I blink the image clear. Relief hits. It's Jack, one of our trainers. "Ace, you were checked from behind and you hit the boards hard. We just put a C-collar on your neck and are going to take you for evaluation, but first I need you to do something for me. Okay?" he says.

"K," I garble out, my mouth full of blood. I grimace.

Jack touches my mouth and then quickly turns to someone next to him. "He's missing his front teeth. After we move him, I need you to find them and put them in milk."

Giving his attention back to me, he explains, "Before we move you, I need to quickly assess you."

Removing my gloves, he has me squeeze his fingers. I do, although I notice it's much weaker than I would have expected. Then he asks me to wiggle my feet. Nothing happens. Fear washes over me as I try desperately to move my feet. My legs. No matter what I tell myself, the fuckers aren't moving.

"I can't," I weakly admit. Jack senses the anxiety tearing through my body. A cold sweat covers my skin, and I'm nauseated again. *Will I walk again?*

He sets a firm hand on my shoulder and says, "It's okay. Try not to panic. We're transporting you to the hospital to have an assessment done. When it's safe, they will remove your gear and do some imaging."

My teammates come up to me after I'm strapped to a transport board. Thankfully, I'm not dealing with much pain on top of everything else. Josh stays near me the entire time, a silent support. Before they transport me off the ice, I look at him and say only two words. "Win this." He nods at me and smiles. I give the team a two-finger wave before I'm rushed down the tunnel and to a waiting ambulance.

Listening to the EMTs on the drive, they mention things like spinal cord injury and concussion, and a shiver rocks my body. When they mention the missing front teeth, I run my tongue around my mouth, and sure enough, I have a giant window in the front. The song "All I Want for Christmas is My Two Front Teeth" gets stuck in my head.

With lights flashing, the ride to the nearest trauma hospital is quick. Doctors and nurses rush around me once I'm in a hospital bay. Once they've verified my C-collar is in the correct position, they remove my gear. In mere minutes, I'm lying on my gurney, wearing a very stylish blue hospital gown and cervical collar. Doctors again check my reflexes with my eyes, hands, and feet. This time I can feel them. They order imaging because my reactions and reflexes are still sluggish.

The on-call neurologist arrives with my prognosis. "Mr. Walker, I reviewed your scans, and everything looks great. Considering what happened, I'd say you're lucky to just be dealing with temporary weakness."

I breathe a sigh of relief. "That's good. So how long do I have to wear this?" I ask while tugging at the C-collar.

He laughs. "Those are a necessary evil. But it looks like you don't need one. You have a concussion, though. Recovery from those usually takes seven to fourteen days. You will need to follow the instructions on that in your discharge paperwork. Follow up with your team physician once you're back in Chicago." He moves toward me. "Questions before I remove this and get out of your hair?" He removes the collar and tests my motor strength. I pass, though I notice the weakness in my body.

With confidence, the doctor explains the weakness

will be short-lived. "After what your body's been through tonight, it'll take a few days to recover." He has me swing my legs over the side of the bed, and I feel myself wobble. Frustrated, I growl. "Ace, don't be so hard on yourself. You had your bell rung." I nod my acceptance when all I really want is to ask for another reassurance that everything will be fine.

The ER doctor comes back in. "Ace, we're printing up your discharge paperwork right now. In it, I included information about concussions and what you can expect in the next days and weeks. Regarding your teeth, I gave your trainers the name of a fantastic dentist. I believe they made an emergency appointment for you to see him tomorrow."Returning to my hotel room after hours in the ER, I convinced Jack to help me call home. I knew they'd be worried. I'd spoken to my family the day before and knew they'd be watching. As expected Ma panicked and Dad remained calm when they saw the hit. My brother Graham was so worried he couldn't sleep. During the short call, I reassured him I was fine. Before hanging up, I promised a calm the next day when I was home.

Returning home, I'm glad my teeth are back where they're supposed to be. But just like the neurologist said, recovery takes a few weeks. I miss a few games, but it's a small price to pay for the ability to walk and the opportunity to live a full life.

While recovering, I see the footage of what happened, and thinking about it makes my blood boil. Jeremy Kane was only given a five-minute major penalty for checking me. It was obvious from the video that the severity of the check was intentional. In the days following the *hit heard around the world*, as it's been called, many believed he should have been suspended from the game and given a stiff fine by the league. I agree, but there's nothing I can do about it.

When I'm cleared, I return to practice. The entire time I'm getting dressed, I feel amazing. I'm energized and ready to play, but as soon as I step on the ice for my first practice, I can feel something is different. I find out it's even worse for games. Anxiety like I've never experienced before weaves its way through my body, affecting every moment of the game. Anytime anyone comes at me at speed, my stomach twists with fear. My mind haunted by the *what-ifs*. I become hyper-vigilant.

When others skate up to check me, I flinch a microsecond before they even make contact. Then there are times when I feel someone come up behind me. Again, my body responds before my brain can, and I almost cower.

I'm overly exhausted at the end of each game because of all the adrenaline flooding my body from the elevated responses I'm experiencing. *What is happening?* I can't continue to play hockey like this. But I don't know what to do. *Has anyone else noticed how debilitating this has become?*

"Ace." My name on Coach's lips has my skin prickling and my heart beating out a rushed beat. *Am I in trouble?* No. It's only my second week back. What could I have done? "After you shower, will you stop by my office for a chat?"

"Sure," I croak out, nervous about what he'll say.

Rapping my knuckles on his door frame, he looks up and smiles. "Come in. Will you shut the door?"

Sitting down in a chair in front of his desk, my stomach swims with unease as worry overwhelms me. Twisting my hands in my lap, I wait for him to speak. *Why am I here?*

"I just wanted to have a conversation about how you're doing."

"Sir?" I question.

He leans back in his chair. "I won't kid you, Ace. You took a nasty hit that initially caused a lot of concerns as to what your future might look like." I nod, agreeing with him. "I just wanted to check in with you and see how you're doing and feeling."

Breathing out slowly, I tug my hand through my still-damp hair before confessing, "Honestly, it's been different."

"How do you mean?" he asks, genuine concern stretched across his face.

"I don't know if you've noticed, but when someone

skates up behind me, moving fast, I flinch. Also, I find myself hesitating."

Coach offers me a smile. "I noticed both those things, and I think they are completely understandable. What do you think about going to see the sports psychologist we have on staff? Maybe she can help you work through the hit and how it makes you feel."

A counselor? "Okay," I tell him, wondering how it will go.

Our conversation ends with me getting the contact information for the counselor.

After one session, she diagnoses me with an adjustment disorder. When Dr. Linda explains the dumbed-down version, everything I've been experiencing makes sense. I now understand why my hands sweat every time I get on the ice, and why I struggle to breathe and my mind spins out of control when I feel like someone is about to check me. She tells me it is usually short-lived and treatable.

This gives me hope that I can get back to where I was before the injury.

Chapter 5

Ace

The new season is officially here. Skating onto the ice, I feel strong both mentally and physically. Starting my third year in the league, I finally don't feel like a rookie. And as a bonus, most of the guys have stopped calling me that too. Poor Klause has filled that role now. When I stop in front of our bench to do my stretches, my gaze searches him out among my teammates. I find him easily, as he's the only one who looks green. Tonight is the first professional hockey game of his career. When our eyes connect, I lift my gloved hand off the ice and beckon him over to me. As he skates to me, I holler, "Hey Pete." He grimaces, worry clear in his expression, and drops next to me.

"Ace, can I ask you a question?" he says, his voice shaky with nerves.

I move into my next stretch and say, "Shoot."

"Why don't you call me Rookie like everyone else?"

I laugh. "Well, Pete, I figured that since I didn't like it when they called me that, you might not either. So I went with your name. Do you want me to call you Rookie?"

He shrugs, his shoulder pads lifting beside his ears. "Honestly, it doesn't matter to me. Both fit."

I nod. "Are you ready for this?" I ask as I look at the now full arena.

"Nope. I haven't eaten at all today because I don't want to throw up." His confession reminds me of myself years earlier. I'd done much the same, and by the second period, I was gassed. No food meant no energy. Thankfully, Josh had some energy chews in his locker that he gave me in between the periods.

"I have some energy chews in my locker if you need them." I smile at him. The one he returned looked more like a grimace than anything. "Listen, man. I know this is nerve-racking, but you've got this. You've earned a spot here, so let's show everyone what Pete Klause is about." His nod is hesitant, but I'll keep encouraging him, just like the guys did for me.

With the first game in the books and a W on record, we head to Dallas to take on the Coyotes, the newest expansion team in the league. From what I've heard, they made solid choices for their roster. They still have many things to work out, like chemistry and compatibility. The Coyotes secured an elite group of veterans whose previous contracts hadn't been protected.

We're dominating the game. I've already scored two goals. Then, in the middle of the third period, I drop to the ice after being hit by Coyotes defenseman Lyle Jeffries. Writhing in pain, I lie as still as possible. Lucas skates up to me and drops to his knees. "Ace, man, what hurts?"

Gritting my teeth, I spit out, "My left leg." Through clouded eyes, I watch as Lucas scans my legs. His expression is something I will never forget. At first, he tilts his head as if he's getting a better view, then his eyes go wide and his mouth drops open. He mouths, *"Oh shit,"* and immediately looks to the bench. His arm raises and he frantically waves for help.

Within seconds, one of our new team trainers, Matthew, is next to me. "Ace, it looks like we need to get you to the hospital." The lack of emotion in his voice sends a chill down my spine. *Not again.*

"Tell me, Matthew. What are we talking about?" I ask as pain radiates through my legs and my stomach swirls with nausea. I swallow hard, waiting for his response.

He scratches his head. "Without an X-ray, I can't say with one hundred percent certainty, but I think you broke your leg."

"Fuck," I mutter as I pinch my eyes closed. I'm desperately wishing this was all a bad dream. Especially after the last time. I dislike hospitals, tests, procedures, and therapy.

A transport team arrives with a backboard, and under Matthew's direction, I'm carefully moved. My teammates gather around me before I'm rushed off the ice. The pity on their faces is enough to make me want to scream.

In no time, my stretcher is pushed through the doors of the ambulance bay at the Dallas County Hospital. The powerful smell of antiseptic tickles my nose, and I can hear the squeaks of multiple pairs of shoes as they rush through the emergency department. The EMTs with me stop at a nursing station. "Twenty-one-year-old male. Professional hockey player suffered an injury to his left leg during a game. The witnessing trainer suspects a probable fracture. Nine out of ten leg pain when moved. BP 135/80, HR 75, temp 98.7."

"Put him in bay four; Dr. Thomas will be there in a minute," a gruff sounding woman answers. And then we're moving again. I close my eyes and focus on my breathing while pushing out the sensations of my swirling stomach and throbbing leg.

The sound of my bay's curtain being opened encourages me to open my eyes. "Hi, Ace. I'm Dr. Thomas. Looks like you'd had a tough night."

Swallowing hard, I rasp, "You could say that."

He laughs. "Well, I see your sense of humor is still intact, so that's an excellent sign you'll be fine. From what I understand, you were hit during a hockey game and went down with leg pain. Can you tell me anything else?"

I shake my head, finally noticing that I'm no longer wearing my helmet. "The hit happened so fast, I don't remember it. All I know is that my leg is killing me, and from everyone's reaction, I'm guessing it doesn't look right."

"You're right. It isn't lined up the way it should be. We need to get your gear off so we can get some X-rays to get a better idea of what we're dealing with. Once those are ready, I'll call an orthopedic surgeon for recommendation on treatment. Does that sound okay?"

I frown. "No, but do what you have to do. Will someone help me get my gear off? And can I bother to ask for some pain meds? My leg is already screaming at me, and I can't imagine it will get better when it's moved."

He offers a kind smile. "I can do that. Your nurse will be back in with some pain meds and she'll help you remove your gear."

Before he ducks out of my bay, I remember my manners. "Thank you, Dr. Thomas."

My nurse, Larrissa, pops in with Matthew in tow. He gives me a wave. "I overheard the doctor, and figured you might need some help to get out of your gear."

I take the pills she gives me and lay my head back on the gurney. "Thanks."

The process of undressing takes longer than any of

us likely expected. Every time my leg jostles, pain halts me and my stomach twists and turns like it's trapped in a stormy sea.

Getting my skate off is the worst pain I have ever felt in my life. "Fuck," I mutter with my teeth bared. Sweat covers my skin and my hands turn ghostly white from squeezing the gurney's plastic mattress. "Get it the fuck off," I growl. The poor nurse probably thinks I'm moments away from committing violence. I'm not, it's just this motherfucker hurts. I hate being that guy. I was raised never to swear in front of ladies, and Larissa reminds me of my mom, which makes me feel even worse.

Pain meds have dulled the excruciating pain, and the X-rays are performed without a hitch.

I'm lying back on my bed with my face tilted to the ceiling as we wait for the X-ray results. "Who won the game?" I ask Matthew, needing a distraction.

"The Steel did. Your two goals put the team well ahead. The end score was 4-1."

I close my eyes, intending to rest for a few minutes. All the adrenaline has worn off, and with the pain meds still coursing through my body, the exhaustion is more noticeable.

"Ahem." A man clearing his throat startles me awake. Slowly, I blink my eyes open. Standing before me is an older gentleman with salt and pepper hair. His tortoise-shell glasses make him look distinguished. His white coat lets me know he's another doctor. "Hi,

Ace. I m sorry to wake you up, but I'm Dr. Williams. I was called in to consult on your leg by Dr. Thomas." I nod. "I've reviewed your X-rays, and it looks like you've broken both your tibia and fibula. The recommended treatment is surgery."

My mouth falls open. "Surgery?" In disbelief, my eyes fly to Matthew for confirmation of what I heard. He nods. I lick my parched lips. "What does that entail?"

"What we would do is called an ORIF or an open reduction and internal fixation. Basically, we need to stabilize the broken bones so they can heal properly. During the surgery, I would place a plate, securing it with screws to ensure your bones are in the correct position for healing."

After discussing all the risks like blood clots, infections, or nerve damage, Dr. Williams talks about recovery, which is where most of my questions lie. "Will I ever play hockey again?" I ask, my voice wavering. My worries and fears swim around me, making it tough to grasp all he's saying. I'm pretty sure I understood the idea of watching for infections and the importance of keeping it immobile at first. Plus, I'm not supposed to miss any follow-up appointments. Once he's gone through his practiced speech, he looks at me.

"Ace, I can't fully answer your question. I want to promise you that you'll play hockey again at this level, but the truth is, I don't know. Will you recover?" He pauses. My scratchy blue hospital gown tugs at my throat as I lean forward, hopeful for good news. *Please, please, please.* "Yes. I believe you will recover. But I won't make any guesses about any damage you may have sustained to your nerves, blood vessels, and muscles. That can only be assessed following surgery and months of physical therapy."

"M-months?" I sputter as my mind, groggy with pain meds, tries to grasp the idea.

He nods. "It takes four to six months to recover."

My head drops back and I mutter, "There goes the entire season." Panic overwhelms me, sitting like an elephant on my chest. It's tough to get a full breath as I consider my future. My lungs tighten, sweat runs down my back, and my stomach knots as I consider that even in six months, I may not play again. During that time, assuming I recover fully, will I lose my spot on the team?

Matthew reaches over and pats my shoulder, trying his best to comfort me. "We'll talk to the team, but just so you know, they won't bring you back until they think you're one hundred percent again."

Then his words register. *I'm out for the whole fucking season, at least.* And that's if everything with surgery and recovery goes as planned. Otherwise, who the fuck knows? *Could this be career ending?* Coach Tristan flashes in my mind. His knee injury was. Who's saying luck is on my side? Just as my mind is filling with disparaging thoughts and scenarios, Dr.

Williams clears his throat. My eyes flash open and I stare at him.

"Your team management has asked that we stabilize your leg so you can travel home. They've spoken with the orthopedic specialist on contract, and surgery to repair your leg has been scheduled for the day after next. Even though I won't be performing the surgery, I would be happy to answer any questions you may have."

Clearing my throat, I say, "You said recovery is four to six months?"

"Correct. This recovery has many steps to it, and it's important to follow them. I will tell you that about ten to twelve weeks after surgery, you will be full weight bearing again. By then, you'll have started some physical therapy too."

Holding my hand out, I do quick finger math. "So, if it takes six months to recover, I should be good by April right? That's still time to play in the playoffs." I offer my first smile in hours.

The doctor frowns back at me, his gray mustache reminding me of the fuzzy caterpillars we find around the farm. "April is when your bones will technically be healed. Physical therapy swoops in next to help rebuild and reestablish what you've lost. And if I can give you a forewarning, physical therapy is both necessary and tough."

My heart drops. "This fucking sucks," I complain.

Both Matthew and Dr. Williams agree with grimacing smiles and nods.

"Are there any more questions I can answer?"

I shake my head. "No, but thank you for your time."

He gives me a firm handshake. "You've got this, Ace. Next season when the Steel come to play the Coyotes, I'll be eager to see you play."

Once we're alone, Matthew makes a call to management. When they patch him through to Trey, the owner, I know it's serious. Laying my head back on the gurney to rest, I hear bits and pieces of their conversation as I try to sort through the chaos between my ears.

"Ace, I just talked to Trey, and what Dr. Williams said is true. Your surgery has been scheduled. Dallas County sent your X-rays to Dr. Neidleman in Chicago. He also said that he's spoken to your parents and planned to have your mom with you for surgery and a few days after. They also lined up home healthcare workers to come and check on you daily."

I sigh. "Thanks, Matthew."

Back in my hotel room hours later, I feel like the Thanksgiving turkey. I've been laid bare, poked, prodded, and dressed up like I'm the star of the show.

"What do you want to eat? I'll order you Door-Dash," Matthew says after I'm settled in bed.

"Can I have Subway? That's the only thing that sounds good." He opens the app, plugs in the location and my room number, and hands it over to me so I can put in my order. Once I'm done building my sandwich —a toasted American club with almost every veggie and honey mustard dressing—I hand the phone back to him.

"Do you want anything to drink?" he asks.

"Please. Can you grab me a few sports drinks? Any flavor will be fine. Thank you."

While we wait, he makes sure I'm as comfortable as possible. He carefully props my leg up with two thick pillows. The hospital gave me crutches, but I'm convinced they hate me. Every time I use them, I get the rubber stoppers from the bottom snagged. Thankfully, I've been lucky enough to catch myself each time.

Despite the crap situation I find myself in, I appreciate all those who came to my aid, especially Larissa. She was my shining star in the ER. Exceptionally amazing is how I would describe the care she gave me. She hooked me up with a disposable urinal so I don't have to move in the middle of the night. I haven't used it yet, so I'm nervous about the logistics, but it's better than those demonic crutches.

By the time my dinner arrives, I'm exhausted all over again, but my stomach rumbles, reminding me I need fuel. I'm sure I set a record when I power down my sub in minutes. I'm not usually such a fast eater, but I inhale it. It's delicious Licking the sweet honey mustard dressing from my lips, I drain the first of three drinks Matthew ordered for me. It's cold and refreshing, but it barely makes a dent in the cotton mouth I'm suffering with. *Thank you, pain meds.*

"You good?" Matthew asks as he adjusts the navy-blue Chicago Steel ball cap he's wearing.

Flashing a dopey, drug-induced grin, I answer, "I'm good. Once you leave, I'm going to sleep."

Like a nervous mother, he nags, "Do you have your alarm set for your next pain pill?"

"Yes. Now, get out of here." He smiles and then leaves.

Chapter 6

Ace

Once we're boarded on the plane, Matthew reminds me to take my next pain pill. The shuffle, hop move I had to orchestrate while getting onto the plane takes everything out of me. By the time I'm in my seat, I feel like I completed a half marathon. Sweat pours down my back. My leg throbs, and it's almost an hour past my window for taking my pill. Not wasting any more time, I pop it into my mouth, washing it down with a big cup of coffee and the egg, bacon, and cheese biscuit the flight attendant handed to me shortly after I settled in my seat. Before the plane even takes off, I'm visiting dreamland. Left in an aisle by myself, I remain undisturbed until we land.

Matthew must have drawn the short straw, because he's been my shadow for days. Reaching over from across the aisle, he nudges me to wake me up. Groggy, I force my eyes open. Panic sets in. *Where am I?* A quick look around tells me I'm on a plane. Blowing out a deep breath, I take a second to reorient myself. "Are we home?" I ask.

"We are," Matthew confirms, and relief sets in. "I just checked the flight schedule. Your mom landed half an hour ago. I sent her a text, and we agreed to meet at baggage claim. But first, we have to get you off the plane. Can you shuffle and hop again?"

Like a petulant toddler, I want to stomp my feet, shake my head, and yell "No!" at him. When I remain mute, he responds with a tight smile, and dammit, I'm officially an asshole. Matthew didn't ask to be my babysitter. The least I can do is not make his life horrible. "Sorry," I say, knowing I owe him more than that.

Thirty minutes later, I'm off the plane and being whisked through the airport by an expert wheelchair handler. *This guy should teach classes or get a medal of some sort.* I'm not sure how many people are injured by wheelchairs every year, but I'm guessing in those few cases, driver error is probably a factor.

The first sight of my mom makes my nose itch and my eyes water. *Damn allergies.* "Jethro," she croons while grabbing at my hand, giving it a firm squeeze. "Ma's here," she whispers. In an instant, I'm transformed into a broken ten-year-old boy again who needs his ma like he needs his next breath. Desperately.

While the team buzzes around, Matthew grabs our bags and arranges a ride home for us. A chorus of "Bye, Ace" follows me as Ma pushes my wheelchair out to the curb for our waiting ride.

Pulling myself up to standing with help from Lucifer and Beelzebub, my demon crutches, I say goodbye to Herbie, the name I'd given the airport wheelchair. The drive home is uneventful. As we turn onto my street, I have never been happier that I bought a single-level house. No stairs for me to navigate in the next few months as I recover. Or so I thought. "Shit," I mutter as I readjust my hat. I forgot about the front steps. Using my crutches to move over to them, the devils do their best to rub my armpits raw. While trying to determine how to traverse the two small steps without re-injuring my leg, the pulsating, throbbing pain returns. My next dose of pain meds is due soon, but I have so much to do before then. Getting inside is priority number one.

Twenty minutes later, I'm in my sparsely deco-rated bedroom. I'm sitting on top of my downy feather comforter, leaning against the soft leather headboard. My leg is propped up with several pillows, and I have a fresh meal cooling next to me. Ma prepared it and served it with another pain pill and the largest bottle of water I've ever seen. This day has been a whirlwind, and although it's still early, I have a feeling I'll be passing out soon.

Matthew appears in the doorway. "I'll be back tomorrow at ten to take you to meet Dr. Jorgensen. She's the orthopedic surgeon on contract, and she'll be the one doing your surgery. I just got off the phone with her office and was told they plan to run labs, take another set of X-rays, and discuss the procedure."

I nod. "Okay, I'll be ready. Thanks, man, for all your help the last few days and for the days ahead. I appreciate it more than I can say."

He smiles. "Is there anything either of you need before tomorrow?" Both Ma and I shake our heads no. "I'm going to head out, then. Have a good night." With a wave, he disappears.

After dinner, Lucifer, Beelzebub, and I have a battle of the wills on a trip to the bathroom. They refuse to stay under my armpits and I refuse to let them lead. After dropping them on the floor, I'm determined to just hop everywhere. "Stupid fucking things," I holler.

"Jethro Walker!" Ma calls out in an unsavory tone that makes me shiver.

"Sorry, Ma," I call back. "I think these things are trying to kill me." As she enters the room, she laughs, only stopping when she sees the disapproval spread across my face.

"They can't be that bad," she says, and my mouth drops open, mocking her. She places her hands on her hips in a challenging pose.

"I'm not kidding, Ma. These things have rubbed

my armpits raw, and I shouldn't even mention it's impossible to crutch effectively with them."

"How about I help you get to the bathroom and get ready for bed?" I give her a hug, whispering "thanks" into her ear.

Chapter 7

Ace

Dr. Jorgensen's nurse finds a small pillow to use to prop up my leg. After answering at least one hundred questions, she excuses herself, reporting the doctor will be right in. I hold in my snicker until the door shuts. Looking at my ma, I ask, "Should we make a wager on how long she'll be?" My ma smiles. Over the years, we've visited plenty of doctors together, and I can count on one hand the number of them who were on time.

Not even thirty seconds later, I hear a soft rap on the wooden exam room door. "Come in," Ma helpfully calls. A woman in her mid-fifties enters the room, sharply dressed in a silk shirt and black dress pants. She also wears a white doctor's coat. She's tall and trim, built like a long-distance runner.

"Ace," she greets as she slips her thick-framed glasses on her face.

Ma and I listen to all the pre-op instructions and what to expect following surgery. We're given pamphlets talking about aftercare and rehabilitation. Now here we are, ready to go under the knife.

The next day is an early one as I get ready for surgery. We arrive at the hospital a few minutes after five. As George, our driver, moved through the city, I noticed there were hardly any cars on the roads. Seeing that we've done all the pre-registration forms and bloodwork, we're ushered to the operating wing. Once I'm shown back to my bay, I'm given a gown, slip-resistant socks, and a hair cap Then I'm left alone to change.

It soon becomes a madhouse as nurses, doctors, and insurance representatives pop in to ask questions about my health history and my injury. Before I know it, Dr. Jorgensen is marking my left knee and then I'm being wheeled back for surgery.

As I lie on the gurney being pushed through white hallways, my mind whirls with all the intense emotions flowing through my body. Above everything, I'm anxious and scared. The smell of antiseptic tickles my nose and I reach up and scratch it. Seeing my hospital bracelet reminds me why I'm here. My heart is racing so fast, I can hear the whooshing noise it makes as it pushes blood through my veins.

When we enter the operating room, it's different from what I imagined. It's so bright and cold. A shiver rips through my body as I'm transferred to the operating table. The anesthesiologist I met earlier stands above me, dressed head to toe in sterile gear. She lowers her mask to give me a kind word and smile. Her kindness is fresh in my mind as she has me count backward.

"Jethro, can you hear me? Open your eyes." I try to lift my eyelids, but they are so heavy. Feeling sleepy, I promise myself I'll try again later.

Someone rubs my chest. "Jethro, you're done with surgery and everything went great. Can you open your eyes for me?" Again, I try to open them, but all I can manage is a flicker. *Did I see my ma?* I feel someone squeeze my hand. *Ma.* This time, I keep my eyes open for a few seconds.

"Jethro," Ma says, her voice filled with emotion.

"Yeah," I rasp.

"They said the surgery went great. In a few months, you'll be as good as new." I hear the excitement in her voice, and I try to smile. "You need to wake up more before they'll be ready to discharge you, but all your vitals are perfect. So go back to sleep. I'll be here when you wake up."

Not long after, I feel like I can keep my eyes open, and Dr. Jorgensen stops by my recovery bay. She reaches out to shake my hand. "Ace, everything went perfectly during the surgery, and your vitals have been outstanding for the last hour in recovery. I just signed your discharge papers so you can get out of here.

"Remember, do not put weight on it, and keep your brace dry. Watch for signs of infection; redness, oozing, draining, swelling, fever. If you notice any of these, contact my office right away. I'll have you back in a few weeks for another series of X-rays so we can track your healing. Weeks after that, you'll be moved to a brace and slowly you'll transition to weight bearing. Physical therapy starts after that. You have a long road in front of you, but I'm confident in you and the recovery you'll have. Any questions for me?"

I shake my head. "No. I just want to say thank you for taking care of me." Dr. Jorgensen gives me a smile and Ma a side hug before she excuses herself.

"Ready to blow this popsicle stand?" Ma asks as she smiles at me.

When George delivers us home an hour and a half later, because discharging from the hospital is never a quick process, I'm exhausted and ready to crash. Ma helps me into bed. We get my leg propped up with pillows, and I barely mumble a "thanks" before I'm out.

Waking up, I notice I'm not as groggy as I was the last time I woke, but my leg hurts. "Ma," I holler.

"One sec, Jethro," she calls back. "It's time for meds. I'm just heating some soup for you."

When she enters the room, I see her worry before she quickly masks it. "What's wrong?" I ask.

Staying silent, she sets the soup on my nightstand so she can hand me my pill and a glass of water. Tossing it back, I look at her. "Please tell me."

She grimaces. "For the last half an hour you've been moaning, and I figured you were in pain, but I didn't want to wake you even though I knew your pain meds had likely worn off."

I reach for the hand that's hanging by her side and squeeze it. "Ma, it's okay. I'm fine. See," I tell her while giving her a smile. She forces a smile back, but I notice it doesn't reach her eyes. "I have an idea. How about you get another bowl of soup and we can watch a show together? You can even pick."

She squeezes my hand back. "That sounds like a great idea." An hour later, we've finished the first episode of a historical romantic fiction, and Ma is on cloud nine. "Can we watch another?"

I laugh. "Only if you reward me with dessert." Her smile stretches from ear to ear.

"Deal," she exclaims as she heads out of my room with our dirty soup dishes in her hands.

Watching episode two leads to three, and apparently I've created a historical-romance-loving monster. I may or may not nod off during large sections of the third episode. Ma is so intrigued with the show, I don't think she even notices. The only thing that wakes me is my bladder screaming at me. After a not-so-quick hobble to the bathroom, I settle back into bed while my show buddy again immerses herself in the Regency era. Lying back with my eyes closed, the sighs, laughs, and gasps of delight from my ma make my heart happy. It's a rare occurrence she does anything for herself, so having her stop, relax, and genuinely enjoy something, feels monumental. It feels like I'm giving her a precious gift.

At the end of the fourth episode, Ma gently wakes me. "Jethro, it's time for your next pain pill. I have an apple and some peanut butter for you too."

"Thanks, Ma," I say while I move into a seated position. Once I'm done with the snack, I again make my slow way to the bathroom to pee and brush my teeth.

"I'm going to take the dishes to the kitchen and get you more water. Anything else you need before you go to bed?"

"I'm good, but thank you."

She's walking back into the room as I crutch back to the bed. Again, we shuffle pillows and I try to get as comfortable as possible. She drags a blanket over me and kisses my forehead. "Night, Jethro. Love you."

"Night, Ma. Love you too."

My ma has been a saint. She's sleeping in my spare room on a blowup mattress Rocco dropped off right after she arrived. She insisted the couch would be fine, but there wasn't any way I'd have her sleep on it for more than one night.

I don't know what I'd do without her.

Chapter 8

Ace

"**Y**ou ready for this, Jethro?" Ma asks as I crutch beside her. It's been two weeks since surgery, and I have a follow-up with Dr. Jorgensen. Ma's been with me every step of this recovery, and while I love having her here, I know that my younger siblings and Dad need her home. Ma refuses to leave until she knows her "baby boy" is on the right track.

Today is when they'll take new X-rays to show the success of the surgery. I'm still weeks away from being able to put weight on it, but at least I can remove the brace when I'm just lying around. And, shit, this experience has been boring. For someone as active as I am, this is fucking awful.

As we make our way down the long hallway, the repetitive clicking sound of my crutches lures me into a trance-like state. "Here we are," Ma says. Looking up, the doctor's office is before me. Shaking off the mental haze, I follow her in.

"Everything looks great," Dr. Jorgensen says after reviewing both my X-rays and incision. "You'll remain in this brace for a few more weeks and then you'll transition to a walking boot. At first, the boot will be used only as you practice short increments of putting weight on your leg."

"What about the crutches?" I ask. *Please say I'm almost done with Lucifer and Beelzebub.*

"You still have months before you'll be fully weight-bearing. Which means the crutches stay," he says.

"Grrr," I mutter under my breath. If Ma weren't here with me, I'm confident other choice words would have come out of my mouth. I tighten my fists as my frustration boils within me.

The appointment goes smoothly, and Dr. Jorgensen is happy with my recovery. George is waiting for us when we exit the hospital, and he delivers us home. Over lunch, I look at Ma. "Thank you for all your help over the past few weeks. Guess it's time for you to head home." I see her shoulders dip, and my stomach twists. *Did I say something wrong?* Reaching over, I grab her hand. "Ma?"

She wipes at her eyes. *Shit, I made her cry.* My heart sinks. "Ma."

Forcing a smile, she lets out a humorless laugh. "It's tough when your babies don't need you anymore."

"I'll always need you, but right now I'm good, and Dad and my siblings need you more." The smile I give her is filled with love. "Can you imagine what the house looks like or what they've all been eating while you've been here? Dad struggles to make toast." My try at humor wins a laugh from her.

"You're right. I should get back to the farm. I just want to make sure you'll be okay." Offering her comfort, like she's done for me a thousand times, I squeeze her hand.

"Ma, I'm good. I can do almost everything independently. I'm not on pain pills anymore, and I have George to take me anywhere I need to go. I can order groceries or already-prepared meals. And since my teammates are back in town for a few days, they're planning to stop over for a visit."

She nods, accepting my reasoning. "But are you sure? Won't you be lonely?"

Breaking my leg has been a test, and on most days I'm passing, but there are days where I feel like I'm drowning. This experience has shaken my physical and mental health. Thankfully, some of my teammates have been by to see me, and others have texted to check in. Unfortunately, those check-ins haven't been frequent because of the hockey schedule. Ma has mentioned several times I'm not as happy or carefree as usual. She's worried about me, and I get it, but I think I came up with an idea that may be the answer to everything.

"Actually, I think during all my downtime, I'm going to take some college classes online. Last night, I was looking, and I found some that interest me."

She perks up at that. "That sounds exciting. How does that work?"

"I sign up for classes, and they send all the materials to me. I submit the assignments online, and at test time, there is a time slot where the exam is proctored live."

Excited, her eyes brighten. "That's incredible. But what if you have trouble or need to do more research for an assignment?"

Yawning, I cover my mouth. Last night, I stayed up too late reading all the FAQs about the classes at one of the most well-known online schools. "The professors offer office hours just like if you were taking a traditional college class. The only difference is that it's virtual. Chicago has plenty of libraries I can go to if I need to do research or if I need a break from my house."

She squeezes my hand. "I'm proud of you, Jethro. Instead of letting your broken leg get you down, you're embracing the opportunity to better yourself." Her corresponding smile makes me feel a hundred feet tall. "Well then, I guess I need to book a flight home," she says as she gathers our dishes. Watching her, I feel my heart dip. A tinge of sadness wraps itself around me. *I'm sure going to miss her.*

Two days later, I practically fly off my couch

when I hear my doorbell. *Company*. Ma was right. It is lonely in my house all by myself 24/7. My saving grace is when the guys stopped by two days after she'd left.

"Ace!" the group of teammates huddled on my porch call out when I answer the door. Scooting back with my trusty crutches, Lucifer and Beelzebub, I welcome them in. Looking around, it's still relatively clean since Ma left. Proud of myself, I smile. *I'm killing this lone recovery thing.*

Rocco saunters in like he owns the place, and heads straight for my kitchen. He has a determined look on his face, and I bet I know why. He stopped by a few times while Ma was here, and she always had something delicious to share. Shutting the door, I crutch behind him as fast and effectively as possible while asking, "Where are you going?"

"The kitchen." His clipped answer only makes me more suspicious he's hunting for any treats that were left behind.

"Whoa, Ace, what's the hurry?" Josh calls out as I hobble past him, muttering under my breath.

"Just checking on something," I say as I turn into the kitchen, where I spot Rocco on the prowl. Stopping, I watch as he looks over the countertop and checks the pantry and the fridge. When he doesn't find what he's looking for, he growls. I laugh. He whips around and glares at me while stalking over until we're toe-to-toe.

"Don't hold out on me, Ace. Where are they?" I laugh again, and Rocco grows more agitated.

"What is going on?" Lucas asks.

"Dude, Rocco, calm down," Mika adds.

Rocco turns on them. "Calm down? You don't understand, man. His mom makes the best chocolate chip cookies I've ever had. I mean, melt-in-your-mouth, taste-of-heaven, utter perfection chocolate chip cookies, and I know there is no way she went back to the farm without leaving him a batch or three." Rocco turns back to me. "Where are they?" He sounds deranged, and I grin at him.

"If they're as good as you say, I need to try one," Mika says, and Lucas nods his agreement.

Josh, the health nut, shakes his head. "You guys are ridiculous."

Looking like a junkie who needs his next hit, Rocco's eyes plead for mercy, so I give in and tell him, "They're in the freezer, but you can only have a few. That's my stash, and I need it to last me a while." Other than Josh, the guys each pull several from the freezer and have them demolished within minutes. Sounds of their appreciative moans fill my kitchen. When they're done, they all wear the same sugar-induced, dopey grin.

"What food are we ordering while we play the PlayStation?" Josh asks.

"Wings," we all answer.

Rocco whips out his phone. "I got it." After a few

minutes, he says, "They'll be here in thirty. You guys get the gaming system set up? I have to take care of a mattress."

Our afternoon is filled with games, wings, and laughter. When the guys are heading out, I get a fist bump from them each. "Thanks, guys. This is just what I needed after being homebound for weeks. Good luck with the game tomorrow. I'll be watching."

Lounging in my bed after they leave, I feel exhaustion setting in. It's been a while since I exerted that much energy. But even then, my fatigue doesn't dampen the happiness I feel in my heart. I have the best friends.

Chapter 9

Janica

"Fiddlesticks," I exclaim as I hustle up the granite stairs of the library. It's the second day in a row that I've been late for work. And when I say that never happens, it's true. In the two years I've worked here, I've only been late... A quick look at my watch shows it's five minutes past nine, and my heart drops. Twice now. I grind my teeth together as I swipe my badge through the time clock. It flashes the time brightly, almost mockingly.

"Trevor," I growl under my breath as I head out to the circulation desk. Because I was running late this morning, I didn't have the chance to do my hair or even make myself a to-go coffee. I run my fingers down the plum-colored corduroy overall bib dress I have on. Because it's winter, and the library is drafty, I wore a creamy white turtleneck underneath it.

"Don't you look adorable," Veronica, the library's

head librarian, clucks as soon as she sees me. Adjusting her glasses, I grimace. *Adorable?* Any woman in her mid-thirties should know better than to call me that. At only twenty-one, I hate being referred to like I'm a child.

Quickly wiping the displeasure from my face, I reply, "Thank you. I'm sorry I'm late again."

"Trevor?" she questions as she tosses her red hair over her shoulder.

I roll my eyes and groan. "He turned off my alarm... again. It's a complete mystery to me. And when I asked him about it yesterday, he just shrugged. I mean, he's been coming to bed at zero dark thirty almost the entire year we've lived together. Being a gamer, most nights he plays online late into the evening. I've accepted it, but I don't understand why it's now an issue and why he suddenly thinks our phones look alike."

Veronica gasps. "How can he get into your phone to turn off your alarm? Don't you have face ID or a passcode set up?"

"Of course I do," I defend myself.

"So, he knows your code?" she asks, her face pinched in disgust. *What's that about?* I know Veronica is a man-hater, and rightly so after what her ex put her through, but Trevor and I have been together for two years, living together for one. Of course he has my code.

I look at her, confused. "Yes, so what? I trust him. We share things like that."

She puts her hands on her hips, reminding me of when Mom would question me when I was a teenager and she didn't believe me. Suddenly chilled to the bone, a shiver runs down my back and my shoulders drop. "I'm just curious. What other things do you share?"

Nervous and feeling like I'm being interrogated, I stutter, "Y-you know, the usual things like N-netflix or DoorDash accounts."

"I see." Her tone is laced with emotion, but when she folds her arms across her chest, her disproval is unquestionable.

Silently, we just look at each other, and finally, I speak up. "Veronica, what are you trying to say?"

"Janica, do you have the code for his phone?" My stomach churns. Why would she be asking that? What is she alluding to? I don't answer because I don't know what my answer means. "Well, do you?"

I forcibly swallow past the discomfort lodged in my throat, and lick my dry lips. When I open my mouth to tell her no, nothing comes out. Staring at her for answers, I don't miss the flash in her eyes or the way her shoulders fall. She's disappointed. *In me?* Shaking my head, I answer my question with a no. I pause. Her words have made me question things. *Why don't I have access to his phone?* I have nothing to hide from him, so I never cared if he was on my phone.

My mind works overtime as I consider him and our relationship. My heart plummets. There's no use arguing. It's been one-sided for a long time. Realization of that slaps me in the face. *Why is that? Is he hiding something?* Suspicion rises in me. I need to sort this out. If it's nothing, Trevor won't have any trouble explaining why he's never given me access and then my brain will be satisfied.

What would he be hiding? Things are making little sense, so I confront the facts Trevor is my first actual boyfriend. In high school, I'd dated some, but the boys were so juvenile. I longed for someone more mature. Someone I could have a normal, thoughtful conversation with.

Not long after graduation, I met Trevor at my job. A few times a week, he would come into the diner where I worked the lunch shift. Each time, he found his way into my section. Over a few weeks of basic get-to-know-you conversation, he asked me out. He's a few years older than me, and he'd finished college in Wisconsin and moved back to Chicago to be close to family. *He was a catch.* College educated, gainfully employed, living on his own, and handsome. He was everything I'd been dreaming of. He supported my dreams of working in a library and seemingly loved everything about me. It didn't take long for me to fall head over heels for him.

Since my parents didn't support my career aspirations of being a librarian, I'd taken a year off college to work and save money. Shortly after we started dating, I saw a job posting for a library assistant and I jumped at it. Veronica practically hired me on the spot. With my new job that paid more than waitressing, I quickly saved up for a part-time course load.

At that point, Trevor and I had been dating for a year and things were serious. He asked me to move in with him and, of course, I said yes. I also enrolled in some online general courses. It seemed like the pieces of my life were falling into place. I had a great job. I was taking classes to earn the degree I wanted, and I had an understanding and supportive boyfriend.

"What?" I choked out in disbelief. She couldn't mean what she was suggesting about Trevor. *My Trevor.* The man who's been by my side through it all. Who packed me a sack lunch on my first day of work at the library. The man who always has my favorite study snacks in the pantry. Well, sometimes.

"M-my ex..." Veronica stumbles over her words. "He... umm... he didn't let me have his code either. And one day he'd mistakenly left it unlocked when he went to the bathroom, and I discovered why." Tears fill my friend's eyes, and my heart breaks for her. *But her Mike is nothing like my Trevor.* I go to say something and she holds up her hand. "I know my past clouds my judgment on men, but recently you've mentioned ways that Trevor has been acting strange, almost secretive, and I can't help but wonder."

She's right. Trevor has been pulling away and

acting strange, but every time I ask him about it, he deflects. He told me he's been stressed over a new classified project at work. On multiple occasions, he explained that was why he was working longer, later hours and having hushed phone conversations.

Worry swims in my gut. *So what's going on?* Shaking my head defiantly, I push her argument aside. "I don't have any evidence of what you're implying, and until I do, I'm choosing to believe there are other explanations to consider."

Her expression falls. "I hope you're right, Janica. For your sake." I force a smile. *Me too.*

"I trust Trevor..." My hesitant voice drops off as I consider all my friend has said. Doubt has my stomach knotted with anxiety and fear, a near-constant nagging weighing on my heart. I hear a click, click, click noise echo through the library.

"Excuse me, ma'am," someone says, the deep, sexy timbre of his voice stroking the unknown desire in my core.

"Ma'am?" I question. "How old do you think...?" My words stop dead, and the question I'd been asking falls flat when I turn to find the most gorgeous man I've ever seen. He's taller than me, which isn't saying much considering I'm only 5'2". His chocolate-brown hair is short and spikey. When he smiles at me, I notice he has dimples that are accentuated by the barely-there beard he has. Even though it's faint, I can tell it's well-kept, making him look rugged and sexy. Standing next to our high-topped desk, I take in his impressive build. He's wearing an athletic-fit shirt that hugs all his muscles. He is in amazing shape. I wonder what he does for a living. My gaze traces over his form, noticing he looks incredibly strong. The last thing I notice is that he looks close to my age. Maybe he's a college student.

Composing myself, I offer him a smile and say, "Is there something I can help you with?"

He smiles back. "Actually, yes. I'm taking a few online college classes and I need someplace quiet to study. Can you point me to a good spot?"

Stepping around the side of the desk, I say, "I can do you one better. I'll show you a hidden gem."

"Thanks." He holds his arm out. "Ladies first." *What a gentleman.*

Seeing that he's on crutches, I make sure I take things slowly. Pointing to his leg, I ask, "Can I ask what happened?"

He laughs. "Sure. I broke my leg in two places playing hockey."

"That sounds painful. I'm sorry."

Shrugging, his response surprises me. "It happens. But now I have unlimited free time to take some classes."

"Were you not enrolled in classes before?" I ask, confused. I was sure he was a college student.

Shaking his head no, he replies, "I didn't have time before I broke my leg. Hockey is my job, but with a broken leg, I can't work."

Hockey is his job. I stop because we're at the spot, and my mouth drops open. "Wait. Do you play professional hockey?"

He smirks, making one of his dimples pop. "I do. I'm Ace Walker of the Chicago Steel. It's nice to meet you..." This guy and his manners. I've never met anyone so polite.

My palms go sweaty. "I've never met a famous person before. My name is Janica Anderson. It's nice to meet you too." I point to the table and chair off in the corner, mostly hidden from view. "This is it. I'll get out of your hair so you can get to work. If you need anything, I'll be at the circulation desk." He gives me a blank stare. I smile and say, "Where you first found me." He nods.

Then he rests his crutches against the table, shifts, and lifts his backpack off his back. The loud reverberated clunk it makes when he sets it on the table makes me laugh. "Let me guess, you have a Stanley in there?"

He laughs. "Is it that obvious?"

I just smile at him. "Okay, I'm going to get out of your hair. If you need a bathroom or a refill, just go down that way and you'll see the bottle-filling station and restrooms."

"This is a magnificent spot, Janica. Thanks for all the library insider tips. I appreciate them. I can guarantee I'll be spending a lot of time here over the next few months, and I look forward to running into you."

Then he smiles again and adds a wink. *Danger. Retreat.*

Before I give myself any time to process that, I turn and leave. Quickly. When I'm out of sight, I practically run back to Veronica at the circulation desk. Flushed and out of breath, when I move behind the desk we share, she purses her lips at me. But she says nothing.

"What?" My voice comes out high and squeaky as I question her.

"Dear, you're blushing. Who is that guy?"

"Who?" I feign confusion.

She rolls her and puts her hands on her hips like she's challenging me. "The hunk with the incredible body who you took to your secret study spot?"

"It's not my secret study spot. It's just out of the way and overlooked," I defend.

Veronica clucks her tongue. "In the two years you've worked here, I don't think you've ever shared that spot with anyone. Why today? Why him?" Her waggling eyebrows tell me everything she's thinking.

I go to defend myself, but I can't. She's right. I don't share my spot with anyone. So then why did I this time? Maybe it was his kind face or his polite demeanor. He seemed like a genuinely nice guy. In fact, after our brief conversation, I've already learned so much about him. But I'm excited about the opportunity to learn more. It's nice to make new friends.

Chapter 10

Ace

When I decided to go to the library today, I didn't know my life would change. Walking up to the circulation desk, I see two women, neither of which fits my image of the stereotypical librarian. One looks to be in her early thirties and the other is probably about my age. Neither is wearing a sweater or orthotics. I notice the older one does wear glasses, but they're stylish and don't hang from a chain around her neck. The other woman caught my eye right away, though. She is hands down the most beautiful woman I have ever seen.

My heart pounds in my chest as I explain why I'm here. She leads me to her secret study spot. While I follow behind her, I memorize the sway of her hips. She has the most perfect ass—high and tight. Her smooth, long brown hair swishes as she makes her way through the stacks.

"This is it," she announces when we arrive at a small maple table that's tucked away in the back.

When she tells me she has to return to work, I'm sad to see her go. She's so friendly, and after being trapped in my house with just my ma, it's nice to talk with another adult.

I remove my laptop from my bag, setting it on the worn wooden table in front of me. As I power it up, my gaze roams around the space, noticing the age of all the furniture in this sacred tucked-away study spot. The dull colors of the fabric on the chairs suggest they've been here since way before I was born.

Settling in, I begin my first assignments. They aren't especially hard, just time-consuming. Rolling my stiff shoulders a while later, I flinch. A crick has formed in my neck from the way I've been sitting hunched over my computer. I lean back and rub at my sore muscles, trying to release them. When I move to neck rolls and stretches, I see Janica nearby. With her unaware of my perusal, I watch as she gracefully rises on her toes to return a book to its designated spot. She looks like a ballerina in pose. Her body is a dream, full of lines that scream beauty and grace. I watch her file several books, and no matter how many times I tell myself to stop gawking at her, I can't. She's mesmerizing.

After she finishes the section she's in, she returns to the cart of books and pushes it toward me. Panicked I've been caught staring, I quickly switch my attention back to my laptop. The screen's black, like it's in sleep mode. I slam it shut, not wanting her to know I was paying more attention to her than my classwork. Looking guilty, I flash her my best smile.

"Hello, Ace. Are you getting a lot accomplished?" she asks.

"I am," I reply while nodding my head. "Thanks for showing me this spot. You were right. It is special."

Chapter 11

Janica

He keeps coming back. I wasn't sure he was serious when he said he'd be here often, but he wasn't kidding. I think he's here almost as often as me, and I'm an employee, paid to be here. Just thinking about that, I question if he's struggling with his courses.

Peeking around the shelf, I look to see if Ace is in our spot. *It's not our spot. We don't have a spot. We aren't a we.* Clearing my head, I slowly approach the table he's occupied for days. "Hi, Ace. Fancy seeing you here again," I whisper, being mindful of the library's noise rules. *Why did I just say that?* Instead of sounding cool, I sound like a creepy stalker who's been lying in wait. I haven't been, mind you. It's just it's tough to be stealthy with crutches. Seeing that the library is notoriously quiet, my ears are well-trained to notice out-of-the-ordinary sounds. Or when Ace arrives.

Ace laughs. "I've been working on an Introduction to Psychology assignment that's taking longer than I expected. When my professor explained the assignment, I thought it sounded like a piece of cake. But that hasn't been the case." With a furrowed brow, he pulls a gummy worm from a bag and tosses it in his mouth. His lips pucker and he shivers.

"Sour?" I ask with a grin, and he nods.

After he's finished chewing, he explains, "I got them so they'd keep me engaged in my work. I'm discovering the quiet of the library is like a pillow luring me to naptime."

Pointing to the bag, I ask "Is it working?"

He frowns. "No, not like I planned." He holds the bag out. "Want a few?"

"These are my favorite. Thank you," I say as I reach for some. The bag quickly closes around my hand and he makes aggressive chomping noises. Startled, I shriek. Ace laughs at my reaction. I laugh too, knowing it wasn't scary, just unexpected. Once he releases my hand from the snack monster, I shake my candy worm at him. Smirking, he leans forward and bites it in half. I drop the other half in my mouth, then cross my arms. Mocking disgust. I say, "That was the butt end you just ate. I hope you enjoy it."

He pats his belly. "Delicious."

Laughing, I dramatically roll my eyes and ask, "So, what's your assignment?"

Flipping through the composition notebook in front of him, I see the pages are packed with what looks like illegible handwriting. "How do you read that? It looks like scribbles."

He just smiles at me. "It's my sleep journal. I've had to record my dreams both in the middle of the night and in the morning. Then I look for patterns. It's messy because I'm half asleep when I'm writing the dream."

"That sounds neat. What have you learned?" I question before I put another gummy worm in my mouth. The citric acid and sugar combination makes my mouth water.

"I actually had a lot of dreams about the game where I broke my leg. I guess they're more nightmare. I wake up all agitated, breathing heavily, and sweaty. Honestly, it's been tough to relive. But in the morning, when I'm able to look back, I see the opportunity it has gifted me."

"What do you mean about an opportunity?" Looking at him, I need further explanation. It isn't tough to recall the last person who had something bad happen to them. But they didn't look for a blessing or lesson in it. They just complained a lot about how life wasn't fair.

Ace motions to another chair at the table, inviting me to join him. I twist my hands in front of me, nervous that I probably should get back to the circulation desk. But I really enjoy talking to Ace, and I'm curious to hear what he has to say. Justifying to myself that it's the only break I'll take all day, I sink into the hard wooden chair he's offered. I can't explain why, but it feels downright decadent, and a moan falls from my lips. Embarrassed, I peer up at him. His eyes have gone wide and his Adam's apple bobs. *Is he nervous?* A few seconds pass and he still has said nothing.

Worried I've misread the situation, I whisper, "Am I bothering you? I didn't mean to disturb your studying, but what you were saying sounded interesting."

He grimaces. "You weren't disturbing me at all. I like it when you stop by." He shifts in his chair like he's uncomfortable. My anxiety gets the better of me. *Should I leave?* I look at him for other signs of discomfort. I see his cheeks turn pink. "Uh, what were we talking about? I lost my train of thought."

Unsure if he's appeasing me or not, I let out a nervous laugh. "You were going to tell me about why you think breaking your leg is an opportunity."

He adjusts his ball cap, flipping it backward, and our eyes lock. Before me are the darkest brown eyes I've ever seen. If you stared at them for too long, it would be hard not to get lost in them. The heat of being under his intense focus is mindboggling. Unidentifiable thoughts stir up chaos in my mind. Shaking my head to clear it, I break our connection. Just as if someone dumped a bucket of ice-cold water on me, I shiver.

Ace clears his throat, and my gaze flicks to him. He still looks nervous. Then a thought hits me. *Maybe his explanation is embarrassing.* Before I can ask, he starts talking, explaining that breaking his leg has allowed him to pursue college. I must have had a confused look on my face because he adds that college wasn't an option for him because the Steel drafted him straight from high school. *He must be an incredible player.*

"The coolest thing about it is when I'm finally able to put weight on my leg and am no longer in need of Lucifer and Beelzebub, I can spend some hours volunteering in the community." *Wait, what?*

"Lucifer and Beelzebub?" I mumble. Did I miss something? He's too nice to be into devil worship, so how does that fit in?

Ace lets out a hearty laugh that makes me smile. "I call my crutches Lucifer and Beelzebub because they're devils who torture me constantly." He pauses, and I remain quiet. Smirking, he says, "Wait. You didn't think I worshipped Satan, did you?" The only thing I can do is shrug my shoulders. "Rest your mind, dear friend. I am not a pentagram-wearing Satanist, just a cowboy from Minnesota."

Dramatically, I wipe my brow. "What a relief."

Looking at my watch, I notice I've taken a longer break than I planned. "I need to get back to work. It was great talking to you. Good luck with your paper.

Thank you for the sour worms. I haven't had them in forever. I forgot how much I love them."

"I really enjoyed talking to you too. Maybe after work, we could grab a coffee?" He follows his request with a sexy smile that really shouldn't make my heart beat faster, but it does. *What does that mean?*

"I... I have a boyfriend," I mumble before I tuck my tail and scoot away. As I'm fleeing, one thought fills my mind. *I wish Trevor looked at me the way Ace just did. Has he ever?* The more I push that question, the tougher it is to deny the truth. I've been ignoring it for too long, but after meeting Ace, I'm suddenly aware of it. It's glaringly obvious Trevor doesn't look at me the way he used to. But even then, it was never as intense as Ace.

Standing there only inches from him, I'd felt my body grow warm under his perusal. The smile he wore spoke of his enjoyment of what he was seeing. His eyes had darkened as they tracked over my body, and even though I'd felt on display, I liked it. I liked his attention. He didn't hide his attraction. His focused look made me feel wanted. *When was the last time I felt that?*

Confronting that question is painful. I know I deserve to feel wanted, and I also know I haven't been getting it from my boyfriend, the man who is too occupied with video games or working all night long. His interest in me has waned, and I feel stuck. If he isn't going to love me, I need to do it for myself. I just have to figure out how. It's going to take some courage to demand what I deserve.

Thankfully, Veronica isn't at the desk when I return; I'm not ready to handle any sort of inquisition. And that's exactly what I know it would be. She isn't Trevor's biggest fan, but Ace has her swooning. I understand why, but that doesn't sit well with me. I'm jealous she can look and fantasize without guilt, and just thinking that makes me feel incredibly remorseful.

After my shift, I drag myself home. "Trevor, are you here?" I call out when I shut the door. The silence of our apartment is deafening and not what my overactive brain needs. When we first moved in together, Trevor used to beat me home. That was until six months ago when he started working late on some "top-secret" projects. When he first told me about them, I was incredibly proud of him for everything he was accomplishing at work. Now, it's become the reason we hardly see each other. When I try to ask about the extra hours he works, he becomes defensive and pushes back, explaining to me how important it is. How important *he* is. I've tried to get him to tell me about it, but it's so complex, and my mind just spins.

Leaving my shoes by the door, I head into the kitchen, wondering if he'll be home for dinner tonight. Most nights, I'm eating and going to bed alone. It's become quite lonely. It seems like I hardly see him. Even on the weekends, he's different, taking work calls from his assistant and making spontaneous trips to the office. It's all become a bit too much, and it's something I know we need to talk about. And soon. I'm not willing to live this way anymore. I deserve better, and it's time I did something about it. *But when am I going to see him?* My thoughts drift back to my conversation with Veronica, and my stomach twists. Trevor is up to something. My gut agrees, and I'm going to figure it out. After a quick text to him I have my answer.

ME

How was your day? Will you be home
for dinner? Love you.

TREVOR

Shit day. I'm working late again. I
don't know when I'll be home. Got to
get back to my special project.

Reading over Trevor's text, Veronica's recent comments pop up like the thought bubbles in comics. And my mind can't help but question. I know I'm missing something, but what?

Chapter 12

Ace

Shortly after I finish my dream paper, I pack up my backpack and slide it onto my back. Groaning, I grab Lucifer and Beelzebub and wedge them under my armpits for the slow crutch through the library. Right now, I wish I could power walk because I'm avoiding running into Janica. I'm mortified. After my failed attempt to ask her for a coffee date, I need to save face. Things became awkward between us when she told me she had a boyfriend and then bolted away. Because, surprise, surprise, the utterly gorgeous woman I met only weeks ago, whom my body already craves seeing every day, has a boyfriend. *Fuck me.*

Dodging around enormous stacks and trying my best to avoid her desk is a bit of an art, but I manage without further injuring my leg. Only my ego is bruised from my daily activities. Veronica, her coworker, whisper shouts, "Bye, Ace. Have a good day.

96

See you tomorrow," when I pop out of an aisle a foot away. I give her a nod and then Janica moves into view, a frown covering her beautiful face. My chest aches like I've been punched in it repeatedly. When our gazes connect, I feel like I've been burned, and panic rears its ugly head. As quickly as I can manage, I retreat, moving away with my head buried between my shoulders, feeling defeated.

Outside, as I wait for George to arrive, I suck in the dry winter air. The crisp breeze is refreshing, but it does nothing to still my mind. Thoughts of Janica overwhelm it. Cataloging all the information I have about her makes me smile. *She has a boyfriend.* Even though it's only been a few weeks, I feel like we have an undeniable connection. But where do we go from here? *She has a boyfriend.* Since dating her is obviously off the table, I decide I can be the next best thing—a friend. Maybe she won't want that, though? Over the next few days, I'm going to define what that means before I do anything. Or at least before I show back up at the library.

Almost a week goes by, and my homework is piling up. While I've been home, hiding out, I've binged so much Netflix. Only one series actually held enough of my attention to finish. Knowing I need to get back to the library to do multiple assignments, I text George, asking for a ride the next day.

Lying in bed, my thoughts drift to the off-limits, gorgeous, curvy brunette whose smile electrifies every part of me. *Just friends.* I can do that. Although, I suspect it will be harder than I think.

Following a sleepless night, I make my way through the front doors of the municipal library at ten thirty. I wave at Veronica. Her expression moves from stunned to smirking in seconds. *Why?* Confusion covers my face, and she lets out a laugh, shaking her head. *What am I missing?* Seconds later, Janica walks up to stand next to Veronica, her arms laden with thick textbooks, a soft smile on her face, whispering something so quietly I can only see her lips moving. When Veronica nods in my direction with a raised eyebrow, I watch as Janica lifts her head, glancing my way, surprise covering her beautiful face, like she wasn't expecting to see me here again. I shouldn't have missed her as much as I have. Happy to see her, I smile. Veronica elbows her and says something out of the side of her mouth. Janica's cheeks turn pink. Is she embarrassed? Instead of going to their shared desk, I bypass it and head over to the spot she showed me a few weeks ago. *Man, these chairs suck.* After living on my microfiber couch the last few days, my ass is looking for a soft landing, not a bone-crushingly hard one. *How the hell did I spend so much time on these the past month?* As if a slap in the face, realization sets in. I wanted to see Janica. Knowing I need to get to work, I shrug off my backpack. I've barely pulled my laptop from it when Veronica appears.

"Hey, Ace. Haven't seen you in a few days," she says.

I scratch my head. *What do I say?* I can't admit I have an intense crush on Janica and I was avoiding her. Stumbling through my words, I answer, "I needed a break... from... umm, homework."

Looking over at her, I see she has her arms crossed over her black pantsuit and her eyes are slitted, making me feel like I'm being interrogated.

"What's up, Veronica? Do you have something you want to say?" She doesn't seem to mind confrontation and gives me a humorless chuckle. Resting back in my chair, I'm ready for whatever she's about to dish out.

In a hushed tone, she answers, "As a matter of fact, I do. I'm aware you asked Janica out on a coffee date and that she said no. She has a boyfriend who, between me and you, is a piece of work and not good enough for her. But she has to figure that out on her own. Pressure from either of us will do the exact opposite of what I think we both want to happen." Then she smiles like the Cheshire cat. *Damn. I need to remember to stay on her good side.*

I swallow hard, then rasp, "What do we want to happen?"

"I've seen the way you watch her. Hell, I've heard the way you make her laugh. I don't even know you, but I sense you are a thousand times better than Trevor." I force a smile at her compliment, but inside, my anger is building. *That's the asshat's name? The* one who is completely undeserving of the most incredible woman I've ever met?

"Why are you telling me this?" I ask. My mind is desperate for her to say that Janica likes me too.

Leaning in, she confesses, "I care about Janica. She's my friend, and even though I don't think relationships are worth it, I know she does, and she deserves better than what she's got. Maybe that's you, maybe it's not. But I sure as hell know it's not that sniveling weasel." Then she walks away.

My laptop remains closed in front of me as I stare into the void, questioning what to think, feel or do regarding Janica.

"Morning, Ace." *Speak of the devil.* Her sweet, almost dreamlike voice fills my ears, making my chest warm. When the smell of citrus hits my nose, my brain registers how close she is. Blinking my eyes into focus, I turn and there she stands in tight black leggings that show all her heavenly curves. She's got on a flowy white cotton top that reminds me of an angel. I bite my lower lip, fighting back the urge to groan. I almost drop to my knees in thankful prayer when I notice the calf-high black and white cowboy boots. *This woman is perfect for me. Made for me.*

Swallowing down my emotion, my simple response of "hi" comes out deep and gravely. A blush appears, covering her cheeks and making her even sexier. I can almost picture her in my bed, wearing nothing but those boots as I continue to stain her gorgeous body with blush-worthy acts. *We're just friends.* Try telling that to my cock, who's trying his hardest to bust through my athletic pants. I shift myself forward in an attempt to fully hide my overactive waist under the wooden library table. Normally, thoughts of studying and homework are a boner killer, but not when she's around. She invades all my senses, making it tough to concentrate.

"I haven't seen you here in a couple of days. Is everything okay?" she asks, her voice heavy with concern.

Before I answer, I force my body to relax. "After spending almost every day here since I started my classes, I needed a few days to chill." My heart flinches when I see her shoulders fall. *Did she make the connection that I needed some space after she told me about her boyfriend?*

She wrings her hands together like she's nervous or uncomfortable. And at that moment, I want nothing more than to grab her, pull them apart, and interlace them with mine. But I don't. I just sit and stare at her, reminding myself repeatedly that she's taken. It doesn't matter if her boyfriend is a douche or not, she's his, and there's nothing I can do about that.

Lost in thought, I barely hear her speak. "Oh, okay. I just wanted to say hi and say it was nice to see you here again." She goes to walk away and I call out her name. When she turns back, she crosses into a shaft of sunlight coming through a nearby window. It makes her appear angelic. I temporarily forget why I called her back. "Yes?" she says, her voice filled with hope. My eyes trace over her glossy pink lips. *Are they as soft as they look?*

"I got you something," I mumble, reaching into my bag. Her eyes glisten as she sees what I've pulled out. It's her very own bag of sour gummy worms. "Here you go. I remember you said they were your favorite, and you hadn't had them in a while."

Stepping closer, she takes the bag from me, and our fingers brush. Chills run up my spine from our first touch. It feels amazing, but it doesn't even compare to the smile stretching across her face. It's more beautiful than any sunset I've ever seen.

"You got me a pack of my favorite gummy worms? Why?"

Her confused tone disappoints me, and I hang my head, admitting, "I know it's lame, but I hoped it would make you smile."

"Ace, this isn't lame at all." When I hear her surprised response, I lift my head. She's smiling at me and my heart soars. "It's one of the nicest and most thoughtful gifts anyone's ever given me. I don't have the right words to tell you what this means to me, but thank you doesn't even come close."

Hearing her say that giving her a bag of gummy worms is the nicest thing anyone has ever done for her makes me angry. That can't be right. This woman is amazing. She needs to be adored, showered with love.

My heart hurts knowing that hasn't been the case. Needing a connection, I look deep into her eyes, and what I see surprises me. There is so much emotion swirling in her beautiful brown orbs. *What is she thinking? Feeling?* It's easy to get lost in them. I notice they aren't as dark as mine, but if you look close enough, you can see a black speck in her left iris. It's unique and special, just like her.

"I'm glad you like them. Your smile is thanks enough" Her cheeks turn from pink to red, and my heart skips a beat. I just discovered my life's goal: To make this woman blush, repeatedly.

Chapter 13

Janica

I wasn't kidding when I told Ace that giving me a bag of sour gummy worms was one of the most thoughtful gifts I've ever received. My childhood had been average. During the summers or other school breaks, when my peers were running around and exploring, or doing whatever they pleased, I was enrolled in whichever camp my mom could find at the last minute. It didn't matter if it interested me or not. Her social life was too busy to be interrupted by a child at home. My parents weren't bad people. They just looked at having a child as a check to be marked off some prestigious list that their social group revered. I learned at a young age not to expect things from people because they often let you down. Instead of waiting for the proverbial shoe to drop, I just had very low expectations of those around me. I guess that's why a bag of my favorite candy lit me up inside, making me feel like I'd won the jackpot.

Riding the train home that day, I pull the bag from my purse and trace my fingers along it. I can't get over how kind Ace was to think of me. I know it's not an extravagant gift, but to me, it means so much more. Maybe that's why it feels like I have a thousand butter-flies flittering in my stomach and every time I think of the smile he'd given me when he handed them to me makes my heart beat faster. Perhaps it's the burst of electricity I felt rush up my arm when our fingers touched. I didn't imagine that, did I? Rubbing my fingertips together, I swear I still feel the slight tingle.

But in addition to the excitement, I also feel guilt. *Trevor.* I have a boyfriend, and I shouldn't feel this way. The trouble is, I don't know if all these new feel-ings I'm experiencing are because of the thoughtful-ness of the gift or who the giver was. "It doesn't matter, Janica," I reprimanded myself. Great, now I'm one of those people riding the train, talking to herself. *Ugh.* Not wanting to think about it anymore, I slip the gummy worms back into my bag and stare out the window until my stop.

Heavy with guilt, I feel weighed down as I drag myself into the apartment I share with Trevor. Silence surrounds me, making me feel even worse. Uncertainty tugs at my heart. Trevor's behavior over the last few weeks has me questioning things. I struggle to remember the last time we had dinner together or even slept next to each other. Having sex is another thing.

Two weekends ago, Trevor came home drunk on a Saturday night. I woke up to him stumbling through the apartment.

"Hey, babe," he'd slurred as he walked toward the bed, peeling off his shirt. "I've missed you and I want to show you how much." At his words, my stomach dropped. With my suspicions heightened, there was no way I was going to be intimate with him. Muttering a string of curses, he struggled to get his pants unbuttoned.

As calmly as I could, I say, "Trevor, I think you just need to go to sleep. You're drunk."

"I'm fine," he growls, and goose bumps covered my body. My pulse picked up.

Pulling my knees to my chest, I firmly say, "No, you're not."

His head snapped up, and he glared at me. "You're telling me I'm not fine. I came home wanting to have sex with my girlfriend and you're saying 'no, go to bed'? What am I, a fucking child?" Spittle flew out of his mouth as he yelled at me.

Shaking my head, I tried to calm him down. "I think it's late and you've had a lot to drink. It's better just to go to sleep and see what tomorrow brings."

His face turned red. "What tomorrow brings? What the fuck are you talking about? I just came home to get my dick wet. What a waste." He grabbed his shirt off the ground, muttering as he stalked out of the room. What the hell? Assuming he's pissed and going to crash on the sofa, I rolled my shoulders, trying to get myself to relax from our heated exchange. Before I could even change positions, the front door slammed.

That night, Trevor had blown in like a tornado, demanding sex, and when I said no, he stormed out. It's just another thing to add to my growing list of suspicions against him. I got up out of bed and walked to the window. I saw Trevor's car parked in the lot. Even though it's dark outside, I can see he's in it, likely passed out. Breathing a sigh of relief, I'm relieved he won't hurt anyone else tonight.

Feeling confused is a constant lately when it comes to our relationship, and I'm at my limit. I know I deserve better. Staying with Trevor is familiar, despite how uncomfortable it's been making me feel recently. He was my first everything and I don't know how to shut my feelings for him off. It's like he'll always hold a part of me, and until I know how to survive without that piece, I'll always be tethered to him. I know changes need to be made, but I have to get strong enough first.

Lying down in bed, I give myself a little pep talk. *You'll be okay. Stay true to you.* Recently, I started giving myself pep talks about what I want in my life. I know I have to do more growing before I'll be able to make changes, but they'll happen, eventually.

As I embrace my new mantra, I feel something

prickle against my skin. Looking out the window, I see the rain falling. In the distance, lightning flashes. A shiver zips down my back. There's something in the air, and I have the feeling a storm is coming, but like I learned when I was little, a rainbow always follows. But weeks later, nothing has changed.

"Janica, can you work this coming Sunday in addition to your normal hours?" Veronica asks while staring at her computer the next morning.

Reaching over, I grab another stack of books that need to be shelved, and start arranging them in order. "Sure, that's fine," I answer. "I have nothing planned, so I might as well. With all the overtime hours Trevor is putting in, he likely won't be home either."

Veronica makes a disapproving noise in her throat, and I look at her. Her face is pinched tight. "Why does it look like you just sucked on a lemon?" I ask.

Removing her leopard-print cat eyeglasses, she frowns at me. "You and Trevor aren't doing anything leading up to the holidays?"

I shake my head. "He didn't mention anything other than having to work late." Suddenly cold, I pull my cranberry sweater tighter around me. I'm feeling vulnerable under her intense gaze.

Clucking her tongue, she mumbles something under her breath. I only catch "no good P.O.S." and I freeze. She isn't unwarranted in her dislike of him. If the roles were reversed, I'd be saying the same thing. In the two years I've known her, Veronica has always seemed more intuitive than most. It's obvious she doesn't like him, and I'm afraid I've armed her with enough ammo to fuel that fire. *Have I been unfairly representing him or us?* Weighing that thought carefully, I come to some conclusions. No, even though I probably overshared a few too many times, I tell her what's truly going on. I mean, come on, what are friends for if you can't be honest? Most of the time, it's just my feelings I share.

Over the last weeks and months, his lack of attention, touch, and presence have become undeniable. If he isn't willing to love me, I need to love myself and move on.

Veronica finishes her grumbling about my no-good boyfriend and turns to me. "So, what are you doing for Christmas? Are you going to see your parents?"

"Pfft." I snort, startling her. Her back goes ramrod straight as she side-eyes me. Unable to hold it in, my laughter bubbles up out of me. I pinch my lips, trying to hold everything in.

"Why are you laughing? What is so funny?" she questions.

Leaning over at the waist, I try to stop laughing and regulate my breathing. Once it's controlled, I straighten back up. "What's funny is you think my parents want me to come spend Christmas with them."

Her questioning look tells me she needs further explanation. "On Christmas Eve, they get together with their friends at their club. They drink and dine on an elegant duck dinner with all the fixings. It's very high-brow, and if you ask me, it isn't something I'd be interested in attending. Not that they'd invite me anyway. On actual Christmas Day, they're usually recovering from the holiday party hangovers, and I'd rather not be around for that."

She removes her glasses and gives me a sympathetic look. "Fine. What about plans with Trevor?"

I wave my hand in the air. "I don't care what he's up to. He's mentioned nothing to me, so I'm going to spend the day reading and pampering myself."

"On Christmas Day?" she questions, and I nod.

Her mouth falls open, and I'm tempted to push it closed when she says, "And you don't care what Trevor's doing?"

"Honestly, Veronica, I have plenty of suspicions about him and what he's been up to. And if my hunch is correct, I'd rather not spend my day with him anyway. I'm taking care of me."

"Why don't you just break up with him?"

I know she means well, but I'm tiring of her always acting like it's so easy. For me, it's not. After all we've been through, I feel like the decent thing would be to at least have a conversation with him. I'm not naïve and holding out hope that Trevor still wants me. I just want to walk away with my head held high. Unfortunately, time with him is so scarce that finding that right moment is proving difficult.

"It's complicated," I say before I push the book cart away.

Later, when I stop by the employee break room and check the schedule Veronica had been working on, I breathe a sigh of relief when I saw she's taking a few days off during the holidays. No doubt visiting her family upstate. I think she mentioned that, but I've been so distracted with my own worries, that I forgot to note the exact dates. Feeling like a terrible friend about how I left our last conversation, I head back to the desk we share, but she isn't around.

Sitting down, I busy myself indexing some new mafia romance. The series looks amazing, and it's by one of my favorite indie authors. I wonder if I could check them out before I have to shelve them. I mean, my nights are pretty quiet. I could use some spice to heat them up. Who doesn't love a trip to the underworld of the mafia to meet some powerful, dangerous, sexy alpha men?

By four, I still haven't seen Veronica, and texting her is my best bet.

ME

Hey, V. Sorry about how I handled our conversation earlier. I'm really stressed out. And I know I need to talk to Trevor, but it never seems to be the right time. I shouldn't have taken my frustration out on you. I'm sorry.

VERONICA

Hey, babe. No need to apologize. I understand you're in a difficult position. I shouldn't have pushed. I just want the best for you, and I hate to see you hurting. I hate you're spending Christmas alone.

ME

I won't be alone. I just unpacked several new romances that sound intriguing. I'm saying yes to a pair of dangerous alpha mafia men. Don't feel bad for me.

VERONICA

If you insist, but I want full book reviews when I get back. Love you, lady. See you in a few days. Call me if you need me.

ME

Call you for what? More batteries.? <hysterical laughing emoji>

VERONICA

<heart emoji>

The last hour of work passes quickly as I get myself set for the next day. With it being Christmas Eve, I'm scheduled to work half the day, and I know the library will be dead.

Today I wore my ugly Christmas sweater. It's a tribute to the eighties. In video game font, the text across the chest says *I closed my book to be here*, and it's surrounded by video game characters in holiday dress.

A few hours later, as I'm adding bar codes to new books, a noise draws my attention, and I stare into the familiar handsome face of my new friend. "Ace! Merry Christmas Eve. What are you doing at the library today?"

"Merry Christmas Eve, Janica. I was hoping to run into you."

My cheeks heat. "You were? Why?"

He laughs and places a gift bag in front of me. "This is for you. Merry Christmas."

Placing my hand on my chest, I say, "You shouldn't have." Pulling out the tissue paper, I find a five-pound bag of sour worms. And I let out a laugh. "You know you're helping me eat these, right?"

Nodding his head, he answers, "Definitely. It'll be fun to see how long the bag lasts."

"Where did you find a bag this big?" I ask.

Ace grins. "Amazon, of course." A few seconds later, he shuffles his feet like he's nervous.

One of my coworkers walks by on her way out, and says, "Bye, Janica. Merry Christmas," I wave at her, but my focus remains on him.

"Shit, are you closing? I need to get out of your hair," he says. His face looks sad, and I hate that.

"Yes, we're closing, but I was planning to get a cup of coffee at the café next door if you'd like to join me." His eyes light up and a smile spreads across his face.

"I'd love to, if you're sure."

"It'd be great to have company," I say while depositing the enormous bag of sour worms into my desk drawer before I log out of my computer and tidy up.

"Why didn't you go home to Minnesota for Christmas?" I ask him once we've ordered our drinks and are sitting in the deep-purple, crushed-velvet-covered chairs.

He takes a drink of his holiday roast before he answers. "I thought it would be too much of a hassle traveling, and I didn't want to make extra work for my folks."

Sniffing my peppermint mocha, because it's too hot for me to drink, I ask about what he'll miss most about Christmas on the farm.

Hanging his head, and with emotion thick in his voice, he whispers, "Everything." My heart aches for both of us. For what he's missing this year and what I've longed for my entire life.

"I'm sorry to make you sad."

He looks up at me. "It's okay. I'm just feeling sorry for myself. I miss my family. They're the absolute best, and the holidays won't be the same without them."

"I understand. If I had a great relationship with my parents, I'd be sad if I missed out on something too."

Looking confused, Ace tips his head sideways. "Aren't you from here? Won't you be spending tomorrow with your parents?"

I grimace. "I am from here, but growing up, my Christmases were probably the polar opposite of yours. My parents would rather celebrate the holidays with their society friends than me." I see him frown, and not wanting any pity, I say, "It's okay. I much prefer knowing how they'll behave, rather than being disappointed year after year."

"That's sad, but it makes sense. Besides, don't you celebrate with your boyfriend?"

Sure. I nod but say nothing. I take a drink of my peppermint mocha, and the rich flavor dances on my tongue. Sighing, I say out loud, "I don't know why I only order this during the holidays. The mix of mint and chocolate tastes good all year long."

Ace chuckles. We sit there for hours, talking and laughing. Before we head different ways, we exchange numbers after he insists he wants to check in and make sure I have a merry Christmas. *He's too sweet.*

After coffee with Ace, I stop off at the mom-and-pop store near my apartment, and grab a dipped beef sandwich for dinner. Standing in my kitchen and unwrapping the deli paper, my stomach growls in anticipation as the heavenly scents of oregano, basil, and onion fill my nostrils.

Trevor isn't home again. I'm not even surprised. "After the New Year, you'll have a conversation about this with him. You owe it to yourself," I tell myself as I settle on the couch. Picking up book one of this yummy new series, I snuggle in, wrapped in a soft fleece throw.

Many hours later, I turn the last page on my newest book boyfriend. Tracing my fingertips over the beautiful maroon cover featuring the well-dressed, dangerous-looking man, I'm not ready for his story to be over. His strong, surly, sexy, alpha demeanor has me gobsmacked. A protector through and through. *What would it be like to have a man like that love me?* Aside from his wealth and prestige, he's hiding a fiercely loyal heart of gold behind his impenetrable walls. It's a true masterpiece, and I can't wait to start the next book in the series. But I should go to bed. I can indulge in the next one after I've had some sleep. Like I suspect, a quick look at the clock on my microwave informs me it's already well into the next morning. "Merry Christmas," I tell myself as I fold the blanket, then toss it back onto the couch.

Sleep comes easily. My dreams are thick with mafia-related scenarios.

Cuddled deep into my down comforter, I slowly crack my eyelids open, then grab my phone from its charger when I'm finally awake enough to join the land of the living. I see I have exactly one text. And it's from Veronica.

VERONICA

Just wanted to say Merry Christmas.
Hope you enjoy your quiet day and
the hot men you plan to fill it with.
<heart emoji>

Her comment makes me smile, but then I remember there's nothing from Trevor. My heart sinks as disappointment floods my veins. After years of dealing with similar behaviors from my absent parents, it would be easy to justify his behavior with hypothetical excuses, but I'm tired of doing that. *I deserve better.*

ME

Merry Christmas to you too. I finished
the first man last night, and he did not
disappoint. His best friend is tonight,
and if I were a betting woman, I'd
guess he's even more. <heart emoji>

Seeing it's after noon, I send a generic message to my parents, wishing them a Merry Christmas. Feeling like I fulfilled my familial obligation, I get out of bed and pad my way into the kitchen to make some coffee. Scrolling through social media, I roll my eyes at all the people opening gifts. I've officially morphed into the Grinch. *This sucks. I hate feeling this way.* Unfortunately, my mood doesn't get better when I remember the expensive Christmas gift I purchased for Trevor months ago. It's still hidden in our closet. Since I'm unsure about where we stand, I don't know if or when I should give it to him. Ignoring all the warning bells screaming in my head, I again ask myself, *Where is he?*

ME

Merry Christmas, Trevor. I know you mentioned working today, but are you at least planning to come home?

Pouring myself a cup, I head over to the couch to start the second book of my new favorite series. Before I even wrap the blanket around me, my phone dings, alerting me to a message. My heart stalls when I see it's from Trevor. *Will it be good or bad?*

TREVOR

Merry Christmas to you too. I know I've been working a lot, but this project is so important and sucking up all my time. I won't be home tonight, but next week is looking lighter.

Rolling my eyes, I question if I should even reply. Grumbling because he doesn't deserve it, I just give him a thumbs up. Then I set my phone down, ready to dive into the next book. But before I do, my phone dings. I reach for it and am surprised by what I see.

ACE

Merry Christmas, Janica. I hope you're having an excellent day.

ME

Merry Christmas, Ace. My day's looking good. I'm spending most of it reading. How has your day been? Did you talk to your family?

ACE

I just got off a two-hour FaceTime with them, and boy was it loud. My brain is still rattling, but it was incredible.

ME

That sounds awesome. I'm so happy for you.

ACE

Thanks. It's been great.

Not knowing what else to say, I leave the thread open and set the phone next to me while I grab Sergio's book. Hours later, when I get up for a bathroom break and to grab a snack, I realize Ace never texted me back. My heart sags and I don't know why. Feeling unsettled, I sink back into the pages of another sexy alpha male who seems even more guarded than the last. *I can't wait to experience his fall. It's going to be epic.*

The pages fly by, and before I know it, I'm sitting in my dark apartment, crying happy tears over a beautifully written, headstrong mafia hero who's determined never to fall in love and embrace his fate as his carefully constructed walls crumble to dust. Now I just need Veronica to read these beauties so we can gush about them.

Chapter 14

Ace

When I decided to stay in Chicago for Christmas instead of traveling back to Minnesota, I assumed it would be easier. Logistically and physically, it is, but emotionally, I'm at a loss. I didn't realize until now how much I enjoyed spending a few uninterrupted days with my parents and siblings.

My mom reminded me a few days ago to order a pre-made holiday dinner from the healthy supermarket a few streets over. I paid extra to have it delivered because the idea of how I would transport it gave me hives. This morning after they opened presents together, my family FaceTime me. It fills my heart to hear all the laughter, but it makes me miss them more.

A little while later, I send Janica a Merry Christmas text because I don't want to forget to do it. My stomach is in knots the entire time I wait for her reply. Thankfully, it's only five seconds. Yes, I was counting. Even though she's hinted at having a quiet day reading, I wonder if she's sad. The thought of that guts me. *Where is her fucking boyfriend?* Needing not to get involved because it's none of my business, I set my phone down on my coffee table and pick up my gaming controller. Distracting myself with *NHL '24* is just what I need to work out my frustration.

An hour later, my phone signals a text. *Janica?* Disappointment weighs heavy when I see it isn't her.

NICOLE

Hey, guys. Big news. Jasmine is moving to New York City before the New Year to start a new job. Come say congratulations and goodbye to her this Wednesday from five to seven at Matec's. I know you're heading out on Thursday for your next away series and she'd love to see you before she leaves. Please RSVP so I can get a head count. Thank you.

What? Jasmine's moving? Rocco cannot be cool with this. *Did he know?* He sure as hell didn't tell me.

Pulling up his contacts, I ask.

ME

Jasmine's moving?

A minute passes with no reply. My stomach drops.

What if he didn't know? Fearing for my best friend, I try again.

> ME
>
> Dude.

Another minute goes by and he still doesn't respond.

> ME
>
> Rocco...
>
> ME
>
> Are you there?
>
> ME
>
> Are you okay?
>
> ME
>
> Need me to come over?

I'm about to call an Uber, because I am not ruining George's Christmas by demanding he drive me somewhere, when Rocco finally answers.

> ROCCO
>
> No, I don't want you to come over. I'm fine.

"Bullshit," I mutter. He's anything but fine. But I'm going to give him some space, let him cool off.

Wednesday, the day of Jasmine's goodbye party, or the day of reckoning, arrives. Rocco has been off the grid since we found out about Jasmine's move. I'm tempted to text him and see if he's removed his head from his ass. But he hasn't listened to me in the past, so I ignore the ache in my chest nagging me to try again. Instead, I press forward.

Before the party, I plan to go to the library to submit a few assignments that are due before the first of the year. The image of Janica's face bubbles up in my mind, and my heart beats faster. I was sure a few days spent away now that I know she has a boyfriend might decrease my crush on her. However, it's done the opposite. Thoughts of her make me smile like a lovesick puppy.

As I approach the circulation desk, my hands sweat. Memories of the last few weeks dance through my mind, distracting me as my eyes desperately search out the most gorgeous woman I've ever seen. *She isn't here. Wait.* Janica's brown hair is tied in a messy bun on top of her head, revealing her sexy-as-fuck neckline. I want to pull her close, kiss the soft spot behind her ear, and then, with my tongue, trace the skin down to her collarbone.

Overwhelmed by my lust-fueled daydream, my "hi" comes out raw and raspy.

Her cheeks turn pink and her eyes blink wide. "Hi, Ace. It's great to see you. Did you have a good Christmas?"

Shrugging, I answer, "It was okay. After I Face-Time'd with my family, I played video games."

Veronica steps over, joining the conversation. "You

should have spent it together since you were both alone."

Where was her boyfriend? I look at Janica in disbelief. "Really? If I'd have known, you could have come over and hung out with me."

My offer is sincere, but anger swirls in my gut. I want to know why her boyfriend wasn't there. I should have asked her when we were texting, but it didn't seem appropriate.

With the flick of her wrist, she waves me off, and snaps, "I was just fine. I got some pleasure reading done."

Feeling like I've been dismissed, I hang my head. "I better get to work. I need to finish a few assignments." I crutch off to my spot before she can say anything.

When I'm finishing up the last assignment, Janica approaches, giving me a hesitant smile. "Hey, Ace. I'm sorry I was a little short-tempered earlier. Since coming back from her mini-vacation, Veronica has been giving me non-stop commentary about how I shouldn't have been alone for Christmas. Except I chose that. I knew there was a chance I was going to be alone, and I filled it with books."

"You know you could have texted me and we could have hung out." She nods her head. "I'm always free to grab coffee."

"I'm just so confused why anyone cares if I was alone for Christmas. It was the first time in a while that I could do what I wanted without worrying about anyone else or making sure I made the best impression. There was no stress... just me, my books, and some great sex scenes."

She stares off, lost in thought, as she continues to chatter. My eyes go wide and I sit back when the words "sex scene" register. *Hello.* I'd kill—okay, I'd maim—for an opportunity to act out any sex scene with Janica. If I ever meet Trevor, I won't hesitate to beat him to a bloody pulp. He's not good enough for her. I don't know him, but I know how incredible she is, and any man would have to be an idiot to not spend his time worshiping her. But for right now, I'm just going to hang back and offer Janica my friendship, and hope she'll gain some clarity soon. In the meantime, I'll be here, waiting.

Reaching out, I place my hand on her arm. Startled, she jumps. "Sorry," I say pulling my hand back. "You don't owe anyone an explanation of how you choose to live your life. Least of all me. It sounds like the quiet, stress-free Christmas is just what you needed. And I'm glad you got it." Her kind smile affirms that what I say is what she needed to hear.

The alarm on my phone goes off, and I quickly silence it. Grabbing my backpack, I close my laptop before I shove it inside.

"It looks like you're getting ready to leave, so I'll stop bothering you," Janica says, stepping to the side of the table. I reach out, grab her hand, and cradle it in my much larger one, despite wanting to interlace our fingers and pull her to me.

"You, Janica, are never a bother. I enjoy talking to you. If there wasn't someplace I have to be, I'd stay longer." A blush covers her cheeks, which makes me happier than I can admit. *She has a boyfriend,* I remind myself. And just like that, as if a bucket of ice-cold water was poured over my head, I'm put in my place. I drop her hand, grab my crutches, and say, "Maybe later this week we can grab coffee?" Her nod and wide smile are everything. My phone chimes again, and I laugh. "I really have to go. Good night, Janica."

"Night, Ace. Hope to see you around," she says as I force myself not to look back at the first woman to ever intrigue me.

George swings by my house so I can drop off my school bag and change clothes. Then he drops me off at Mateo's and I assure him I'll grab a ride home from someone or order an Uber.

When I walk inside, I'm pointed to the back room, which is already full of people, most of whom I recognize. It looks like Nicole ordered some finger foods and all the guests have helped themselves. She and Jasmine are talking to an older couple, who, I assume, are Jaz's parents. If Rocco were here, I could ask him. But I haven't seen him yet, and considering he's punctual as fuck, if he isn't here already, he's probably not coming. *That dickhead.* I can't believe he isn't going to show up to his best friend's goodbye party. I can guarantee I'll be pounding down his door later and giving him shit for this major fuckup.

During the time I've known Rocco and Jaz, I have always suspected they had feelings for each other. So his absence tonight both makes sense and doesn't.

An hour into the party, I catch Jasmine's eye, and she mouths, *"Where's Rocco?"* I don't know, and I wouldn't lie for him even if I did. Truth is, because I'm still recovering and haven't been to the arena at the same time, I haven't talked to him in days. I move over to her so we won't be having our private conversation across the room.

"Hey, Jaz," I say as I hug her. Her resounding frown tells me she isn't happy, which I completely understand.

"Thanks for coming," she says before we part ways.

Pointing to my leg, she asks, "How are you feeling? How's your recovery going?"

I smile at her. "It's going... slowly."

She laughs. "I bet. Thanks for coming. It's great to see you."

A few silent seconds pass between us and it's incredibly tense. "Is he coming?" she whispers.

I stare at the floor, unable to make eye contact.

"Ace." When I look up, I know she can see the disappointment on my face

"I don't know. He's refused to call me back all week. I went by his house a few times, but he never answered. I'm sorry." I'm hoping my words offer comfort, but I'm not sure they do.

She forces a smile. "It's okay. I appreciate you being here and saying goodbye."

"But is this truly goodbye? Are you leaving Chicago for good?" I ask, worried Rocco has fucked this up beyond repair.

"For now," she replies, shrugging her shoulders.

Nicole walks up to us. "Okay, you two. Stop with the sad faces. We're celebrating that Jaz is going to kick ass at her new job. And then she'll come back and visit us."

Jasmine stands there silently, and my stomach drops. "Right?" Nicole questions, her tone demanding.

"Yeah. Right. Of course." Jasmine mumbles and I wonder with Rocco's no-show if she actually will come back. Those two have danced around their mutual attraction for too long. Maybe this stunt he's pulled has finally tipped the odds, but not in his favor. I guarantee he'll wise up in a few days and realize he's made a terrible mistake. Hopefully, it'll be one he can repair. I'm just glad I'm not in his shoes.

<hr>

After thinking about it all last night, I'm sick to my stomach. Rocco's being an ass, and he needs someone to tell him that. Might as well be me, right? Knowing he won't answer when I call, I have George drive me over to his house. While still in the car, I call him. No answer. Because I want to be bothersome, I try again. He still doesn't answer. Peering out at his house, I know he's home, so I climb out of the SUV and crutch my way up his walk. When I'm at his door, I knock. But he doesn't answer. So, I move on to plan B. If subtle isn't working, go for loud and proud.

"Where to Ace?" George asks after I'm buckled in.

I open my phone to check the time. I still have that one assignment to finish, so I say, "Can you take me home to grab my school work and drop me at the library?"

He smiles at me in the rearview mirror. "I wish my kids were as studious as you."

If only he knew the real reason I spent so much time at the library, he'd probably change his tune. A brunette in the stacks has me all twisted up. I only wish we were twisted up in other ways. *She has a boyfriend.*

Half an hour later, I'm seated at my table, working on my final assignment for the semester, when a text comes through.

NICOLE

Hey, Ace. I'm worried about Jaz and Rocco, and I need to talk to someone about it. Are you home?

ME

I'm at the library finishing some homework. I won't be home for a few hours. I can text you when I get there.

NICOLE

Jasmine and I are going out to dinner later with her parents. I'm about five minutes from the library. Can I stop by? I promise I won't stay long.

ME

Yeah. Sure. When you get here, text me, and I'll come get you from the circulation desk. My study spot isn't the easiest to find.

NICOLE

Thank you. See you soon.

Ten minutes later, I hear the sweetest voice approaching from behind. I smile, but then it registers she's talking to someone. I turn slowly, hoping to catch a glimpse of Janica. I haven't seen her yet today. Hoping she was working; I styled my hair and brushed my teeth again before coming in. She looks radiant. The sun coming through the window highlights flecks of red in her brown hair. Wearing a long, flowy skirt that covers most of her legs, the creamy alabaster skin of her ankles stands out. My fingers itch to touch her and find out if she's as smooth as she looks. The cranberry cardigan she's wearing is buttoned tight over her perfect-sized breasts. White lace peeks out from below it, a tease if you will, and I find it makes her even sexier. It's then I notice the person she's talking to is Nicole, and I put my hand up to wave.

"Ace, I found a friend of yours." Janica smiles at me. My heart beats faster and my smile grows wider the closer she gets.

Nicole steps closer, a smirk on her face. I cock my head at her, and she flicks her gaze at Janica, then waggles her damn eyebrows. *Are you together?* She's asking, almost as if she said it out loud. I frown, shaking my head no. Her smirk fades and she says, "Hey, Ace. Thanks for letting me crash your study session."

Looking at Janica, I notice her watching Nicole and me. *Interesting.* I turn back to answer Nicole. "It's no problem at all. I'd do anything to resolve this thing between Rocco and Jasmine."

"Same." She sighs while forcing a smile. Our best friends are being ridiculously stubborn, and we get to deal with the fallout.

"Janica, this is Nicole. We know each other because our best friends are also best friends. And they're kind of not talking right now. It's making our lives miserable."

Nicole laughs. "Nailed it, Ace. It's so good to meet you, Janica. Obviously, you work here, but what do you do?"

Janica smiles. "It's nice to meet you too, Nicole. For the past few years, I've been a library assistant. I was taking online classes but have stopped. I really enjoy my job and don't need any higher education for it. For now, I spend my day shelving books, organizing materials, and helping people like Ace, research and locate the books they need for life, school, etc. Oh, and the librarian is one of my best friends... so, bonus."

"I can't stand my boss," Nicole says with a frown. "As soon as the ink has dried on my business degree and I'm official, I'm getting a new job."

Janica smiles. "We have a job posting board, so I'll keep an eye out for you. If I see anything, I'll pass it on to Ace."

Nicole beams and then wraps her arms around Janica. "Thank you so much."

I'm jealous. I want to be that close to Janica.

Janica chuckles. "It's no problem. I should get back to my desk, and you two can get to scheming on how to get your friends to talk."

Just as she's stepping away, I grab her hand and squeeze it. My body lights up from the contact. "Thank you. I'll see you later?" Without a word, she nods and then turns to leave.

Once Nicole and I have complained to each other about Rocco and Jasmine and still haven't come up with any definitive idea to get them to talk, she leaves and I get busy finishing my final assignment. When it's done and submitted, I make sure that the classes I enrolled in for the next semester appear on my student portal. Then I set a reminder to order books and materials.

After packing up my backpack, I head out to the

circulation desk and see Janica sorting through a stack of books. Clasped tightly in her hand, she's reading the back cover of one. Her lips move as her eyes flick back and forth. I notice her cheeks are pink, and she has a sexy smile on her face. Clearing my throat, I ask, "What book has you so enamored?"

"What?" she squeaks while pushing away the book. Her blush grows darker. *Is she embarrassed? Whatever is happening is cute as fuck, and I want to know which book caused it.* "W-why?" she stutters nervously.

Leaning against the desk, I smirk. "Maybe I'd like it. What do you think? Should I check it out?"

"You can't," she practically pants. *Did the thought of the book or me reading it get her out of breath? Is she turned on right now?* "It's not, umm... been entered into our system yet. No one can check them out."

Dropping my voice and leaning in, I say, "But you've read it, haven't you?" *She has a boyfriend. I* know I'm playing with fire that will probably end with me being scorched, but I can't help myself. I saw the cover when she was trying to hide it. It's a romance, and just the thought of that gets me excited. All the blood in my body rushes south. I press my hard cock against the desk, wishing it were her, and I hold in a groan. *It feels so damn good.* In fact, I've caught myself daydreaming of laying her out across this desk and pleasuring her until she screams my name repeatedly. Every time I think of it, it not only makes me rock hard, but it also makes me laugh since being silent in the library is rule number one.

Dipping her head to hide her face, she traces her finger over the book intimately. "Yes," she whispers. A minute later she looks up, her eyes focused, and she clears her throat. "But Veronica hasn't, and she likes to read most of the books before we put them into circulation."

The moment has passed, and I know I should go. I shouldn't have been flirting with her since I know she's in a relationship. Feeling terrible for putting her in that position, I hang my head. This minor break in classes is probably what I need to get her out from under my skin. When I come back in the new year, things will be different. At least I hope so, or I might have to find another place to study.

"I better go. I'll see you in the new year when classes start back up."

Janica frowns. "Oh, okay. Hope you have a Happy New Year, Ace." With a last wave, I crutch out to the lobby to send George a text that I'm ready to be picked up. The next time I come through these doors, I'll be without Lucifer and Beelzebub, and in a walking boot.

Later this week, I have a meeting with the team's head physical therapist to work on my treatment plan. I also need to get new X-rays and get fitted for the boot. The thought of putting weight back on my leg is both exciting and scary. But I know doing it puts me one step closer to getting back onto the ice.

Chapter 15

Janica

"Happy New Year, Miss. J," a little girl with pigtails singsongs as she walks up to the circulation desk.

Giving her a big smile, I wish her the same and ask, "Are you ready for school to start again, Gracie?"

Thoughtfully, she flips through the sticker box we have. "Yes, I've missed my friends so much."

Her mom, standing next to her, sighs. "If that was all we had to worry about, right?" Gracie looks at her mom, confused.

I nod at her and reply, "Life would be simpler." I look at the clock on the wall, then say to Gracie, "Are you here for story time? I already saw Stacey come in. I bet she's saving a seat for you."

Excitedly, she looks at her mom, who says, "Let's go, kiddo."

"Bye, Miss. J," Gracie chirps as she heads off toward Kids' Land.

Her mom mouths, *"Is there coffee?"*

I give her a smile and a thumbs up as she follows her seven-year-old daughter.

While Veronica is away doing story time, I busy myself with applying scan codes to some newer paranormal fantasy books we just received. Veronica has given them all her seal of approval. They aren't a genre I enjoy, so I don't know what they're about. Even if the stories don't entice me, the beautifully illustrated covers do.

"Read any good books lately?" a deep voice asks. My head whips up, and a smile stretches across my face. There, standing before me, is Ace. I haven't seen him in weeks, and despite the time apart, my pull to him seems just as strong.

"Hi, Ace. Happy New Year," I say, testing where we stand. I'm uncertain because our last conversation left me with many unresolved emotions. Foremost, I felt guilt. Although I didn't think I had given off the wrong signals, I couldn't help the way my body responded to his flirting with me. Out of respect for Trevor, I kept it innocent, but it seemed like Ace wanted to keep pushing the envelope. *What would he do now?* Maybe my feelings were confused because we'd seen each other so often in such a short period. He'd gotten under my skin and, with Trevor being so absent and dismissive, I'd latched on to Ace's kind personality. Yes, that's it. It was nothing. We're just friends.

His sweet smile warms my heart. *He's such a nice guy.* "Happy New Year to you too. Did you do anything special to ring in the new year?" I shake my head no. "Me either," he replies. "Actually, that's a bit of a lie."

If he tells me he went to party and hooked up with some lady, I think I'll just have to walk away. Even though he's not my boyfriend, the thought of him with another woman makes me sick and angry. *Why is that?*

He taps the counter with his hands. "I got rid of the crutches, and I now have a walking boot."

Leaning over the counter, I see his big black boot and exclaim, "Whoa, that's something."

He laughs. "It's big and bulky, but I get to take it off when I'm resting my leg or sleeping. I'm not driving yet, but it won't be too much longer."

"When can you skate again?" I ask, assuming his frequent trips to the library will decrease rapidly once he's back to playing hockey.

"It'll be a while before I'm back to skating. This boot is helping me learn to put weight on my leg again. I'm also starting pool work to help build strength and gain flexibility back. It's additional support to speed up recovery while reducing pain and supporting bone joints."

I laugh. "You sound like the audio version of the book *An Idiot's Guide to Physical Therapy Needed for a*

Broken Leg." He laughs too which makes me feel warm all over.

"You're right. I have no other choice but to know my recovery inside and out if I ever want to play professional hockey again," he says. "Just the thought of getting back out there brings a smile to my face. Hockey is my first love, and I've missed her so much over the past few months. It isn't the same watching it. Not being able to lace up my skates and get out there with my buddies has been agonizing."

Pointing to his backpack, I ask, "How many credits are you taking this semester?"

"Because my physical therapy schedule is going to be intense, I only signed up for nine. It isn't a full load, but I'm not trying to earn a degree in a set timeline, so I'm doing it at my speed. Once I'm fully rehabilitated, classes will go on the back burner. I'll still probably try to take one class per semester, but we'll see how that goes."

I smile and say, "That sounds like a grand plan. I need to get these shelved. Your spot should be empty. Get to work."

Giving me a salute, he replies, "Yes, ma'am. See you around, drill sergeant."

week later, toward the end of the busiest day I've had in months Ace appears at my desk. "Hey, Janica."

Surprised to see him, I reply, "Hey. What are you doing here?"

He looks around. "In the library? I'm pretty sure everyone is welcome."

Laughing, I shake my head. "No. Yes. Everyone is welcome, but I didn't see you studying, and I'm surprised to see you."

Removing his hat, he scratches his damp head. *Why is his hair wet?* "I wasn't, but today's been a rough day and I wanted to see a familiar face."

I hate that he sounds so sad, but it's nice that he sought me out. Standing from my computer, I go to him. "Is everything okay?"

"I just got done with physical therapy. I was in the pool today, and everything they asked me to do was difficult." He frowns, and my heart squeezes.

Wanting to be supportive, I reach out and touch his arm. "Oh," I gasp when I feel a charge pass between us. A shiver rocks his body and his eyes go wide. *Did he feel that too?* My body tingles. Sucking in a breath, I wait for his next words. Our eyes lock and he tips his head to me in question. Silence holds us hostage to the heated moment.

"Hi, Ace," Veronica calls as she approaches. And just like that, the spell is broken.

His gaze darts away from mine. "Oh, hi, Veronica. How are you?"

"I'm great. How are you?" She looks between us with piqued curiosity.

"I didn't have a great day, so I stopped by to see if Janica wanted to grab a cup of coffee or dinner with me." With his focus still on her, I feel myself panicking. My heart thumps in my chest and my hands sweat. An internal conversation wars in my head. *Is he asking me out? He knows about Trevor.*

Veronica clears her throat, and my eyes flash to her. With a mischievous smile, she says, "I think that's a great idea. Obviously, as friends, it's important to support each other when you've had a tough day. I know from experience that Janica is always there for me in those times." Then she winks. *What is she trying to do?*

Ace turns to me. "Do you have time for coffee... or dinner?" Behind him, Veronica nods repeatedly. Dipping my head, I consider it all.

"Sure. I'd love to have coffee with you. Let me grab my bag and log out." The smile he gives me could power a city block, and the way it makes me feel... whoa.

Over coffee, he mentions more about therapy and how he has good and bad days.

Loving the taste of my peppermint mocha, I moan.

He laughs. "That good?"

"You don't even know. Want to try it?" I offer. He

makes a face and shakes his head. Shrugging my shoulders, I taunt him. "Fine, but it's your loss."

He smirks at me. "You're ridiculous."

I jokingly frown at him, and he holds his hands up in defense. "Just teasing."

I smile. "In all seriousness, do you think today was so tough because you were trying something new?"

He settles back into his chair. "Yes and no. Working in the pool wasn't new, and neither were the exercises. The only difference was that I was doing the exercises *in* the pool, and for some reason, that made them more difficult."

"Did you talk to your physical therapist about it?" I ask, concerned for him.

"Yeah. He said it'll get better. It just takes time. But that's just it. I feel like I've been recovering forever. When will I be done?"

"I wish I had the answer for you. Mentally you're ready, you're just waiting for your body to catch up. That has to be frustrating."

He grimaces. "Yes, that's it exactly."

I encourage him to talk to his physical therapist about his frustrations and see if they've got a better idea of when he'll be ready to get back to skating.

Ace leans forward. "I'm going to grab another coffee. Do you want anything?"

"No, thank you. I'm going to use the restroom. I'll be right back." He smiles at me as he heads to the counter.

Excited to continue our conversation, a wide smile is on my lips as I depart the bathroom. When I get to the end of the short hallway, I see Ace engaged in conversation with a petite, curvy woman. My smile falls as she laughs at something he says and tosses her strawberry-blond hair over her shoulder. My stomach drops and my steps slow. Looking past the woman, Ace catches my eye and his smile morphs into concern.

He steps to the side, ending their conversation, and says my name. The woman turns around quickly with a bright smile on her face. *Nicole?*

"Janica. It's so good to see you again. I didn't mean to interrupt your coffee date, but I stopped in for a drink and saw Ace, and had to say hi."

Now that my jealousy isn't overwhelming me, I smile. "Of course. Would you like to join us?"

Before she can respond, the door of the cafe swings open, and a group of gorgeous ladies enter. They're all laughing. *That must be nice. A close-knit friend group.*

"Ace?" a tall lady with striking brown hair says, and the entire group goes quiet. *What's going on? Is she a past girlfriend?* For the second time in five minutes, jealousy I have no right to feel spins in my stomach.

"Hey, Samantha. Ladies," he says, greeting the group with a neutral look on his face. "What are you all doing here?"

Nicole answers, "That was just what I was about to tell you. The ladies and I are catching a movie while the guys are out of town." She turns to me. "Janica, you should totally come."

Feeling incredibly uncomfortable as the entire group of them stare at me, I force a smile and say, "I have something to do. Next time?" I doubt I'll ever run into them again, and if I do, they probably won't remember me. The ladies go back to chatting with each other.

As if he can sense my anxiety, Ace steps closer. "Are you okay?"

"Yeah, I just don't know any of those women except Nicole," I whisper.

Ace claps his hands together. "Ladies, this is my friend Janica. Janica, these are the Steel Ladies. They're married to or dating my teammates." He runs through their names, and they each give me a smile. They seem nice, but I'm glad I'm not being evaluated for my recall. Needing to get off to their movie, they order their drinks and are gone.

After we finish our drinks, I give Ace a hug and remind him again, "You're putting in all the hard work. Skating and hockey will be back in your life soon. But in the meantime, if you need to grab a coffee or a meal with a friend, you have my number and you know where I work."

"Thanks for today, Janica. I really appreciate you and value our friendship."

I'm floating on a high as I ride the train home. But the empty apartment I arrive to, taunts me. It's like

Trevor knows I want to have a conversation to end things, so he's purposefully avoiding me. He comes home when he knows I'll be gone. I see evidence he's been here. I don't know where he's been sleeping and I don't care. We're through, and if I weren't such a nice person, I'd call him and break up with him over the phone. But no matter how pissed off I am, I can't seem to bring myself to do that. Being decent is just about to kill me, especially when I walk into my bedroom. A faint, unfamiliar scent hangs in the air and it makes my stomach cramp. Grabbing my phone, I reach out to the one person who won't think I'm crazy.

ME

You'll probably think I'm crazy, but I think Trevor is cheating on me. My apartment smells different.

VERONICA

I don't think you're crazy. What do you want to do about it?

ME

I need proof.

VERONICA

Then we'll find it. We're going to end him. Know a good place to bury a body? <angry emoji> <knife emoji> <skull and crossbones emoji> <shovel emoji>

ME

He wasn't here when I got home, no
surprise there, so he doesn't know I
suspect a thing.

VERONICA

Now we just have to catch him in the
act. Any guess who it's with?

ME

If I were a betting woman, I'd guess
it's his assistant. He puts in a lot of
hours at work. Or so he says.

VERONICA

Sounds plausible. Let's start there. I'll
brainstorm tonight and we'll have a
pow-wow tomorrow to plan his
takedown.

ME

You know, you're kind of scary.
Remind me never to piss you off.

VERONICA

I'm fueled by my own selfish anger for
my ass of an ex who drug me through
it too. I never got to inflict revenge on
him. Trevor will be my stand-in. He's
going to wish he was never born.

ME

I'm angry and hurt, but I'd rather not
end up in jail at the end of this. Okay?

VERONICA

Message received. Dialing back my
intensity. Love you, girl. I am so
fucking sorry. But I have your back.

ME

Thanks. Love you too. No other woman I'd rather be in the trenches with.

VERONICA

Night. Go get some rest. We need fresh brains and ideas for scheming.

ME

Night.

Chapter 16

Ace

When I head into the library to get a paper done today, I notice Veronica and Janica are huddled around a notepad while Veronica wildly explains something. It seems intense, so I don't disturb them. By the time I leave, the desk is empty. I'm bummed to have missed talking to Janica, but I have to come back later in the week to finish a unit for my math class.

I make a mental note to check in with her. She looked sad today, but I didn't want to intrude. We're friends, but Veronica is one of her best friends. If something's going on, she'd know and know how to handle it. The thought of something being wrong stirs up my protective nature, and I fight the need to sit at that desk and demand answers from them. *She has a boyfriend.*

The realization that it isn't my job to protect or defend her is tough to accept. Ever since I met her, I've felt we have a special connection. It's what keeps me coming back and fuels my intense attraction to her. It's caused me to not care at all about openly flirting with a taken woman, which is something I normally wouldn't condone. But she makes me insane and has me doing all kinds of I things I wouldn't usually do.

Chapter 17

Janica

Veronica and I have designed the perfect plan to catch Trevor in the act. We named it Trevor Watch. Veronica threatened to make t-shirts with her Cricut, but she could never give me a suitable answer as to when they'd be appropriate to wear.

He doesn't work too far from the library, so she and I have been taking our lunch at different times and sitting inside the café in the lobby of his building. So far, during our week-long investigation, we've seen Trevor leave his office building twice. Both times he'd had his assistant with him and he carried a briefcase. Our assumption is they were headed off to a business meeting. In our observations, there had been no inappropriate touches exchanged between them. They grabbed a cab both times. There was no way we could have followed them. We weren't professional private investigators. Scorned women, armed with anger and an hour-long lunch break, we were doing the best we could. Week two fell flat, and either Trevor didn't leave the building for lunch or we missed him each time he did.

On Valentine's Day, I wake up with what feels like a head cold. I haven't seen Trevor in days, even though I know he came by our apartment. Other than a few random texts between us, we don't communicate. Who cares if it's the day of love? I don't care to celebrate it. Not with him.

I spend the day in bed, trying to drink plenty of fluids. After work, Veronica brings me chicken soup from the Vietnamese restaurant near the library. The heavenly smell makes my stomach growl. Not caring about being ladylike, I slurp an enormous bowl down after she leaves. It warms my insides, making me feel the best I have all day. Afterward, I take a hot shower, dropping in eucalyptus oil to open up my sinuses. When I climb back into bed, relaxed and warm from the soup and the shower, the tight band around my head is finally releasing.

Stopping by the corner mart near my apartment the next morning, I grab a box of tissues with lotion. My cold has moved on to the next phase, and my sinuses are draining, making blowing my nose a regular occurrence. I don't look like Rudolph yet, but I suspect unless I use softer tissue, I'll have a very sore and chapped nose by the end of the day.

Veronica laughs when she sees me walk up with my trusty box of tissues. "How are you feeling?"

I force a smile. "A tad bit better than yesterday. I brought my tissues, sanitizer, and a megadose of vitamin C."

She puts her hands on her hips. "You know, you could have stayed home today. We would have been fine."

I sigh. "I know, and if I get worse, I'll go home, I promise. I was bored at home. You can stick me on the other side of the library, filing books. Oh, and look, I brought a mask and disposable gloves so I don't spread my germs either."

She chuckles. "Okay, but if you get worse, you're going home."

Nine hours later, and at the end of my shift, I'm dead on my feet. I don't feel worse, but I'm exhausted. Veronica walks up to the desk we share and tsks at me. I don't even have enough strength to lift my head from where it's pillowed on my folded arms. "Janica, it's time to go home. You look miserable, and I don't want to catch whatever you have."

"Okay," I whisper. All I want is to take the next dose of my cold medicine and pass out for hours.

"You weren't kidding," a familiar masculine voice says from next to her. Moving my head slowly, I shift my focus and see Ace, and I grimace.

"Ace," I rasp.

"Veronica told me you were sick, and we decided

you needed to go home to rest. I'm giving you a ride there. We can stop at the store if you need anything." Usually, I don't like people deciding for me, but my head is so stuffed up right now, that simple things perplex me.

"Okay," I answer.

Veronica helps by grabbing my things from my locker. When she has me all bundled up, she hands me over to Ace. "Thank you for taking her home," she says to him. To me, she says, "I'll check in with you later. Let me know if you need anything. Do you need any more of that soup?"

"I've still got some. Thanks, Mom. Love you." She hands my bag of tissues and cold products to Ace before he leads me out of the library.

"This way," he instructs as he leads me over to a luxury SUV.

"Wow. Nice car," I say.

He laughs as he helps me in. "The team hooked me up. Janica, this is George, my driver."

"Where to, ma'am?" George asks, giving her a smile in the rearview mirror.

Stunned, I give him my address while I buckle myself in.

"Do you need to stop anywhere first?" Ace tenderly asks.

I shake my head. "I did it on the way to work before my head puffed back up."

The ride to my apartment is comfortable and

smooth. I think I doze off for a second or two, but Ace never mentions it when we arrive.

"Here we are, ma'am," George says.

While Ace is coming over to my side, I look at George. "Thank you so much for the ride."

"I hope you get to feeling better soon," he tells me before Ace helps me from the SUV.

Tucking my coat tighter around myself to fend off the wind, I look at Ace. His beautiful brown eyes are filled with concern. "I'm okay, Ace. It's just a head cold. In a day or two, I'll feel better. Thank you for the ride home."

He hands over my bag, saying, "If you need anything, you have my number."

Giving him the best smile I can while feeling terrible, I thank him again before I head inside. All the way to my apartment, I think about how sweet he is.

Letting myself into my apartment, I hear an odd sound. It's like something scraping against a wall. *Maybe a neighbor is moving*. I'll ask Mr. Henry across the way when I'm feeling better. He always knows what's happening in our building.

Kicking my shoes off, I see a pair of Trevor's by the door. I'm sure they hadn't been there when I left for work. Maybe he's home grabbing something. I shut the front door and then I hear that scraping noise again. It's unnerving, and goose bumps cover my body. Worry fills my mind and my stomach drops. *What is that sound?* My mind plays tricks on me. *Was it coming from inside my apartment?* Maybe Trevor is moving something. I move toward the bedroom, and the door's partially shut.

"Trevor," I say while I push the door open. My heart squeezes and my brain short circuits, trying to make sense of the scene in front of me. My stomach twists in disgust.

"Babe." His voice makes me want to rage. I grind my teeth together. *Bastard.* Even though I suspected him of cheating, it still hurts to have him put it on display. They are in my fucking bed. On my favorite sheets. Now I have to burn them.

"Are you fucking kidding me?" I growl.

The woman riding him screams and tries to shift off him. But he tightens his hands around her hips, forcing her to stay still. Her head drops, and I know who it is from the color and cut of her hair. It's his assistant. *Asshole.*

My fists clench. I want to hit something. And there he sits, smugly relaxed, and unbothered by his choices. He never deserved me. He'll get what's coming to him. He doesn't know I've had weeks to wrap my mind around the fact I suspected he'd been cheating.

I have questions I want answered, and I know the only way that will happen is if I force the conversation right now. It's uncomfortable as fuck, and I suspect from his lecherous smirk that he's getting a thrill out of it. The sick bastard is probably still hard inside of her, seeing as how I interrupted their good time. *Joke's on her*. During our time together, he'd never pleased me. Regarding Trevor and what he's packing and able to deliver, I'm sure there aren't many, if any, good times in her past or present.

Tired of this shit show and still exhausted from my cold, I growl, "How long, Trevor?"

His assistant drops her head more, trying to hide her face behind her hair. And now I'm pissed at myself.

"Six months, sweetheart," he replies.

Gnashing my teeth, I try hard to rein in my temper. Glaring daggers at them, I force out, "Six months?" *What the actual fuck?*

Pieces slide into place, and a calm washes over me. He's no longer my problem I'm free. Not being able to stand sharing the same space with them, I'm ready to get out of here, but I have one more thing to say.

"You deserve each other. You make me sick. You never deserved me. I wasted too much fucking time on you." Looking at his assistant, I laugh. "Oh, and honey, he's a lousy lay and you've been screwing him long enough to know that, so the joke's on you. Have a nice life, assholes."

Then I leave. I need two things right now: to get far away from Trevor, and to have a drink. I'll give myself one night to deal with my hurt and then I'll move on. I've already wasted too much time settling for something that wasn't worth it. I'm ready to live my life and embrace the things that make me happy.

Hopping back on the train, I plan to ride until it stops near The Dragon's Lair. A fellow passenger bumps into me as they are trying to find a seat. Scattered, I blink out of the haze I've been in, and realize several hours have passed. Listening to the announcements, I recognize the stop I'd been looking for is coming soon. When I get to the sidewalk above, the sky has darkened; I look down the street and my eyes find my target, The Dragon's Lair. I once visited the bar with Veronica. If memory serves me correctly, it has great drinks and music. I'm saying yes, please, to anything that will drown out the thoughts in my head. And bonus, the brandy or a hot toddy will probably ease the last of my cold symptoms.

Chapter 18

Ace

Physical therapy kicked my butt today. It was pool work, and so I assumed that meant it would be easier. Boy, was I wrong. As soon as I seemed to master a skill, my therapist would make it more difficult. His favorite, I think, was adding a weight belt to me before I completed jumping jacks in chest-deep water. As I continued to work on rebuilding strength and flexibility, my therapist pushed me to the limits. It's incredible to think in such a brief time span, I've lost so much strength in my leg. I know I'll have to work hard to rebuild my strength just so I can get back to hockey. One good thing is, at least I'm not a goalie. I'm less flexible than I was before I broke my leg.

After the rigorous session, Robert gives me some handouts of stretches that I can easily do at home. Because I'm still weeks from being weight-bearing, I have to start everything slowly and work my way back to what I was before. This entire process has been incredibly frustrating and discouraging. Instead of heading straight home after my session, I detour to the library to see Janica. I'm in desperate need of the calmness only she can deliver to my overworked body. Something feels wrong as soon as we arrive and Veronica informs me that Janica is sick and needs to go home. Seeing her weary and weak body using a library book as a pillow, I offer to get her home. When George and I drop her off, I'm convinced all she needs is adequate rest.

When I arrive home later, my phone rings just as I'm about to sit down and start an assignment. I answer right away when I see who it is.

"Rocco, what's up, man?"

"Ace. How do you feel about grabbing beer and dinner?" he says over the noise of the locker room. Man, I miss my teammates.

I push my books away. "Sounds great. What time?"

"I just got done with practice. I'll head home to change and then I can come to get you at six."

"Sounds great. See you soon." After I hang up, I see I have plenty of time to shower. When I was planning to stay home, the chlorine smell didn't bother me, but if I'm going out, I want to smell more like a man than a pool.

Sitting at Meat & Potatoes, Rocco and I drink beer while waiting for our food. "Any plans for the weekend?" I ask.

"I'm going to see Jasmine tomorrow," he says, and I smirk.

"Are you going to tell her how you feel this time?"

He remains quiet, taking a swig of his beer. The server delivers our food, and it looks amazing. I'm sick of the prepared meals I've been eating for weeks. Rocco takes a bite of his loaded potatoes, still refusing to answer my question. I stare at him. "Well?" I demand.

When he's finished chewing, he finally answers. "Yes, I plan to tell her." Then he whispers, "I just hope it doesn't fuck up our friendship."

His concern makes me sad. I frown. "I don't think that will happen. I think you both have been fighting your attraction to each other for a long time. And I think one of you needs to bite the bullet and come clean."

"I hope so, man. I don't want to waste any more time," he confesses.

"It'll be fine," I say, hoping to convince us both. The rest of our dinner is enjoyable and we devoured our Wagyu steaks. They're amazing and melt in your mouth like butter.

This place is incredible; the ambiance is top-notch. I watch as Rocco looks around in awe, pausing for a second before he asks. "Who told you about this place? It's amazing."

"Do you remember Janica from the library?" I ask. "She's a big reader and saw a review a few weeks ago in the paper. She told me she wanted to visit, but her boyfriend, Captain Dickface, won't bring her."

He mutters, "Captain Dickface," and laughs. "Well, he sounds like an asshole."

"He is," I agree. I've never met him, but Veronica says he is. "I wish she'd just break up with him. She deserves so much better."

Rocco's tone drops as he asks, "Like you?"

Shaking my head, my voice strains as I confess the truth. "She's incredible, but she's too good for me." I care about her so much, and I wish I could be the man she deserves.

Rocco catches my eye. "There's no one better than you."

Then my phone rings. Seeing Lucas's name, I answer it, putting it on speakerphone in case it's team related. "Hey, man. I've got you on speakerphone. Rocco's here with me. What's up?"

"I just got off the phone with Samantha. She and the girls are at a bar celebrating her first drink since Chloe was born, and they ran into a friend of yours. Janica."

"Oh yeah? That's nice. So, is that why you're calling?"

"Well... I'm not sure how to tell you this, but she's

really drunk. The girls have tried to get her to leave, but she refuses. She doesn't really know them. Could you maybe stop by and help get her home?" I look at Rocco, and his eyes are wide. Words don't come because my mind is spinning. *What happened?* I just saw her.

Rocco jumps into action. "Hey, Lucas, it's Rocco. What bar are they at?"

"They're at Dragon's Lair. I'll let the ladies know you're on the way." Then he ends the call. I'm frozen.

Rocco grabs my arm and shakes it. Startled, I look at him. "Let's go get your girl," he says as he stands, then tosses some money on the table.

All I can do is mumble. 'Okay."

Dragon's Lair is a very popular bar. Most of the interior of the establishment is black. Red lights are strategically placed, giving the space an eerie, haunted feel. It doesn't take long to locate the ladies. They're circled up around Janica, who is crying. Her makeup is running down her blotchy face. Her eyes are red and swollen. Seeing that I have a sister, I'm proficient in crying women. It breaks my heart to see her like this.

I move to her side and whisper, "Janica."

Whimpering, she wipes away tears and squints her deep brown eyes at me. "Ace, is that you?"

"It's me," I say, opening my arms. She stands up and rushes into them. Wrapped tightly against my chest, she sobs. *This is the first time I'm holding her. I wish it were under better circumstances.* Gently soothing her, I tell her everything will be okay. And it will be. I'll make sure of it.

After a while, she quiets down and I pull back. "Janica, what happened?"

Sniffling, she wipes her nose on her sleeve. "I just found out Trevor has been cheating on me for six months. After you dropped me off, I found them in our bed."

I'm livid. My body shakes with an excess of adrenaline. I want to hurt him. "That asshole," I growl. He just became my enemy number one. Tipping her chin up, I look into her eyes. "And what is your plan now?"

"Tonight? Well, I just wanted to forget it all. Tomorrow, I can move out. I'll just need to find a place to stay," she says, then her body slumps against mine. All the drinking has done her in.

"Rocco, can you give us a ride to my house and then I'll put her in my room for the night? Tomorrow, if she agrees, I can rent a van and help her move out." *Not sure how that's going to go with a walking boot on, but I'll figure it out. For her, I have to.*

"I got you, man. And I can help tomorrow too," he says.

"But you're supposed to go see Jasmine. That's important," I argue.

"Ace, Jasmine will understand. I promise. I'll make it up to her," he insists, emotion heavy in his voice. He's doing this for me. What an incredible best friend I have.

Samantha and Shiloh step forward. "We just texted the guys, and they can help tomorrow too."

"Thanks so much. I'll let the guys know if she's good with it," I say as I support Janica's dead weight.

The drive back to my house is quiet as I hold Janica close to me. Once we park, Rocco carries her inside for me and lays her on my bed.

It's eerily quiet as I walk him back to the front door, then he breaks the silence. "Let me know about tomorrow. We've got her back."

He pulls me in for a quick hug.

"Thanks, man. I appreciate it." He nods before he turns to leave. Shutting the door, I question what to do now.

I head to the kitchen to grab a glass of water and some Tylenol. When I get to my room, I have to hold back a laugh. There, in the middle of my bed, is the woman of my dreams, channeling a starfish. Her arms and legs are cast out as far away from her body as possible. I set the water and meds on the nightstand. Stepping over to the bed, I carefully remove her heels. Grabbing the blanket from the bottom of the bed, I lay it over her. Reaching down, I push the hair covering her face off to the side. I assume she's sleeping soundly from the light snoring and the drool seeping from the corner of her mouth. Once I'm convinced she's okay, I close the door and head back out to my living room, hoping I can catch a few hours of sleep.

Creak. The bedroom door hinges protest their

displeasure at being opened. Then I hear the not-so-quiet noises of someone with a hangover trying to move undetected through an unfamiliar space; mumbles of "ouch" and "oof" on repeat as she tries to navigate the space in the dark.

I quietly call her name, and she startles, her arms flying up like they've regressed to the Moro reflex of a newborn. She spins around and drops her heels, which thunk on the wooden floor. "What are you doing? It's five in the morning."

Grabbing at her head, it's obvious she has a headache and probably will for a while. "Ace, is that you? Where am I?" I turn on the flashlight on my phone and point it at the ceiling. The room is bathed in a faint light.

Smiling at her, I pat the couch cushion next me. My boot still lies on the floor, abandoned. I'm not ready for it yet. "Yes, it is me, and you're at my house."

Her brown gaze darts left and right as she analyzes my words. "Umm... why?"

Stepping over her shoes, she comes to sit next to me.

"What do you remember from yesterday?" I question.

She looks at me, her eyes wide. "I went to work but wasn't feeling well, so I came home right before the end of my shift. Your driver dropped me off. And when I got into the apartment..." She stops talking.

"What?" I prompt.

She hides her face behind her messy hair and whispers, "Trevor was there with his assistant in our bed."

Hearing it again, rage surges through my veins and I twist my hands together. "I'm sorry, Janica. He doesn't deserve you."

She sniffles. "I know, but what am I going to do now? We live together."

"Did you co-sign the rental application?"

She shakes her head. "No, it was his apartment. After we'd been dating a year, he asked me to move in with him, and I did." She sniffles again. "Now I have to find another place."

Move in here. Last night, while lying on my couch, I came up with the perfect solution, a win-win for both of us. She needs a home, and I want to help my friend.

I let go of the tension in my hands and reach for one of hers. "You know, I have a big house. You can move in here until you find another place," I offer.

Janica's mouth drops open and her hand flies to her chest. "I couldn't ask that."

I laugh. "You didn't. I offered."

"But, Ace, you barely know me. I could be a robber or a murderer and you wouldn't know," she protests, her nose squished up like she's disgusted with the thought.

She is fucking adorable. "Are you a robber or murderer?" I ask.

"Well, no," she tells me. I smirk at her. She hums,

then adds, "But my being here would cramp your style."

"Cramp my style?" I laugh. "Never fear, the boot has already done that." Clapping my hands together, I state, "It's settled. My teammates and I are moving you out of Dickface's apartment today and into my house for as long as you need." *My confidence is unwavering.*

"Are you sure about this?" she asks.

Nodding, I meet her worried gaze. "It'll be nice to have a roommate."

I just hope I can keep my hands to myself. I may have just set myself up for a permanent case of blue balls.

Chapter 19

Janica

Ace wasn't kidding when he said his teammates were going to help me move out of Trevor's apartment. Before today, no one had ever come to my aid. It's kind of amazing.

"Janica, these are some of my teammates. This is Lucas, Mika, and Rocco," Ace says, introducing me to the three buff hockey players standing in front of me.

Smiling at them, I say, "Thank you for all your help today. I don't have a lot of stuff, so this shouldn't take long."

Surrounded by four taller-than-average, outrageously handsome professional athletes, I walk into the aging brick building I called my home for the past year. People openly gawk at us. You'd think from all the attention I'm getting that I'm someone special.

Although I don't want to see Trevor, I'm curious about how he'll react to my bodyguards. I unlock the door to the apartment I shared with the cheating asshole. Ace stands next to me with his hand resting on my lower back. At the faint brush of his fingers, my body flushes with heat. It's only subtle contact, but it lights my body on fire. But like being sprayed with cold water, all the happy feelings dissipate when Trevor comes strolling out of the bedroom wearing only a pair of sleep pants. They sit dangerously low, as if he rushed to put them on. My heart sinks. *Is she still here?* Mortified that Ace and his friends will not only see Trevor, but also possibly the woman he cheated on me with, is enough to make my stomach swirl with unease.

"Janica, I wasn't expecting to see you so soon. What's with the goon squad?" Trevor says while puffing out his chest.

"Trevor, are you coming back to bed?" a woman's voice calls from the direction of our bedroom. Trevor smiles like the cat who got the cream, and I want nothing more than to throat punch him. Instead, I just dip my head in embarrassment.

Ace turns to me, pulls me closer, lifts my chin, and makes eye contact. His brown eyes are swimming with emotion. "That's Trevor?" he growls while looking at me. *Is he angry at me? Is he wishing he didn't volunteer to help?* Nervous, I lick my lips and nod.

"Why are you here, Janica? As you can hear, I'm kind of busy," the smarmy asshole says while smirking. *What did I ever see in him?*

Ace grinds his teeth and turns away to glare at

Trevor. "She's not here for you, dickhead. She's moving out."

Trevor gets a wild look in his eyes, and I feel the guys step closer to me. It's like they're forming a protective wall.

"Yeah? Where are you going to go?" He knows I don't have any options and I don't make enough to afford anything decent. "How about your parents? Oh wait, I forgot how excited they were to have you move out." His mocking words slice deep, but I can't deny the truth in them. I never fit into their lifestyle, and they'd been more than pleased when I told them I was moving out. With me gone, they didn't have to fake interest in my life. It feels like I've been sucker punched. All the air in my lungs escapes and my shoulders fold in.

Like a knight in shining armor, Ace answers him in a deep, gravelly voice. "Not that it's any of your business, but she's going to be living with me."

Trevor's eyes bulge out, and he sputters, "Y-you're joking, right?"

Putting his hands on his hips, Ace states, "Not one bit. Janica and I met a few months ago, and in that short amount of time, I've already learned she's kind, funny, thoughtful, generous, honest, encouraging, and beautiful." Standing beside him, my mouth gapes as he talks about me. In the months I've known him, it seems I discovered much of the same about him.

"Trevor, baby, what is going on?" his assistant

whines as she prances out of the bedroom dressed in a gaudy piece of lingerie. When she sees us, she stops and then stares.

I scoff. "Trevor, I have one question for you." Motioning to the assistant, I ask, "If you wanted this, why didn't you just end things with me? What was the purpose of keeping me around?"

Because he's a certifiable dick, I know his answer is going to upset me even before he gives it. He smirks, and I glare at him. "Because I could."

Pain slices through me, but it's not at losing Trevor. It's that I was so easily duped by him.

I can sense the anger rolling off Ace like heat emitting from freshly laid asphalt. Rocco must notice it too, because he puts his arm in front of Ace, stopping him from moving toward Trevor.

Rocco looks at Trevor, huffs, then asks, "Are you two going to stay out of the way so we can pack Janica up?"

Trevor moves toward his assistant, avoiding Ace and his friends.

Two hours later, we have all my things packed into the few moving boxes we brought and the suitcases I had at the apartment. Before I leave, I remove my key from my purse and set it on the counter. Once I'm outside, I take a cleansing breath, knowing I'll never have to deal with Trevor again.

"Ace, are we heading straight to your house to drop everything off?" Lucas asks.

He smiles, replying, "That would be great. Thank you."

"Can I buy you guys pizza or something as a thank you for today?" I ask.

Lucas steps forward. "I have orders to have you and Ace come over to the house tonight for dinner. The Steel ladies want to officially meet you. Everyone is going to be there."

Swallowing hard, I look at Ace. He shrugs, so I say, "Officially meet me? That sounds so serious."

Lucas laughs. "Sorry, it's just most of the ladies were there last night at The Dragon's Lair, and they didn't know if you'd remember them. This way, they can get to know you under better circumstances."

Groaning, I cover my face. "They all saw me drunk and weepy? Shit, that's embarrassing."

Ace tugs my hands away from my face. "Janica, my guys and their ladies are the greatest people you'll ever meet. There's no way they'd hold last night against you. More than likely, they'll pull you into a hug, and after five minutes with you, they'll pick up their pitchforks, ready to inflict revenge on Trevor."

The guys laugh, nodding their heads in agreement.

Rocco speaks up. "He's right. Each one of them has their own story. And no doubt, you'll hear them all."

Mika looks at Rocco. "Can you take Ace, Janica, and the luggage with you? I'll meet you at Ace's with Lucas and the boxes."

After we move all the boxes and luggage into Ace's

garage, Lucas and Mika head out. Before Rocco does, he tells us he'll be back to pick us up for dinner.

When we arrive at Lucas's house for dinner, Nicole's the first one to greet me, her arms wide open and ready to pull me in.

"I guess they told you what happened," I whisper, still embarrassed about my state at the bar.

"They did, but they also told us what a jerk Trevor is, and we're happy you left him. Ace is a much better catch."

Her words stun me. *How did they know I've got more than friendly feelings for Ace?* Sputtering, I say, "Oh, w-we aren't together. I-I mean, I literally just broke up with Trevor last night. Ace is just a friend."

Nicole winks at me. "I know, but things change." She reintroduces Samantha and Shiloh when they join us. I look over at Ace, considering her words. *We're just friends.* I just broke up with Trevor and I'm not ready to jump into another relationship, even if it's with the perfect guy. I don't want him to be a rebound. He's worth more than that, and so am I. *He's my friend.*

He must feel my eyes on him because he looks over at me, and when our gazes connect, he gives me the widest smile. It creates feelings in me I'm not ready to acknowledge, as I'm still trying to process the implosion of my last relationship. *It's too soon.*

"Janica, I was just about to make some virgin strawberry daiquiris. Do you want one?" Samantha asks, a baby in her arms.

"That sounds amazing. Between the head pressure from my cold and the bender last night, I'm giving up alcohol for a while," I say, following them.

She laughs. "Me too, but for a whole different reason. Breastfeeding and alcohol don't mix." When she goes to gather everything she needs, she realizes she'll need both hands. Looking at me, she asks, "Would you mind holding Chloe while I play bartender?"

Shiloh and Nicole stand next to me with empty arms. "I'm getting over a cold. I really shouldn't," I say.

She smiles and nods. "I appreciate you telling me. I would hate for her to catch something." She sets the baby in her bouncy chair on the counter, turning on the vibrating butt pad. In no time, she's asleep.

Chloe sleeps through the racket the blender makes and the ornate doorbell, alerting us dinner has arrived.

"Pizza is here," Lucas calls before he walks into the kitchen, his arms full of boxes. He places a tender kiss on the exposed skin of Samantha's neck. "Damn, you smell good," he growls. Assuming those words were just for her, I turn away, a blush covering my cheeks, mentally fanning myself. *What would it be like to have a man behave that way around me?* Shut up, brain. You aren't being helpful. *Stay in the moment.*

Focusing on the sweet baby, I grin. I lift my head, and my gaze catches Ace's across the room. He smiles at me and butterflies dance in my stomach. My pulse climbs. He approaches and says, "I've never seen you look so happy, relaxed, and..."

"And?" I question, wanting to know what he's holding back.

He pauses, taking a moment before he tucks a strand of hair behind my ear and whispers, "Beautiful." I gape at him in disbelief. *Did he just say that, or did I dream it up?*

"W-what?" I stutter, feeling off-kilter.

"Wings are here," Lucas announces as he strides out of the kitchen, returning minutes later with multiple bags filled with to-go containers. *How many people are eating?*

Still stunned by Ace's confession, I almost miss Samantha's next directions. "Tonight, we are doing this family style. Load a plate, grab a drink, and find a seat wherever."

I step back, watching everyone move about. It's like they're a well-organized and choreographed machine. Obviously, they've done this before.

Like a champ, Shiloh helps her two kids with their plates. And then she leaves them at the dinner table with Mika before fixing her own plate.

Still on baby watch, I stand near the counter, making sure Chloe is fine. "I'll grab Chloe so you can eat," Lucas tells me as he and Samantha approach. Moving over to Samantha, she hands me a daiquiri.

"This looks delicious. Thank you," I say before taking my first sip. Smooth and icy, the strawberry-flavored drink soothes my overheated body. Licking my lips, I ask, "Do I taste lime?" Samantha just smiles and then flicks her gaze at Ace. I look back at him, and under his intense focus, I feel myself grow excited. *What is happening?* Ace has never looked at me like this before. His heated stare is unnerving, but in a good way. Standing here, lost in the moment, I find I enjoy being the object of his interest. The hungry look in his brown eyes makes me question if I'm also the object of his desire.

"You two going to eat?" Rocco asks. His question breaks the private moment we'd been sharing.

"Are you hungry?" I ask Ace.

He nods, then answers, "Always."

Chapter 20

Ace

Dinner tonight at Lucas and Samantha's had been great. My Steel family is incredible, and I knew Janica would fit in perfectly.

Returning to my house, it's still early, so I turn to Janica and ask, "Do you want to watch a movie before bed?"

"Sure. Do you mind if I hop in the shower quickly and change into something more comfortable?"

Just thinking about her in the shower, wet and soapy, causes my brain to misfire. *Down, boy.* I will the semi in my pants away as I think about the situation I'm in. Above everything, I want Janica to feel safe and comfortable. In the meantime, I'm going to have to figure out how to keep my attraction to her under control. *This is going to be hard.*

"That gives me time to make popcorn," I say. "I think the guys moved all your boxes and suitcases into the spare room next to mine. There should be clean towels under the sink in the hall bathroom. Or at least that's where I think my ma put them when she was here. If you can't find them, let me know and I'll hunt around."

"Thanks again for letting me crash at your place. I can't tell you how much I appreciate it. As soon as I can, I'll get out of your hair."

"It'll be nice to have you here. There's no rush for you to find a place. Please stay as long as you need." *Or forever*. She nods, then turns down the hallway and enters the spare room. In moments, she's standing back in front of me.

"Howdy, darling. Did you find the towels?" I ask.

"I did, and they are so soft. But I found one thing missing." I hear the distress in her voice and panic sets in.

"What's missing?"

Fumbling with her words, she finally asks, "Umm, do you have another bed?"

Somewhat embarrassed, I answer, "No. You can sleep in my bed."

She blanches at my suggestion. "I couldn't do that. It's your bed, plus you're recovering from a broken leg."

"It'll be fine. I promise," I insist.

She looks over to the couch, frazzled. "You can't sleep there. You're way too long. I can just grab an Uber and go to a hotel tonight. I can see if I can crash with Veronica for a week. Can I keep my boxes in your spare room until I can figure it all out?"

"Really, Janica, the couch will be fine." Or I could always have Rocco bring back the air mattress my ma used when she was here.

She places her hands on her hips. "The only way I'm staying is if we share the bed. You need to continue to heal, and you won't be able to get the rest you need if you're trying to squish yourself onto a too-small couch. Your bed is massive. And seeing that we are mature adults, we can set extra pillows in the middle like a barrier. Would you feel comfortable with that?"

I nod. "It would be nice not having to move a few more times. Are you sure it won't be an inconvenience to you?"

Ace laughs. "It'll be nice to have one of my friends here all the time."

She rolls her eyes. "After living with me, you may reconsider that friendship label."

Smirking at her, I ask, "Why? Would it be because I'd want something more?"

She scoffs. "Not likely."

Her words make me angry. Clearly, she doesn't see what I do. Not only is she breathtaking, but she's kind, thoughtful, genuine, funny, and smart. It's going to be my mission while she's here to get her to accept that she's all that and more. Instead of acknowledging her personal dig, I ask, "Aren't you going to shower? I have a movie to pick and some popcorn to pop." Once she shuffles off, I grab the remote. It's a good thing I have to focus on a movie selection because thinking of her naked would certainly make the evening hard. And not in the way I'd benefit from. Having her as my roommate is going to test me greatly. Am I up for the challenge? We'll see.

Sitting down on the couch, I set the bowl of popcorn on the coffee table before I pull a blanket over my lap. I hear the chime of a text message and I retrieve my phone from my pocket. "Not mine," I say to myself. Leaning forward, I set my phone next to the bowl of popcorn and hear another text chime. "Must be Janica's." At least three more texts come through before she appears.

"Ready?" she asks as she walks into my living room with her wet hair tied up on top of her head. She has no makeup on, and her soft peach skin glows. She's wearing a matching black cotton sleep set that is making it tough for me to swallow. Absolutely fucking gorgeous is how I would describe her if I was asked. She is a vision, or at least the best of my spank bank material. Before I can even answer her, her phone chimes again.

"It's been doing that the last few minutes," I tell her.

"I'll just silence it so it doesn't interrupt the—" Her words cut off, and I look up to find a panicked expression stretching across her face.

"What is it?" I ask, concerned.

Slowly walking toward me, she flips the phone around so I can see. It's a half-dozen messages from Trevor. "I'm not sure I want to open them," she mumbles, hesitancy laced in her voice.

Pulling back the blanket, I say, "Come here. If you want to open them, I'll be right here. If you don't, I'll still be right here. Remember, he doesn't have any power over you. You ended things with him because he was awful. You don't owe him anything."

Janica settles into my side, and I feel her shiver against me. "Do you have enough of the blanket, or do you want me to go get one of my sweatshirts?"

"No, I'm good if you stay right there," she replies. *There's no place I'd rather be.*

Having her snuggled into my side is incredible. It's where she's meant to stay. I want to wrap my arms around her and pull her even closer. *She just broke up with her cheating boyfriend.* The truth of her situation slaps me in the face, sobering me. I watch her as she stares at her phone.

"Do you regret moving out?" I ask through tightly clenched teeth. *Please say no.*

Turning toward me, her eyes wide, she says, "Are you kidding?"

"People make mistakes. Maybe he's realized that." I shrug.

Her hands start fidgeting, straightening all the folds out of the blanket we share. "Yes, people make mistakes, but he didn't do it once, regret it, confess, and apologize. He cheated on me for months. He knew what he was doing."

"So why do you think he's texting now?"

Her laugh holds no humor in it. "You got me. Maybe he has no clean clothes, or he's taken a massive, messy poop and run out of toilet paper, or he can't find the dishwasher pods. Who knows? Trevor is helpless, and he got way too comfortable letting me do everything for him. Serves him right. He has to figure it out himself or ask his assistant." *Well said, beautiful.*

Tossing the blanket back, I stand. "I forgot something. I'll be right back and then we can watch the movie." I feel her gaze follow me to the kitchen, and my body heats. It's amazing to be the focus of her attention.

Pulling the bag of sour gummy worms from the pantry, I also grab two water bottles from the fridge before making my way back out to the couch, where Janica is snuggled into the blanket. "Are you sure you're warm enough? I can go grab a hoodie for you."

Reaching out of her cozy cocoon, she pats the seat next to her. "Just missed your heat. I'll be good now that you are back." Smiling, I sit back down and hand her the treat I'd brought to share. "Sour gummy worms. Ace, you're spoiling me." Her cute squeal makes my heart soar. *If that's all I have to do to make her feel spoiled, she'll be feeling like royalty in no time.*

I laugh. "You have to share them. They're my favorite too." We settle in and turn on the movie. I picked *Jurassic Park*. I mean, who doesn't like dinosaurs? Plus, every time she's surprised, she jumps into my arms. Holding her tight, feeling her curves tucked into mine, is a definite highlight for me.

When the movie is done, we clean up and get ready for bed. When she comes into my room, she's still dressed in her plain sleep set. Some would probably say it's boring, but I swear it's the sexiest thing I've ever seen. Add in that her long brown hair is down, the wavy tips dancing above her perfect breasts. My gaze traces over the lines of her tank top like a parched man who's stumbled upon a lake. Greedily, I suck in labored breaths as I imagine what's underneath the thin, soft cotton. Is her skin soft and freckled like I've imagined? Overheated, I nervously reach up to adjust my shirt. When my hand comes in contact with skin, I remember I opted to go shirtless, pulling only athletic shorts on for bed. Janica's brown eyes go wide in surprise, and I watch her slowly peruse my body. Unsure of what to say or do, I remain still. An awkwardness fills the surrounding air. My gaze flicks to the bed, jarring my memory. "I, uh... I already set up the pillow wall in the middle of the bed, and I grabbed another blanket for you."

Janica nods and goes to the other side of the bed. She lies down and pulls the blanket over her. She's stiff and unrelaxed. I sit down on the edge of the bed, turn toward her, and say, "Is there anything else I can get you?"

"I'm fine," she whispers as she tugs the blanket higher. *Is she as miserable as she looks?*

"I can sleep on the couch if it will make you more comfortable," I offer.

She sits up. "I'm sorry, Ace. I've only ever slept with Trevor. And I'm not saying we're going to "sleep" together. It's just... I know we aren't sleeping together. Ahh. I'm ruining this. What I'm trying to say is, I don't want you to sleep on your couch. I'm just nervous because you aren't my boyfriend and I'm sharing a bed with you." Her rambling is adorable, but I understand her trepidation.

"You're my friend, Janica. And yes, we're sharing a bed, but I'm not expecting anything in return. Believe it or not, I've never shared my bed with anyone. You're my first." *I'd like you to be my last.*

She gasps and rolls over toward me. "A bed-sharing virgin? How is that possible? You're a good-looking guy who's also a professional athlete. You aren't a virgin, are you?"

I dip my head, and she loudly sucks in a breath of surprise. Then I laugh. "No, I'm not a virgin. I just don't host sleepovers. I'm picky about who I invite into my space. Not just any lady can sleep in my bed."

She gives me a side-eye and asks, "But you're letting me?"

I smile at her. "You, Janica, are my friend. And for friends, I would do just about anything. Including sharing my bed." She nods, then lies back.

Assuming the conversation is over, I turn away and remove my walking boot. Before I lie down, I turn off the bedroom lights with my phone before setting it on the charger. Into the dark room, I say, "Good night, Janica. I hope you sleep well."

A quiet sigh comes from the other side of the bed. "Good night, Ace. Thank you again for letting me stay here. I appreciate it."

Chapter 21

Janica

My alarm goes off and I reach for the nightstand to silence it. As soon as I move an inch, I feel an arm tighten around my waist, tugging me backward. In a nanosecond, I'm plastered to a hard, well-defined chest. *Ace?* Panicked, my eyes fly open and my heart pounds out an unsteady beat. He lets out a small snore behind me. *What happened to the impenetrable pillow wall?* Lifting my head, I find my answer. The pillows are strewn about. Some are still on the bed and others have disappeared completely. They're probably on the floor. One of us apparently plowed through it during the night. But who and why? From the way Ace's arm is anchoring me to him, my guess is he is responsible, but then I notice I migrated too. In fact, I'm much closer to his side of the bed than my own.

I try to squirm away from him, but I have no luck.

Every time I move, his hold tightens on me like he's a boa constrictor squeezing its prey. As I lie there, thinking of ways to escape, I can't help but wish this were real. I know I just broke up with Trevor, but our relationship had soured months earlier, and apparently, he's moved on, so why couldn't I?

Being snuggled in Ace's arms is a dream come true. Since I'm stuck, I might as well enjoy it. Right? I melt into him, savoring the heat of his hard body against my much softer one. I notice immediately that our curves fit together perfectly. His muscular forearm hugs around my soft waist, and he pulls me against his hips. As I shift my hips to get more comfortable, I brush against something long and hard. *Is that his penis?*

I close my eyes, listening to the quiet cadence of his breathing. My body relaxes further, and just as I'm about to fall back asleep, my alarm goes off again. Ace's arms tighten around me again and then he tenses. I can tell the moment he's awake enough to realize that during the night, we crossed a line. I remain still, curious about what he'll do. When he gently slips his arm from around me and rolls onto his back, my heart flinches. As soon as his body disappears, I shiver from the lost heat and connection we'd been sharing. I crave his touch like I do my next breath.

Ace pushes out a deep breath and then sits up. I can just barely hear him adjust the Velcro straps on his boot over my pounding heart. As soon as he's done, he rises from the bed. Not wanting to face him yet, I pretend like I'm still asleep. *Stupid girl.* I'm mortified. I'd enjoyed our connectedness so much, and it seems like he couldn't get away from me fast enough.

My alarm goes off for the third time, and I try to pretend like I'm just waking up. Stretching my body over to the nightstand, I turn it off. Sitting up, I look around the room. He isn't here. Not only did he run from the bed, but he ran from the room too. *Shit.* Had we just messed up our friendship? What if I pretend it never happened? Then all he has to do is get over it. *But is that possible?* I don't know if I can pretend. I now know what it feels like to be held by him, and I never want to forget. Bringing my knees up, I hug them to my chest while I consider what to do. *I can't stay here with him. I have to move.*

Opening my phone, I pull up an apartment finder website. I put in one bed, one bath, and hit search. Almost ten thousand hits come back, and I'm instantly overwhelmed. *There's got to be something here.* Looking at the first ones, I see the rent listed at about two thousand dollars a month. *What?* Looking up, I see I didn't specify a monthly rent. I quickly change it to something in my price range and run the search again. Thirty hits return, and I look at the map to see where the apartments are located. They're all over the city. Guess I know what I'm doing this weekend: pounding the pavement and finding an apartment. Maybe I can find a pull-out couch at the Goodwill store so I don't have to spend money I don't have on furniture. It's just me, so I don't need anything fancy. Plus, Goodwill also stocks basic kitchen items and bedding.

Just as I'm bookmarking the page for the apartment results, Ace comes back into the bedroom. He's wearing a confused look on his face. "Morning," I say, trying to break the tension. He looks so uncomfortable with me in his space. I knew this would happen. I don't give him any time to respond to my greeting before I've launched into the swirling chaos of my mind. Afraid he'll see through my thinly veiled disguise, I lower my head, refusing to make eye contact.

"I appreciate you opening your house to me, but I just don't feel right about staying here and invading your space. I've already looked up some promising apartments, and I'm going to get dressed and contact the rental offices to see if I can tour them today. Maybe by the end of this weekend, I'll have found a new place." I chance a look up, and the confusion on his face has morphed into a scowl. *What's that about?* Is he mad I might need the weekend to get out? "Or I can get a hotel room if you'd like me out sooner," I offer, worry strangling my voice.

"Out sooner?" he says. My heart drops. I don't register the question in his voice. Standing up from the bed, I walk toward the door, and he grabs me and growls, "Where do you think you're going?"

"You said you want me out sooner, so I'm going to get myself packed up, find a hotel room, and call an Uber. I'm sorry for imposing, Ace."

Still holding my arm, he turns to me and, in an authoritative tone, says, "No " His voice sounds rough and incredibly sexy. A shiver runs down my back. *Stop it, Janica.* He's not trying to seduce you.

"No? What's that supposed to mean?"

He pulls me closer, the thumb of the hand holding my arm, stroking my skin as if he's trying to comfort me. *That feels nice.* "It means you aren't going anywhere. You are not looking for another apartment. You are not packing up. You are not moving out. I want you here, and I won't accept you leaving."

I swallow hard, not sure I heard him correctly. "But you seemed upset when you left the room this morning, and I assumed I did something wrong. I don't want to do anything to mess up our friendship."

"Friendship?" he growls.

Flustered, I just nod.

"You weren't still asleep when I left?" His gaze burns into mine. "When exactly did you wake up, Janica?"

Oh no. Worry about how he'll react churns in my gut. *I can't tell him, because if I do, I'll have to admit I knew we were snuggling and I liked it.*

"Janica." His voice is deeper and more unnerving. It's not scary, per se, but it's definitely demanding. It sends unfamiliar tingles through my body... and I shiver with pleasure.

Unable to lie, I lower my head and mumble,

"When my alarm first went off, I was awake before you were, and I pretended to be asleep when you woke up."

He drops my arm and scratches his head. "Why?" I understand what he's asking, but I would do just about anything right now not to answer.

"Why?" I parrot.

He lets out a breath like he's frustrated. "Why did you pretend to be asleep?"

Staring at my feet, I wiggle my pink-painted toes, waiting to see if he'll keep pushing me. *Please don't. Just drop it.* Unfortunately, my silent pleas are ignored. He tips my chin up. "Please talk to me, Janica."

When I look up, I'm met with a smile that makes my knees weak. His mocha-colored eyes beg me for an answer. Pushing down the unease I'm feeling, I answer, "When I woke up, we weren't on separate sides of the bed anymore." I pause, letting that sink in. I watch his reaction to my words. He swallows hard and nods his head as I add, "You were holding me like I was..." I force out an uncomfortable laugh, hoping it will diffuse the tension circling us.

Ace's gaze is intent on mine, like everything hinges on my answer. "Like you were what?"

"Like I was *yours*."

And that's when Ace's cheeks turn an adorable shade of pink. *He's embarrassed.* "I'm sorry, Janica. I didn't know what I was doing. But you were nice to snuggle with," he admits, then grins at me. His eyes go wide with realization. "Is that why you were going to move out? Because I used you as my personal stuffed animal? Did I hurt you or make you uncomfortable?"

Shaking my head, I say, "It was actually the best sleep I've gotten in a long time. You're a great cuddler." Then, from my admission, I feel my cheeks grow hot.

He smiles widely, but then it dims. "I don't understand, though. Why did you pretend to be asleep?"

"Because I thought you'd be mad about how we ended up." *I wasn't, though.* Being snuggled up to Ace was the best I've felt in months.

He frowns. "I wasn't mad at you. I was disappointed in myself. We're friends and I crossed a line. Last night before we went to bed, I reminded myself to stay on my side of the mattress, but my subconscious had other plans. I'm really sorry."

"Stop apologizing. We're both responsible for what happened. Can we just move on? I mean, nothing happened." *Though, I wouldn't have complained if it had.* Thoughts of what could've happened fill my mind and my heart begins to race. My body grows warm, and I can feel myself sweat. *Stop it. He's told you that you're just friends.* That thought instantly sends a chill racing through my veins.

He pulls me into a hug. *Just friends.* And squeezes. *Just friends.*

"So, enough talk about moving out. What do you want to do today? Since it's the weekend, you don't have to work, and I'm all caught up on homework."

"Since I'm staying, I should probably unpack. Do

you know if there's a store nearby where I could buy some hangers and inexpensive stackable containers? I'd like to get my clothes out of my suitcases and boxes."

"Did you look at what is already in the spare room? Whatever's there, you can use. I know Ma got a few things. And I know the perfect store to go get anything else you might need." Leading me to the spare room, he opens the closets, and he wasn't kidding. Inside are plastic stackers that will work perfectly for some of my clothes. I just need a few more to unpack everything.

"That's great. Thank you. I know of a few things I'd still like to get." Smiling, I ask, "Do you want to come with me?" *Please say yes.* I enjoy spending time with him, talking and laughing. In the short time we've known each other, he's already become one of my closest friends. When it comes to sharing, he's an open book, telling me all about hockey, his family, and the farm. I'm much more reserved. I've yet to tell him anything more than surface-level stuff. It's not that I don't trust him. I don't want him to either look down on me or with pity for the life I've had.

"It's a date," he says, and my heart flutters. *Can you imagine?* A second later, the balloon pops when he corrects himself. "I mean, yes, I'd love to come, but I need breakfast first." I force a smile after what feels like my heart's been trampled.

"I'll meet you in the kitchen in a few. I need to take a shower and get dressed first."

"Me too," he answers.

Chapter 22

Ace

When we enter the store later that morning, I'm not sure what Janica is looking for, but I'm fairly confident we'll find something. While she's looking for the best storage containers for the bedroom, I get distracted by the custom spaces section and I get thinking about my disorganized closet.

"Can I help you with something, sir?" a woman asks as she approaches. The way she's looking at me makes me uneasy.

I force a smile. "I'm just looking while a friend shops."

"Are you sure there isn't anything I can interest you in?" she says while stepping closer. Her proximity and voice put me on edge.

I take a step back. "I'm all good here. Thanks."

"Ace, where did you go?" I hear Janica say from a

few aisles over where I left her. *Thank goodness. Maybe the saleslady will leave me alone.*

Taking another step back, I turn as fast as I can with a walking boot and call back to Janica, "Don't move. I'm coming to you." Striding off, I assume the saleslady will get the hint.

The sound of heels clicking on a hard surface follows behind, and I feel my shoulders creep up in annoyance.

"Found you," I breathe out as I step up close to Janica and wrap my arm around her. Lowering my lips to her ear, I whisper, "Warning: clingy saleslady. Please play along. You'll be saving my ass." She nods, and excitement floods my veins, wondering how far she'll take this. Just having her tucked into my side has my body buzzing like an electrical outlet has shocked me.

"Babe, I just found the cutest containers that'll work perfectly for what I'm planning at home," she exclaims, pointing to the containers in front of her. "But I need your opinion on what color you think we should get."

The lurching saleslady, who is testing all my patience, steps closer to me. She puts her hand on the arm that isn't around Janica and leans in. She's staring at me while talking to Janica. "You have a good eye. Those containers are buy one, get one fifty percent off today."

Janica does a happy dance. "So, what color do you think we should get?" she excitedly asks me again.

I step closer to the containers and out of the reach of the saleswoman. "I think you should pick yellow. It's happy and sunny and reminds me of you."

"That's so sweet," she says while picking the sizes of containers she wants in yellow. When she has her arms piled high, she looks back at me. "You're sure this isn't too much?"

I tip her head and gaze into her gorgeous honey-brown colored eyes. I've never felt so connected to someone. I feel like I'm staring into her pure, unblemished, vulnerable soul. *Does she feel our connection too?* "Not at all," I answer her. Hearing that, the saleswoman clucks, then retreats. The click of her heels fades into the distance as I'm lost in Janica's smile. *Fuck, she's beautiful.* My heart thumps in my chest, and my pulse races through my veins. Being this close, my body reacts to hers. Feeling overheated, my hands sweat. Dropping the one from under her chin, I wipe it on my shorts before I take the empty containers from her hands. "Let me help you."

"You're so sweet, Ace. Thank you." *I'm not always sweet.* Stirring up fantasies about how *not* sweet I'd like to be to her is not a good idea when I'm out in public with my ultra-sexy roommate who doesn't know I find her irresistible.

"Where to next?" I ask after she's paid for her new

containers. I ordered an Uber while she did that. "Uber will be here in a few minutes."

She peers around the giant stack of bright containers. "I'm glad I went with yellow. They make me happy. Speaking of things that make me happy, I love to cook. After dropping these off at your house, do you want to come with me to the grocery store? I want to make dinner for you tonight as a thank you, and I need to pick up some things for the week."

I laugh. "That sounds great. My pre-made fish dinner in the fridge didn't sound appealing this morning, and I was trying to figure out an alternative." Janica laughs too.

After dropping the containers off, we head to the market nearby. "What do you want for dinner?" she asks as we enter the store.

Shrugging, I answer, "You choose."

Looking at me with disbelief, she whispers, "You really don't care?"

I honestly don't, so I shake my head.

"Okay, I have a lot of questions for you. Is there anything you're allergic to? Anything you don't eat? How loaded is your kitchen?"

I smile. "No allergies. I like almost anything except sushi. I refuse to eat oysters or organs. And my kitchen is fully stocked with appliances, dishes, and utensils."

Janica's bright eyes dance, and I wonder what she's thinking. She's playful and adorable. My fingers flex. I want to touch her, pull her close. *She just broke up with her boyfriend.* That argument loses most of its power when I remember he was cheating on her. *She isn't ready.* That's believable, and I won't be the asshole who pushes anything, despite how badly I want to call her mine. I tighten my hands around the shopping cart, ready to follow her wherever she goes. *Damn, I'm already whipped, and she's not even mine.*

"How do you feel about pork tenderloin?" she questions.

"I'm in, but only if you're also making mashed potatoes," I tease. I'm only half-serious. There's something about the combination of a tender, well-seasoned pork tenderloin and creamy mashed potatoes that does things to me.

She smiles. "How about pork tenderloin, garlic and sour cream mashed potatoes, roasted asparagus, and rolls?"

I swallow hard. *This is the woman of my dreams.* Awkwardly, and looking like I'm an animatronic, I lower to one knee. "Will you marry me?"

Shocked, her eyes go wide. Her head darts back and forth, looking to see if anyone's watching. A blush stains her cheeks. "Ace, get up," she mumbles through tight lips.

I laugh and then dramatically clutch my chest. "So that's a no?" Using the counter for help, I stand before she even responds, pulling her to my side. "I was teasing. We aren't there." I wanted to add *yet*, but I don't want her freaking out. Instead, she just blinks her eyes rapidly, as if she's trying to catch up. "Where to?" I ask, my hands wrapped around the shopping cart handle.

In a half hour, we find everything we need for dinner, plus I find out that every workday for her lunch, Janica has a turkey and colby-jack sandwich. I have flashbacks to packing my lunches in high school when she loads Ziploc bags, a family-size bag of pretzels, and a tray of cookies into the cart. To round it out, she grabs a bag of apples, some baby carrots, sweet peppers, and mini cucumbers.

"Do you need some ranch for all those veggies?" I ask.

"Nope, I like them plain."

Nodding, I push the cart forward, right past the delicious salad dressing aisle. *Where's the fun in that?* I love Ranch. I'm not a believer that Ranch is its own food group, but I dip a lot of stuff in it.

We move on, and I finish my first grocery shopping date, I mean excursion, with the woman of my dreams.

Chapter 23

Janica

After the grocery store run, we head home. *It's not your home.* Well, it's my temporary home until I can find an affordable apartment.

Flashbacks of earlier when Ace told me I wasn't moving out flood my mind. The gruffness in his voice made me hot and bothered. I don't know if he noticed me squeezing my thighs together to dull the intense ache that appeared when he demanded I stay. My brain struggles to function properly whenever he's nearby. In no time, I have discovered he is everything. Kind, funny, sexy, honest, and reliable are just some words I'd use to describe him.

I spent most of the rest of the afternoon organizing my new containers and unpacking. Ace was right about the yellow. They're bright and cheery, and you can't help but smile when you see them.

Having worked up a thirst with all the shifting and shuffling, I make my way to the kitchen. When I pass through the living room, I see Ace, dressed in only a pair of athletic shorts, doing his at-home physical therapy exercises. If I thought I was thirsty before, my mouth now resembles the desert. He is completely unaware I'm unashamedly gawking at him because his eyes are closed and he's wearing noise-canceling head-phones. Tracing all the curves and muscles of his upper body, I knew I was staring, but I couldn't look away.

Holy shit. Ace has undeniably the most incredible body I've ever seen. Not only does he have exquisite arms with defined muscles, but his abs are divine. He doesn't just have a six-pack; he has a full eight-pack on display and they're begging for my touch.

Licking my lips, I remember I was on my way to the kitchen for water. *He looks hot.* Maybe he'd like something cool to drink too. Turning quickly before I'm noticed, I grab us both something to drink before returning to the living room. The cool water I splash on my wrist brings my heart rate somewhat closer to normal.

With my hands full, I step closer. Ace finally notices me. His gaze travels up my body to my eyes, and he smiles before pulling off his headphones. "Hi." His deep voice registers in my overexcited core.

"H-hi," I stutter. "I came out to get some water and saw you exercising, so I grabbed one for you too."

"Thank you. I was just trying to get some PT in while you were busy." Smiling again, his bright white teeth show, and my insides grow giddy. *He is so handsome.* A thousand butterflies take flight in my stomach. *He has the best smile.*

Dipping back his head, he almost drains the bottle, and I'm mesmerized by the movement of his Adam's apple. I have to suppress a moan, because seeing him swallow is so incredibly sexy

After his drink, he wipes his mouth with the back of his hand and clears his throat. "Are you going to need help with dinner?"

"I think I have it covered. I want you to sit back and relax."

"Yes, ma'am," he says before he nods his head, accepting my command.

An hour later, he wanders into the kitchen. "That smells delicious. My mouth is watering already."

Blushing at his compliment, I look up from the tenderloin I'm browning on the stovetop. *Holy hell.* He's still shirtless. *Is he trying to drive me insane?* My libido is screaming, *"Hey, big guy, want to take me for a ride?"*

"I'm starving. Is it almost ready?" he asks as he takes in my outfit. After digging through my suitcase, I settled on a pair of dingy aqua sweats that I've had for years. They are the coziest piece of clothing I own, and I wear them whenever I need an extra dose of confidence. They hide my flaws perfectly. I've always been critical of the way I look, but this afternoon I gave myself a break and wore what I liked. Most of the time, I dress strategically to draw attention to my nicer assets, like my full, high breasts or my well-toned arms. Working at the library and stacking so many books has given me a free arm workout, and I'm not complaining about my definition one bit.

"It'll be about half an hour," I say, while reaching for the baking pan. One look at Ace and my panties grow damp as I see him slowly lick his lips. *I want to feel those lips on my skin.* Glancing down, I notice he's fixated on the cleavage shot I'm providing. *Oops.*

When I peer back up at him, I see his brown eyes have turned almost black. *What does that mean?* He steps closer and again licks his lips. "Did I mention I'm starving?" he husks out.

I nod. The way he's looking at me makes me hot, like I'm going to melt into a puddle of goo right on his wood floor. *Has anyone looked at me like that before? No.* Feeling out of my depth, I switch my focus from the devastatingly handsome man standing next to me to putting the tenderloin in the oven.

"Are you sure you don't need any help? Ma had me help in the kitchen a lot when I was younger until I could be of help on the farm." Just picturing a younger Ace, I smile.

"Were you a cowboy?" I ask playfully.

A stunning smile stretches across his face. "I still am." *Damn, that's hot.* I want to fan my face to cool myself off. Instead, I embrace the fantasy overtaking my brain, and dig deeper.

"You have boots, a hat, and a belt buckle?" I ask, my voice wavering with desire. Cowboy romance is one of my favorite tropes. There is something about a powerful man who skillfully operates huge equipment and wrangles animals that's incredibly sexy.

Ace tips an invisible cowboy hat to me, drops his voice, and says, "Yes, ma'am. I can even country line dance. I'd show you, but this boot would be a hindrance to me stomping, kicking, or grapevining anywhere."

"That's a shame. I guess once you're out of that, you can teach me." My heart squeezes in my chest at the hope I'll still be around and close to him in a few months when he's cleared to engage in full activity again.

"It's a date," he croons, his smile incinerating my already damp panties. "I better get out of the kitchen. I'm distracting you from finishing dinner. If you're sure I can't help, I'll skedaddle."

"Skedaddle?" I laugh at his word choice, choosing not to focus on his date comment. "What does that mean?"

"My ma says it means to get out of your way."

Chapter 24

Ace

Leaving Janica in the kitchen goes against every one of my wants and needs. I want to be next to her making dinner. I want to spin her around the kitchen as our dinner cooks. I need to have her next to me, our heated bodies saying the things we can't. I need to kiss those soft pink lips that have tantalized me for the past few months.

Needing a distraction, I open the music app on my phone. I hit shuffle and the first song almost brings me to my knees. It's a soulful country song where the singer talks about all his love for a certain woman. Every word hits me in the chest, becoming my silent prayer.

As I sit on my couch pondering when I can make her mine, another song comes on. It's about how these lovers met and what he'd do for her. Even though I recognize my feelings are new and intense, if Janica were to ask for anything, my answer would be, *anything for you.* The understanding that I've never felt this way should scare me, but it doesn't. I want more with her. But I also understand she just got out of a terrible relationship and she needs time. I don't want to be a rebound or a regret. I want to be her future.

Needing to get out of my head, I switch to a faster, less emotional playlist that features some of the best songs to country line dance to. Having no one to take or go with, I don't even know if there's a country bar close by. Shortly after I came to the Steel, I tamped down some of my country charm because it made me a target of teasing from my teammates. Nothing they ever did was cruel or mean, it just made me miss home and my family.

Thoughts of my family make me wonder how Janica would fit in with them. It doesn't take long to conclude that she'd fit seamlessly. Graham would be the only brother who wouldn't drool over her, but he'd steal her heart for sure. Melissa would befriend her, and I'm sure in no time they'd be sharing secrets and laughter. My parents would love how sweet and kind she is. Ma would drag her to the kitchen to teach her all my favorites, and Dad would tell her all about the things we grew on the farm. Before introductions would be made, I'd have to be sure she was mine and committed to our future, because if anything changed, they'd never forgive me for not making her part of the family.

"Dinners ready," Janica calls from the kitchen. Sniffing the air, my stomach growls its approval. I don't have a dining room table because I've had no need for one. But that might be changing. "Hope this is fine," she says as she points to the place settings she's set out on the island. At least I have enough bar stools to accommodate a few guests.

"This is amazing. I haven't had a home-cooked meal since Ma was here helping me recover from surgery. Thank you, Janica. Everything looks and smells delicious." An adorable blush covers her cheeks, matching the pink tint of the perfectly cooked tenderloin. She graces me with a sweet smile.

"Mmmm," falls from my lips as I lick away the savory juice from the meat. Her blush gets darker, and she dips her head like she's embarrassed. "Aren't you going to try some? I think it's the best pork tenderloin I've ever had."

She giggles. "It sounds like you're enjoying it." Then she flicks her gaze to mine, and I'd swear her eyes have turned the color of caramel. They're captivating, sucking me in like a magnet.

"I am," I answer, lust coursing through my veins faster than the speed of light. My blood rushes to my groin, and all rational thought evacuates the premises. Can you be so horny you dissociate? Because I swear I'm watching my fucking hand reach for Janica, but I have no control over it. *Stop it. It's too soon.* But no matter what I tell myself, it keeps advancing. Whatever spell I'm under breaks when her phone rings incessantly. "You should probably get that," I tell her while silently reprimanding myself for almost crossing a boundary I'd set for myself.

"Really?" I hear her say as she looks at her phone.

"Who is it?"

The phone stops ringing.

She lets out a breath, but I notice her shoulders have fallen and her smile has disappeared. "It's Trevor," she mumbles.

Jackass. The phone rings again. "Want me to answer it?" I offer, smirking.

She shakes her head. "I think I'm just going to silence it so we can get back to enjoying our dinner. If he leaves a message, I can deal with him later."

My blood boils. He better stay away from her. I may be recovering from a broken leg, but I will still protect her from her ex.

We return to our dinners, but the moment we were having is broken. The delicious sexual tension that had been heavy in the air when we first sat down to dinner, has dissipated. The food is still delicious, but its flavors have dulled since the first bites.

After dinner, I boot her out of the kitchen so I can do the dishes. She cooked, so I'll clean. I even tell her she should go take a relaxing bubble bath in my jacuzzi tub. But while I'm finishing up cleaning the kitchen, I hear the faint whispers of her talking to someone. I can tell she's trying to remain calm, but it sounds tense. I wonder if she called Trevor. Maybe she finally called Veronica to tell her everything that's happened. Although I suspect that conversation would have been much louder than a hushed whisper. Telling myself I just need to use the bathroom, I step into the one across the hall from the spare room that houses all her stuff.

Assuaged with guilt, I'm about to escape the bathroom when I hear her say, "We are done, Trevor. I don't want to see you ever again." Not able to see through the wooden door, I hear Janica drop her voice. "No, you listen here, Trevor. I don't need you or my parents. I'm just fine by myself." *What about me? She has me.* I'm about to storm over to the spare room and remind her of that when she says something that halts me. "Starting today, I am no longer willing to surround myself with horrible people who think they're doing me a favor by being in my life. I'm choosing to surround myself with people who love me for me." A smile spreads across my face. I am so proud of her. On top of all her other amazing attributes, she's strong as fuck too. And I think I just fell even farther for her.

Chapter 25

Janica

Ace offered to do the dishes because I cooked dinner, and it'll be nice to be off my feet. I'm just about to take him up on his offer of using the jacuzzi tub in his bathroom when another call lights up my phone. It's Trevor. "Ugh," I groan quietly. *Just answer it and get it over with.* Letting out a deep breath, I answer the call.

Rapid, heavy breathing fills the line. "Janica, you answered. Oh, baby, where are you going to come home?"

"Home?" I snarl. "We don't live together anymore. There is no 'us' anymore."

"You don't mean that, sweetheart. Can't you forget what happened? Let's move on," he croons. His voice makes my stomach clench, and the contented feeling I had only minutes before turns sour.

"Forget what happened?" I spit. "Are you fucking

crazy? You cheated on me with your assistant. And who knows who else." I clench my fists as I grit my teeth. I'm not a violent person, but I really would like to inflict harm on him.

My heart is pounding in my chest, my shoulders are tight, and my temper is reaching an all-time high as I try to calmly remind Trevor that we aren't together anymore. The more desperate he gets, the squeakier his voice grows.

I've had enough of the conversation when he tries to remind me he and my parents are the only people I have in my life. It's a pleasure correcting him. When I end the call moments later, it feels like a weight that I've been carrying around for too long has been removed from my shoulders. Reaching into my new yellow pajama drawer, I snag a fun and flirty cotton short set that makes me feel beautiful. *Eat your heart out, haters.*

Stepping into Ace's bedroom, I grab my Kindle from the charger and escape to the bathroom. I go to start the bath and remember I left my rose-scented bubble bath in the spare room. Lost in thought about the new cowboy romance I downloaded earlier, I don't notice Ace crossing out of the half-bath until I'm nearly on top of him. "Oh!" I squeak, startled. "I'm sorry. I didn't see you there."

He smiles widely at me. "No worries. I thought you were going to take a bath. It's that way," he jokes as he points back toward his bedroom.

"Funny," I say as I roll my eyes at him. "Actually, I was going to earlier and then Trevor called again."

Ace releases a low growl from his throat but says nothing.

"I answered the call, put him in his place, and hung up on him," I admit with a giant smile on my face. Ace smiles in return, and I know he's happy too. "And now I'm going to take a bath, but I forgot my bubble bath, so I came out to get it. Luckily, I hadn't gotten naked yet. Otherwise, I'd be running around here with only a towel on." *Shit. Did I just say that out loud?* Looking at Ace, his cheeks are flushed and his eyes are wide and wild. *I must have.* Embarrassed by my verbal vomit, my hand flies up to my mouth. "S-sorry," I sputter before I turn tail and run back to his room. Never mind the bubble bath. I can just smell like Ace's body wash. *That won't cause any trouble for me.*

Chapter 26

Ace

Did I just suffer a stroke? My vision's strange, like I can't believe my eyes. I'm dizzy and weak, and I'm having trouble speaking. Oh, wait! Janica just said she could have come out in only a fucking towel. Hold up. I'm changing my diagnosis. Because if she did that, I would for sure have a heart attack. And priapism. Either way, I think I need to go to the hospital for emergency treatment.

After a few minutes pass where I haven't dropped dead or had my dick fall off, I move to the kitchen for a cold drink of water. The refreshing beverage does little to cool my heated body. I've heard that mindful breathing can be beneficial in stressful situations. Walking over to my couch, I sit down and close my eyes. I shift into a comfortable position and relax my shoulders. Then I focus on my breathing. In through my nose for four, out through my mouth for six. I repeat it a half dozen times, then open my eyes. As I reorient to the room, I gauge what I can see, smell, hear, and feel. Feeling better, I sink deeper into the couch, tip my head back, and close my eyes again.

"Ace." I hear my name called, and I grunt.

"Ace." There it is again.

This time I reply, "Yeah?"

"It's early. Are you taking a nap or zoning?" a soft voice that reminds me of Janica asks.

Feeling my lips pull into a smile, I answer, "I was doing some mindful breathing and I must have nodded off."

Janica's laugh rings clear and I force my eyes open. Seated next to me in another sexy sleep set is the woman who has invaded every thought, fantasy, and dream I've had the past few months. She's gorgeous, and the smile gracing her lips makes my resting heart rate climb. Cursing myself internally, I shift closer to her and inhale. *Fuck me.* She smells just like my body wash—like me—and damn, if that doesn't bring out all my caveman instincts. I move my hands to my lap, interlocking my fingers to not only hide my growing reaction to her, but to prevent myself from touching her.

"Want to watch a movie?" she asks.

I nod. "Sure, but it's your pick."

"Do you like Disney movies?" she asks, her eyes bright with excitement.

Grabbing the remote, I turn on the television. "I

haven't seen many. Growing up, Melissa got me to watch a few, though. Pick your poison."

"I would love to watch *Beauty and the Beast*. Have you seen that one?"

I chuckle. "I have, and I enjoyed it. My favorite characters were Lumiere and Cogsworth."

She squeals. "They were great, but I loved the tenderness of Chip and sexy, flirty Plumette, the feather duster."

We pop a bowl of popcorn and share it while a Disney musical entertains us. I hum to some of the catchier tunes, like the mob song led by Gaston. *What a dick he is.* As the movie unfolds, I watch Janica more than the TV, and that stirs up unfamiliar emotions within me. I swallow hard past the lump in my throat. Her perfectly timed sighs when she hears of the enchanted rose or when Belle returns to the Beast after the mob attacks him, make my heart beat faster. *Does she want to be rescued or does she want to be the one doing the rescuing?* I'm not over-emotional, but the magic of this love story speaks to even me. Janica is my Belle and I am her Beast. With her cuddled into my side, I want nothing more than to protect her from those ugly things in the world. But I know I can't rush it. I have to give her space. Until then, I plan to be the best friend she's ever had. And that starts with getting to know her better.

After the final credits, I turn off the television. "I'm not tired. Do you want to play a game before bed?"

She turns toward me, rubbing her hands together. "Which one? I play a mean Skip-Bo."

"I was thinking of twenty questions. You game?" I challenge with my stare.

When she laces her fingers together and cracks them, I know she means business.

Rolling my shoulders, I look at her. "Ladies first." I'm feeling confident until she taps her finger on her chin like she's searching for the perfect question.

"What is your favorite color?" she asks.

"Blue. And yours?"

She laughs and answers, 'Yellow."

I smile, thinking of the containers we picked up. I recommended the color because it reminded me of her. "Have you always loved yellow?" I ask, knowing it's more of a follow-up question than how the quick game is played.

"No. Until recently, I hadn't given it much thought. I've always loved magenta." I store that in my memory. You never know when you need random knowledge.

"Is it my turn for a question?"

Janica smiles. "What do you want to know?" *So much.*

I smirk. "What is your favorite food?"

"That's tough. I'm a mood eater. But my all-time favorites are probably noodles with alfredo and Greek salad. What's yours?"

She's right, this is a hard question. I love food, and

as a professional athlete, I rarely get to indulge in my favorites, most of which my ma makes when I go home to visit. Patting my stomach, I answer, "Chicken pot pie."

"My turn, right?" she asks, excitedly bouncing next to me on the couch. *What's she wanting to know?* I nod. "When was your first kiss?"

I grin. "I was fourteen." Then I waggle my eyebrows at her. "When was yours?"

She frowns, then looks down. My stomach twists.

While fiddling with her hands, she whispers, "I was nineteen."

Silently doing math in my head, I wonder if Trevor was her first kiss. "Was Trevor your first kiss?" Keeping her gaze averted, she only nods.

Knowing I need to distract her, I ask my next question. "Since it's my turn, I want to know what your favorite farm animal is."

Her sad eyes meet mine, and I offer a kind smile, trying to silently reassure her. After several moments pass, she answers, "I like them all. Though it's probably because I don't live with them. Cows are adorable, and I love it most when they moo. Horses are scary, but they're so majestic and powerful. Pigs are funny; they eat anything and are the messiest. They seem like the wildest part of farm life. And then there are goats. I think they faint when they get startled. Watching them tip over is hilarious." Her lips curve up, and she again looks happy. *My mission is complete.*

"Since you grew up on a farm, what is your favorite farm animal?"

"Our farm was the fruits and vegetable kind. We didn't have that many animals because my dad didn't want them eating all the crops. Ma wanted a cow, so for their fifteenth anniversary, Dad bought her a Longhorn. I'm not sure what inspired him to go that route since their name gives away an accurate description of what they'll look like when they're grown. The problem was, we were unaware of how large his horns would get. When we first got him, his horns were tiny. But by the time he was two, they were half the size they would be and already they were huge. By the time he turned six, they were full grown."

Janica repositions, sitting with her legs tucked under her. "I've got two questions for you. How long did the horns get and what is his name?"

"I think his horns measured out at ninety-six inches, and his name is Harold."

She grabs my arm and excitedly says, "Wait. He's still at the farm?" Nodding my head, I laugh. Her brown eyes light up. "Well, I need to meet Harold. I love cows. I need to see that beautiful beast."

"Slow down, tiger. Harold's not going anywhere. Longhorns live twenty-plus years. We have plenty of time to go visit him."

Janica sighs. "Your home sounds amazing. I have to admit, I'm jealous."

"Why would you be jealous?"

"Because you have parents and siblings who adore you. I wanted that my entire life. I wanted to be the pride of my parents, the apple of their eye, but I was just a checkmark on some proverbial list of things you must do in order to be successful. My parents were more concerned with the matters of their social circle than with what was going on with me. I learned early on never to rock the ship.

"Neither of my parents were cold or mean, but they weren't big on giving attention or love. I knew I was cared for, but I always wanted something deeper. That feeling has always been out of my reach, and maybe that's why I clung to Trevor when we first met. He showed me affection and was my first everything. I thought for sure that was love, and I didn't want to give up on it easily. That's probably why I stayed with him so long." She hangs her head, flushing with what I assume is embarrassment.

Placing a finger under her chin, I nudge it up. "Look at me, Janica." I wait until I can see her eyes, then tuck a strand of wayward hair behind her ear. "I'm sorry your parents weren't as loving as mine. I know I hit the jackpot. I pray their love, care, support, and encouragement has made me a better man and friend, and someday, a partner. My dream is to show my spouse and children the same love and kindness that was modeled to me."

She beams at me. "They would be proud of who

you are. You are by far the sweetest, most caring, and thoughtful man I've ever met."

For the next hour, we go back and forth, asking random questions. I learn so much more about this incredible woman. Our conversation drives home how much I like her, and that waiting for her is the smartest move I could make. This is the happiest I have ever been.

Chapter 27

Ace

Two weeks later, when my physical therapist, Robert, arranges for me to meet at the rink with the team's trainer, Matthew, I'm a mess of emotions. I'm both excited and scared. Lacing up my skates requires mental gymnastics and breathing exercises I hadn't been expecting. When I returned to the ice after my last injury, where the initial concern was my spine, I hadn't been as worked up as I feel right now, sitting in the locker room in front of my cubby.

"Ace, you okay?" Robert asks on approach. Glancing up at him, I'm sure my ambivalence shows on my face. "Shit," he mutters, dropping onto the bench next to me. "I understand you might be worried, but we've both seen your X-rays and talked to your doctor. You're ready."

My gaze shoots back to my freshly sharpened skates. I wiggle my left leg, ankle, and foot. Things feel different from what they used to, but I know I've worked hard to recover. There's no way that either Robert or Matthew would let me back on skates if they didn't think I was ready.

"Let's do this," I say, projecting confidence as I stand.

Robert pats me on the back. "You got this." I nod. *Yeah, I do.*

My first steps back on the ice are tentative as I try to remember the feel of my blades cutting and slicing into the surface. It's just like riding a bike. Short glides turn into longer ones, and before long, I'm adding in crossovers. Next, it's backward skating and braking.

It's invigorating having the wind I'm creating blow against my face as I suck in deep breaths of cool arena air. It reminds me why I love this sport so much. I feel free when I'm on my skates. Just as I'm getting more comfortable, I move to the blue line and lower my stance. A shrill whistle blows through the air as I'm about to push off with my dominant foot. My head flies up and I look at Robert. He's shaking his head. *What did I do?* Feeling like I'm in trouble, I skate slowly over to him.

"Why'd you stop me? I'm feeling great, and I wanted to see how my starts are."

"I know you're getting stronger, but we need a few more weeks of building back your strength before I'll feel comfortable having you practice explosive starts. This is your first time back on skates, and you easily surpassed what I have planned. Let's let your leg rest and we'll come back later this week for another session. Maybe I'll even join you and you can have a stick and puck."

He smiles, and I laugh at him, muttering, "Yes, sir."

With therapy accomplished for the day, I head home. I broke out of the boot and resumed full weight-bearing status at four months and have been working on regaining my balance and muscle tone. Today was a testament to that.

Once I'm home, I shower and change into a pair of my favorite blue jeans. They're all worn in the best places, and soft like velvet. Grabbing a Henley, I pull it over my head. "You need a haircut," I tell myself as I attempt to style my wayward hair.

Grabbing socks and my backpack, I head into the kitchen to snag an apple, protein bar, and a bottle of water. I plan to head to the library and finish a paper that's due later this week. I know my odds of seeing Janica are higher because I'll be sitting in our spot.

After pulling my socks and Chucks on, I head out to my Toyota truck. Once I was free to drive, I kindly kicked George to the curb. I was grateful for his months of driving, but I missed the freedom of driving myself.

Janica isn't at her desk when I arrive.

ME

Hey, I'm here in our spot.

Our spot. Every time I'm at our spot, a calmness washes over me. I feel connected to Janica, and that thrills me.

JANICA

Cool. I'll stop by after I finish shelving this section. See you soon. I want to hear all about therapy.

Diving straight into the paper I'm writing, I print off a few articles I need to read before I work on the next section. As I read, highlght, and note my articles, I eat my snack. I don't hear Janica approach over the crunching sound of me biting into my crisp, green apple. A hand appears on my shoulder. "Ace."

Wiping my mouth, I set down the apple and turn toward her. "Hey. How are you?"

She smiles at me. "I'm great. How are you? How was therapy? Why did they have you meet at the arena?"

Rising out of my chair, I stand facing her, ready to deliver the best news. "This morning, I skated," I announce. Her mouth drops open, and she launches herself at me. I catch her awkwardly and pull her in tight for a hug.

While still clinging to me, she excitedly chirps, "I'm so happy for you." Pulling back, I set her on her feet and then she plops down into the seat next to me. Our knees brush, sending tingles up my thighs and straight to my dick. *Down, boy.* "How was it? Tell me everything." Her eyes soften like she truly cares and wants to hear every detail.

I laugh, setting my hand on her leg. The contact heats my blood, and my body goes hot. *Damn it.* I should stop touching her before she figures out I'm falling for her. But no matter what I tell myself, my hand refuses to move from her leg. "It was amazing. At first, I was nervous because everything felt different. But once I adjusted to my new normal, it was almost the same. Robert wouldn't let me push it too hard because we're still working on my strength, but both he and Matthew were impressed by what I was comfortable doing."

Janica reaches forward, setting her hand on mine. "We need to celebrate this milestone."

Running my free hand through my messy hair, I confess, "That's why I came by instead of doing my homework at home. I had an idea and wanted to run it by you."

"Yeah?"

"I want to either take you out to Mateo's or grab takeout from there. Which would you prefer?" I tell her about Mateo's, but I don't think she's ever eaten there.

"It's been a long day. Do you mind if maybe we do takeout tonight and we can go in person the next time?" she says.

What the woman wants, the woman gets. "Sounds great. Here, I'll pull up their menu and then I can order it and we can pick it up on our way home. How does that sound?"

"It sounds perfect," she says, while perusing the menu on my phone. Once she's decided, she gives me another hug before returning to shelving books. The next two hours pass quickly, as I'm immersed in the journal articles I'm reading for my biology class.

At five-thirty, I pull up outside Mateo's. Hopping out of the truck, I note what a warm April evening it is. "Be right back," I say before shutting the door. Our order is ready, and within a few minutes, I'm back on the road.

Living with Janica has been a dream. We spend a lot of time together, and other than minor squabbles over cleanliness—my fault—we get along great and are killing this roommate situation. The one thing that remains a perpetual problem is that my insane attraction to her hasn't waned one bit. In fact, it's grown. The better I get to know her, the more intrigued and obsessed I become.

My mouth is watering as the savory scents of delicious food fill the cab of my truck. "This smells divine," she says as we drive home.

Laughing, I tell her, "It tastes even better." I take a quick peek at her and see her eyes are bright and dancing.

After parking the truck, we hop out and make our way into the house. I carry the bag of food to the kitchen, then get two plates from the cupboard. When the dinners have been plated, I hand her one, grab two bottles of water from the fridge and my own plate, and we head to the living room.

Hunkered down on the couch, we dine on deliciously creamy chicken alfredo. Our dinner conversation is fun and lively, as usual. We even have a faux battle over the last breadstick. Being the gentleman I am, of course, I let her win.

She catches me off guard when she asks, "So, what's next?"

Confused, I turn to face her. "What do you mean?"

"For therapy and hockey. What's next? Will you be ready to play for the Cup next month with the team?" Her hockey knowledge has increased tenfold since moving in with me. She's heard me excitedly cheering on my teammates as they worked hard to battle for a slot in the Stanley Cup playoffs. She's also heard me grumble about my frustration at not being able to be out there with them.

I set my plate on the coffee table and sit back. "Playing for the team is off the table until fall. Our goal is to have me ready for preseason. Right now, I'm working on improving my balance, strength, and eventually my speed."

Standing up, she grabs my plate, stacks it on top of hers, and heads to the kitchen. Over her shoulder, she says, "It sounds like you'll be spending a lot of time at the gym and the rink. What about your classes?" I hear a dip in her voice when she asks about school. *Why does she sound sad?*

Moving so I can keep her in sight, I see her shoulders have dropped, and she's not smiling. "I'll spend a lot of time on recovery, but my classes are still a priority. I'll have time for it all. Like I said before, I'll have to cut down on credits when I return to the roster, though. With practice and travel, my time will again be limited."

She forces a smile, but I can't shake the feeling our happy dinner has turned sad, and I'm not sure why.

Janica finishes washing the dishes and then comes back over to the couch. "Do you care if I use your tub to take a bath? I'm feeling a little blue and I'm hoping that will help."

"Are you okay? Did the food make your stomach upset? Can I do anything for you?" My panic spills out as various questions. I want to make things better for her, and I feel like I upset her.

"I'm fine. The food was excellent, but I had a hard day, and I guess it all hit me once I slowed down. I just want to take a bath, go to bed, and start over fresh tomorrow."

She heads to the bedroom, and I frown. Leaning my head back on the couch, I replay the last half hour, looking for anything that could explain Janica's sudden mood change.

Chapter 28

Janica

Ace's words are on repeat in my head. When I heard him excitedly talk about returning to hockey, I couldn't help but be happy for him. His dream since he was little has always been to play hockey professionally, and because of his broken leg, he's had to sit on the sidelines, working his ass off for the chance to do it again. When he told me he skated today, I was overjoyed. But then, as we ate dinner, I realized that his life would soon change.

Over the last few weeks, we've grown closer, but I question where I'll fit into his life once he goes back to playing. I'm not brave enough to ask, though. Because other than friends and roommates, I don't know what we are. He hasn't said as much on the topic, and neither have I. I know I'm crazy attracted to him and would jump at the chance to be with him, but is it too soon? Trevor and I have been broken up for over a month, and I know I'll never find anyone as good as Ace. At times, he makes me believe he's interested, but at others, he treats me more like a sister than a potential partner. It's all so confusing. My brain's foggy with uncertainty, and I need a few moments alone to find some clarity.

Standing in his bathroom, I let out a deep breath as I turn on the water. My gaze travels the room, and hints of Ace and his recovery are everywhere. But soon, it will all be a distant memory.

As the water rushes from the tap, I travel back to the words of our conversation that struck the hardest. *"With practice and travel, my time will again be limited."* My heart flinches. Will there be any room for me? Will I drop another rung on the ladder of importance? Was I only filling the slot left empty because of his injury?

Feeling sorry for myself, my shoulders dip in defeat until I'm curling in on myself. Questioning my worth reminds me of how I felt growing up and when Trevor and I were together. I seem to be the common factor in my failed relationships. I drive people away so they don't want to stay with me. Then the thought strikes me. Did I do that with Ace? Did I put myself in yet another situation where I'm undervalued and waiting to be abandoned? My heart hurts as more questions fill my mind. How will his life change? How will things change between us? Will he not want my friendship anymore? What about the life choices he's made in the past six months? Will he finish the classes he's currently taking? Will he take more in the fall? Will he pursue an actual degree? It's the first time since meeting Ace that I wonder if he considers his studies a speed bump or a minor distraction along his journey. And if so, is that how he sees me? The uncertainty of it all overwhelms me.

My chest tightens and I can't hold back the weary whimper that falls from my lips as the tub fills up. Just thinking about Ace moving on has me in knots. My stomach bubbles with unease and I rub circles on it, hoping to comfort myself.

Taking my rose-scented bubble bath, I drip a few drops into the swirling hot water. Bubbles multiply quickly as I slip my clothes off, leaving them in a pile near the door. I grab a fresh towel so I can use it as a headrest. Testing the temperature, I adjust it until it's not too hot for me. Leaning over, I breathe the delicate rose scent into my nose. It instantly soothes my soul, like it's a Band-Aid to my cracked heart. Lowering myself slowly into the tub, I feel my muscles relax. "Mmm. That feels so good." I moan as I lean back on my makeshift headrest and close my eyes. *At this moment, I choose to be grateful.* Thinking about all the things I'm grateful for helps distract me from my uneasy feelings about Ace.

Half an hour later, when I've soaked all the heat from the water, I step from the tub, careful not to get water everywhere. *Don't need Ace getting hurt again.*

Dressed in my typical cotton bed shorts and tank, I expect to see Ace already in bed, scrolling through his phone. But to my surprise, he s not.

Walking past the bed on my way to deposit my dirty clothes in my hamper, I see a sheet of paper on the bed. Because it wasn't there when I entered the bathroom, I wonder if it's for me. Sure enough, my name is written in chicken-scratch across the top, and I see Ace's signature at the bottom.

> *Janica,*
> *I have a lot on my mind. I went for a drive to clear my head.*
> *Ace*

Worry sets in. Maybe he's also thinking about where I'll fit in with him after he's fully recovered. Has he concluded I've served my purpose, and he doesn't want me around anymore? The quiet room feels so cold. A shiver passes down my back and goose bumps appear all over my skin. Trying to ward off the chill, I climb into the empty bed and pull the covers up tight. Since we haven't used the pillow wall since that first night, his absence next to me is notable.

Ace

When I left tonight to clear my head, I wasn't sure what I'd been feeling. Everything felt like a chaotic, jumbled mess. At the start of the evening, things seemed perfect, but then, like a storm rolling in, the winds shifted and I could not tell which direction I needed to go in. Janica seemed upset, and I didn't understand why or what I'd done. When I returned home hours later, I hadn't found the clarity I'd been seeking. Still plagued by confusion, I only knew two things. In the future, I plan to keep my focus on both Janica and hockey. It wasn't one or the other.

Chapter 29

Ace

I'm six months post-op, and all my X-rays, reports from my physical therapist, and doctor's appointments say I'm right on track to making my comeback at the start of next season. I'm bummed I didn't get to play with my team for the Cup, but they'd fought hard to earn their spot, so I'm confident they'll give it their best. The first games scheduled are against the Colorado Mountaineers and at home, so I'll be able to watch them from the family box. Maybe Janica would like to come? For the last few weeks, things between us have been strained. Perhaps we need a fun night out together?

ME

When are you going to be home
tonight?

JANICA

Probably around six, like normal. Why?

ME

I needed to talk to you about something. I'm going to throw a steak on the grill. Do you want one?

Ten minutes pass without a reply.

ME

Everything okay?

ME

Hello? Are you still there? Are you busy?

ME

I bet you're busy. So I'm going to throw two steaks on the grill. See you at about six.

"That was weird," I tell myself as I pocket my phone and head to the kitchen to get to work on dinner. Busying myself with food prep, I lose track of time.

"That smells so good," Janica says as she comes into the kitchen, dressed in high-waisted pants that make her legs look even longer than they are. Her gorgeous brown hair is tied in a messy knot at her neck, and I wonder if it's on purpose. My eyes are drawn to the deep V of her silky aqua-green tank top, appreciating the cleavage she has on display. It's been warmer outside lately, so her cardigan is in her hand. She drops it, her purse, and lunch bag on the counter, asking, "What do you need help with?"

I point to the plated food, and she smiles. "Thank you, Ace. It's been a day."

"Why don't we sit down, eat dinner, and you can tell me about it," I suggest as I move her plate in front of her. Walking around the island with my dinner, I notice the stools are incredibly close to one another. Trying to squeeze in, my body brushes up against hers. "Excuse me," I say as she swings toward me. Our knees knock, and we both laugh. Reaching up, I push a loose piece of hair behind her ear so I can better see her face. "There you are." Janica's cheeks turn pink. "Dig in. I doubt it's as good as the pork tenderloin you made, but I hope it's decent."

I watch as she takes the first bite of her steak. "Mmm," she hums as her eyes roll back. Her moan is deep and packed with desire. I love to hear her enjoy her food. Her reaction makes my cock grow hard, wishing the sound was for me. *Settle down.* Controlling my body's reaction around Janica has always seemed to be a problem. *Would she moan like that in the bedroom?*

I want her. No ifs, ands, or buts. But I'm scared. I've never been in a relationship before, so I'm unsure how to approach it. At first, I questioned how much time you're supposed to wait before you pursue someone who just broke up with their significant other.

Then, after a decent amount of time had passed, I was afraid that if I pursued her, I might just mess up our friendship; and that was the absolute last thing I wanted to do. Recently, things have been off between us, and I wonder if I did something wrong. The biggest reason I have done nothing is I'm afraid of the rejection I'll feel if she doesn't have the same feelings. Concern about it has affected all parts of my life, and I don't know what to do.

"Sorry, that is so tender and full of flavor. It's perfect. You are the best, friend," she gushes.

Hell yeah. I made her moan. *Over a steak.* "I love hearing that you're enjoying it." Her moan echoes in my ears, and I wonder what noises she'd make if I touched her. Didn't you hear what she just said? *You are just friends.* Forsaking my fantasy, I ask, "Why was your day so bad?"

Her light, airy laughter fills the room. "It wasn't bad, per se. It was just busy. Veronica was out for an appointment, and I forgot until the very last minute that I needed to do her reading groups with the kids. It was hairy for a moment until I located the books they'd been reading."

"That sounds stressful. I'm glad you got it worked out," I say.

She waves it off. "It was fine. Just some juggling and scrambling on my part, but I survived." She meets my gaze and says, "So, when you texted, you said you needed to talk to me about something."

I nod and am about to invite her to the playoffs when she sputters out, "Y-you aren't going to tell me it's time for me to m-move out, are you?"

My mouth drops open. *That is the furthest thing from what I want.* "Where would you get that idea from?"

Fidgeting with her hands, she says, "Well, I've lived here for months now, and you're mostly recovered. Aren't you sick of me yet? I mean, if I weren't here, you could resume your bachelor lifestyle, right?"

Giving her a skeptical look, I pause for a moment. *What is she trying to say?* "Do you want to move out?" I question, completely blown away.

Janica stops fidgeting. 'No. I just don't want to cramp your style. With me gone, you could have friends over... and women." Anger boils up within me. I don't want other women. I want *her*. But no matter what, I can't bring myself to tell her.

I turn toward her and grab her hand, making sure our eyes meet. "My friends come over now. Rocco was here the other day. And as far as women go... What women? The only women I care to have in my life are you, my ma, and my sister." Nerves wrap around me and my heart gallops in my chest. That felt like a confession. If she reads between the lines, it'd be a tease for sure.

"Ookaaay," she says, drawing out the word. But the question in her eyes makes me short of breath. The words are right there, on the tip of my tongue. *Do I tell her more?* Scared, I seal my lips tightly shut but keep hold of her hand. I'm not ready to let go.

"So then, what did you want to talk to me about?"

I look down at our joined hands and watch as she mindlessly strokes her thumb against my skin. *Does she know she's doing that?* If not, I'm not telling her, because her touch lights me up.

"Do you want to come watch the playoff games with me this week?" I finally ask.

Her mouth drops open. "Really?" she whispers.

"Yeah. You'd have to watch it in the family suite with me. The seats are decent, and they feed you too."

"What? And you're inviting me?" she questions, her brown eyes wide in disbelief.

"Yes."

With her free hand, she hits my chest. "But are you sure?"

Shaking my head at the nonsense, I laugh. "I'm sure."

Her smile is everything. "Thank you, Ace. It would be nice to see your team play. It's a pity you won't be out there."

"I will be soon," I confidently reply.

"I know you will, and I cannot wait to watch you." Flashes of her cheering me on, wearing my jersey, fill my mind. A grin takes over my lips. Seeing her with my name on her back would be a dream come true.

After dinner, I work on some homework due in the next week. With all the time I've been spending in rehab and at the gym, I haven't visited the library recently. Granted, a major distraction works there, but I seem to accomplish a lot, even if I'm listening for her sweet voice and expecting a visit to our spot.

Glancing over at the couch, I see she's cuddled under a thick blanket, reading a book. The smile on her face and the twinkle in her eye tell me it's a steamy romance. When I see her bite her lip, I almost throw my textbooks across the room and demand that she read to me. The only problem is that once she started reading, I'd picture us doing everything her fictional friends are doing. My interest in her would be undeniable, and I still refuse to be the guy who pushes her into something she's not ready for.

Feeling parched, I rasp, "Need anything from the kitchen? I'm getting myself some water."

"No, thank you," she replies, unaware she's torturing me. Really, it's not her fault. She's just being herself. Her adorable, smart, kind, sexy, funny self. Using my laptop to shield my groin, I adjust myself before I stand up. Seeing that my hips are at eye level, I don't need my dick attracting any attention. While I'm in the kitchen waiting for my hard-on to go down, I rummage through the pantry, looking for a snack. Standing back, I run my eyes over all the shelves, hoping something will jump out at me.

"Excuse me," Janica says before she slips in front of me. Before I can step back, her luscious body slides against mine, and I have to bite back a groan. *Damn, I want her.* I want to push her up against the wall and kiss her until she's panting out my name. But instead, I freeze, allowing myself to enjoy the feeling of her butt pressed against my crotch. The delicious pressure is making my skin itch with need. If I lean forward a bit, my nose would be buried in her hair. She moves her head to the side, and we're mere inches from each other, sharing the same heated air. I tighten my hands into fists so I don't reach for her and pull her to my mouth. My tongue peeks out, giving me the go ahead to taste her. She responds by swallowing hard, then licking her lips. In pure frustration, I screw my eyes shut, blocking her out, knowing I can't have her.

Something beeps and ends the moment. She steps away from me, and I swear my body groans.

"Want to share?" Her sweet, melodic voice breaks me from my forced pleasure prison. I'm wound tighter than a coil. Unsure what will come out of my mouth if I respond with words, I just nod my head. "Great." She smiles and dips around me.

Heading back to the couch is a test of my self-restraint. Instead of tossing her on the couch and ravaging her, like I desperately want, I sit beside her and share a snack that encourages our skin to touch every time I reach for a handful. And if that weren't bad enough, my cock couldn't be any harder in my shorts. *This is the worst form of torture.*

Chapter 30

Janica

True to his word, Ace and I attend the first game of round one for the Steel. This is my first professional hockey game, and the air is thick with excitement. Arriving early, I'm alone in the family suite. I look around and see a bunch of chairs have been pushed up toward the glass, presumably for those individuals who want to watch the action. I see comfortable couches closer to the two overloaded food tables, and some spectators stand at the high-top tables they have throughout the space.

Moving toward the glass, I look down at the ice. Thankfully, there is Steel gear all over his house, so I recognize his team right away. Watching, I see the players move around and warm up. There's something about a big muscular man dropping to his knees and hip thrusting the ice. *Holy hell, that's hot.* I giggle to myself, wondering if I'm the only one who fixated on that.

Tonight, the Steel are playing against the Colorado Mountaineers. From what Ace has said, they were a tough opponent during the regular season. He's confident in his teammates but knows these games will be tough. When the guys leave the ice, I grab water and move to a chair right by the glass. My body vibrates as I wait for the start of the first period. Ace settles down next to me. He moves his chair closer so our bodies are touching, and suddenly the ambient temperature in the suite seems to rise. I take a large drink of water, hoping to cool myself down. I'll be sweating in no time and my focus on the game will be questionable. Breathing out deeply, I focus on the team as they return to the ice.

Ace pats my leg and asks, "You ready for this?"

Nodding, I cover his hand with mine and ask, "Are you?" I imagine this has got to be hard for him.

He forces a smile. "Yeah, but I'm sure ready for next season."

Leaning into him, I squeeze the hand on my thigh, and tell him, "I can't wait to see you play."

During the first period, I focus on Ace as much as I do the game. Every flinch and grunt he makes, puts me on edge. As the last minutes of the period tick by, with the Mountaineers already leading by one, I lay my hand on his arm. His whole body is tense, but when he sees it's me, he relaxes and gifts me a half smile.

Leaning in, I whisper, "Is it killing you not to be out there?"

Frowning, he sets his hand on mine. "Is it that obvious?"

"You look like you're in physical pain. Can I do anything?"

His eyes speak before he does. "Distract me, Janica."

I'm not sure how I'm going to do that, but I have a brief intermission to come up with a strategy. "Do you want to go grab some food?"

The clock sounds, and I watch Ace turn to watch his friends leave the ice. He looks back at me with sad eyes and says, "Okay."

During intermission, we stuff ourselves with so many finger foods—thankfully, most of them are healthy—it's embarrassing.

At the start of the second period, even before the puck is dropped, I lean into Ace's space and say, "You know, this is my first live hockey game, and hockey is still confusing to me. So if you wouldn't mind, could you explain the game to me in real—" Ace's beautiful brown eyes light up, and I see specks of amber in them. The most gorgeous smile spreads across his face, making my heart thunder in my chest.

"Okay, you asked for it. So here goes. This is a sport we call hockey. Six players from each team are on the ice at one time. They use their sticks to push a puck around, passing it back and forth while moving down the ice toward their opponent's net. Once close enough, they hunt for an opportunity to score."

Rolling my eyes at him, I fake a ditzy sounding voice. "OMG, you're like some all-knowing hockey god." Then I bat my lashes and sigh.

He laughs. "Was that too elementary for you?"

"Ace, I have watched a few games in my life. I get the gist of the game. I just don't understand the lines, penalties, and power plays/penalty kills," I tell him.

"Okay. So let's tackle the penalties and power plays/penalty kills first. When a player from either side earns a penalty, they go to the penalty box, or what we lovingly call the sin bin. They serve either a two-minute minor or a five-minute major. In hockey, there are quite a few penalties. Some are blocking, checking, hooking, clipping, slashing, spearing, and roughing."

I stare at him. "Roughing?" He nods in answer. "Aren't all the penalties you mentioned rough?"

He tugs his hand through his brown hair and rasps. "You might be right, but the calls are specific to the infraction."

I purse my lips. "How do power plays fit in?"

Ace points across the ice to where the players sit when they aren't on the ice. "Those are the players' benches." He looks at me to make sure I'm following. I nod for him to go on. "A power play is when one team has an advantage of more men on the ice, because of a penalty acquired by the other team. The shorthanded team goes on what is called a penalty kill."

"So, say the Mountaineers get a penalty. Their player goes to the penalty box and they have five guys on the ice while the Steel has six. That's a power play opportunity for the Steel and penalty kill for the Mountaineers?"

Ace smiles widely, pulls me into a side hug, and kisses the top of my head. Butterflies take flight in my stomach as he says, "You got it." His confidence in me feels amazing. But the one thing that really makes my heart soar is, even if I hadn't understood, I know he would've explained it until he was blue in the face.

"So, the lines. What are they? And what are those circles?" I ask him next.

He uses his left arm to explain, the right one still tucked behind me. Pointing to the middle of the rink, he explains how there are five circles on the ice, one is in the middle at center ice and the others are in each team's defensive zone on either side of the net.

"Are those the only places a puck drop can happen?" I ask. He shakes his head.

"Faceoffs or puck drops can take place at any of the five circles, but there are two dots on either side of the neutral zone, just inside the blue line, that can also be used."

I scratch my head. "There are nine places for face-offs? Is that right?"

Ace nods yes, then explains there are three types of lines on the ice. The neutral zone or center ice is the most obvious. The two blue lines separate each team's defensive zone from the neutral zone. The far-red lines that the nets sit on are the goal lines. He also explains that the direction of play determines which side of the rink is attacking or defending zones. By the time he's finished, my brain is mush, but it's the end of the second period and the score is tied. The Steel could still win.

At the end of the game, the Mountaineers win by one. This being my first live game, I wasn't prepared for how fast and thrilling it was. My body feels like it's buzzing from an overdose of too much caffeine.

Sitting in the car on the way home, Ace is unusually quiet, lost in his thoughts. "Thanks for taking me with you to the game. I had a great time," I say. The car remains silent. *Did he hear me?* "Ace," I try again. Nothing. Reaching over, I squeeze his arm, and he jumps. *Did I do something wrong? Had I bothered him with all my questions?* "Sorry. I didn't mean to startle you."

He brushes it off. "It's nothing. What's up?"

"I was trying to talk to you, but you seemed lost in your head. Anything you want to talk about? I'm a good listener."

He turns to me and gives me a half smile. "I appreciate that, but I'm not ready."

"Oh. Okay. No worries. I just wanted to say thank you for bringing me to the game tonight. I had a great time."

Focused back on the road, he taps repeatedly on

the steering wheel like he's feeling edgy. Without looking back at me, he says, "That's great. I'm really glad to hear that. It was nice having you with me."

Really? It doesn't feel that way. It's almost like he can't wait to get home and away from me.

As soon as we pull into the garage, Ace is out of the car. Within seconds, he's opened my door and helped me out. His hand on mine sends a wave of warmth through me and makes me crave more.

"Thank you," I whisper. But I'm not even sure he hears me. He again seems like he's distracted by something. When he drops my hand and strides away, I sigh in dejection. When I finally enter the house, he's stepping out of the bedroom, dressed in low-hanging athletic shorts. *Holy hell. Is he trying to kill me?*

My libido does a happy dance, and my blood races through my body, making me slightly dizzy. *He is divine.* I lick my lips. Tracing my gaze up his gorgeous body, I linger at his Adonis belt for a beat longer than I should if I'm truly trying to keep my feelings locked down. When I continue my perusal and finally reach his face, I breathe a sigh of relief. He's so lost in his head that he didn't notice me staring. It's just another sign he's not ready to learn I have a massive crush on him. Though, by now, it's probably morphed from a crush into falling for him, but I'm not ready to admit that yet.

He adjusts his headphones as he passes by me without a word. When I see him turn into the spare room he's converted into an at-home gym, things make sense. His mood change has to do with not being able to be on the ice with his teammates. I breathe easier, knowing I'm not to blame for his obvious discomfort. *I only wish I could help.* I don't enjoy seeing him upset.

Still too wired from the game, I make myself a cup of chamomile tea and grab my Kindle. I'll read on the couch until I get tired. There's no way I want to lie in that giant bed by myself and stare at the ceiling. Even though we're just friends, having Ace there next to me is relaxing. I don't know if I'd be able to sleep if he wasn't there. He makes me feel safe.

I must've nodded off at some point, because at four a.m. when I wake up to use the restroom, I open my eyes to discover I'm looking at the ceiling in the bedroom. Only I don't remember coming to bed. I turn my head to find Ace sleeping soundly next to me. *Did he put me in bed?* It's definitely something he would do.

After visiting the bathroom, I slip back into bed. Ace rolls over on his stomach and his arm reaches out as if he's searching for something. When he hits my arm, he quickly squeezes it, then releases it and tucks his arm back under his pillow. The whole while, I watch his eyes to see if they're open. They aren't. *Was he subconsciously making sure I was still here? Does he do that often?* It's not like I can ask him in the morning. There's a strong possibility he wouldn't know what I'm talking about and he'd think I'm losing it. Plus, even if he admitted it, would he know why he'd done it?

As I lie here thinking about it, the only thing I'm certain of is that it makes me feel special to know he wants me near. I still don't understand what that means. And since neither of us has raised the subject of getting another bed for the spare room, we both continue on, content with what we have. I have become accustomed to the soft sounds he makes while he's sleeping, and the heat his body emits. I'm not sure how I'd do without them. Plus, I absolutely love knowing he's right there next to me.

Chapter 31

Ace

Bringing Janica to the first two games of round one of the Stanley Cup playoffs was a brilliant idea. She did her best to distract me from the games, which relieved me of some of the guilt I had for not being out there. I know my broken leg isn't my fault, and I have no reason to feel guilty, but I do. Like a record on repeat, I keep telling myself if I'd only worked harder in PT, I would already be back with the guys, fighting for the Cup.

When I mention this to Robert at our next session, he just shakes his head. He spends a lot of our time reminding me of all that I've accomplished so far, and that by taking my time, and not rushing things, I'm setting myself up for a successful return in the fall.

I understand what he's saying. It isn't the first time I've heard it, but my heart aches. I want to be on that ice more than anything, helping my closest friends fight for another championship. But I was forced to watch them lose the first two games of round one, and I fear for the rest of their games against the Mountaineers.

"I'm home," Janica sings as she comes into the house after a day of work. "Are you all right?" She gasps as she enters the living room and sees me sprawled out on the couch.

I laugh and lift my arm. "I'm good. I promise. Robert kicked my butt today. He had me on my skates, doing sprints. I'm not sure what he considers high-intensity if he calls that low-intensity."

She shrugs and says, "I grabbed the mail, and you have something that looks fancy." Handing me the envelope, she gushes about the texture and thickness of the paper. Carefully, I open it and pull an invitation out. It's announcing the marriage of Mika and Shiloh. A slip of paper falls out and lands in my lap. *Janica is also invited.*

"This is also for you," I tell her, flipping around the invitation.

"How kind of them to include me." She blushes.

"Does that mean you'll go with me?" I ask. Her resounding smile is bright and cheerful as she nods.

A week later, the Steel's hope for another Cup is lost. Games three and four were in Colorado. The Steel lose the third game, and the fourth game never happens, as most of the Steel come down with Norovirus and don't have enough players to field a decent team.

Mika and Shiloh are getting married a few weeks after the team returns from Colorado.

"You look beautiful," I tell Janica as she steps out of the spare room where she got ready. She's wearing an emerald-green dress that hugs all her curves. A blush covers her cheeks, only making her more breathtaking. "Did I get the right color tie?" I ask as I step closer. She runs her hand down the green silk tie, and I'm mesmerized by the look in her eye. I've seen it before, but it's been fickle. Here one minute, gone the next. However, this look seems intent on staying, or at least making my knees go weak and breaking down my resolve.

Once she's done smoothing my tie, she breathes deeply. "You look so handsome, Ace. Thank you for taking me with you." Finding it difficult to speak, I just nod.

Our drive to Mika's house, the site for the wedding and reception, is quiet. Both Janica and I keep a hand on the center console between us. The pull to her is almost unbearable. I desperately want to hold her hand and pull her close. The few innocent touches we've shared over the past few months have been combustible. They're always quick, but they knock me on my ass, and it takes weeks to recover.

From the corner of my eye, I see my fingers flex, reaching for her. Hers respond in kind, and we're only centimeters away from contact. I can feel the heat coming off her, and I'm so scared to cross the invisible boundary we have between us.

Before we park, I issue a command. "I will get your door." A laugh is all I get, but she lets me do the gentlemanly thing.

Walking next to her, I wrap my arm around her waist, and my body's humming with need. Every part of her is a genuine mystery, but I can't count the number of times I've imagined touching her everywhere while I've been in the shower. Picturing her naked in our bed makes my cock throb, and I only allow myself to do that when I'm in the shower and she's not home. She, of course, doesn't know I take multiple showers every day to satisfying my insatiable appetite for her. The unfortunate thing is, after coming, I'm still not satisfied because I haven't experienced the real thing. But this is all I can do until I think she's ready for more. She's told me several times how grateful she is for our friendship. I, too, am grateful, but I believe there could be so much more between us. However, until that day arrives, I'm going to steal touches whenever I can, jerk off like a teenager, and fantasize about her often. She is my dream woman. If only I had the balls to say something.

Since Mika & Shiloh's wedding is outside, I'm distracted more than once by the ripples in Janica's dress as they're tousled about in the light wind. Every once in a while, it gives me a peek at the sun-kissed skin of her upper thigh. I want to reach over and see if her skin there is as soft as it looks. But I know one touch wouldn't be enough.

I'm not normally one for weddings, but even I think it's an enjoyable afternoon celebrating two fabulous people. The weather is perfect, the ceremony goes off without a hitch. The food is delicious, and hanging out with my friends, and Janica, at the reception is fun.

"Couldn't you feel their love?" she squeals as we drive home. I shrug, not understanding what she's saying. I haven't ever been in love. The woman who's brought out the most intense feelings in me is sitting in my passenger seat and doesn't know I'm head over heels for her. Looking at me with hearts in her eyes, there's no denying it—she's a definite romantic.

Do I have it in me to be what she needs?

"What was your favorite part?" she asks, a smile spread across pillowy lips.

Laughing, I say, "You'll hate my answer."

Shaking her head, she confesses, "The whole day was perfect. I can't think of one thing I'd change." *Interesting.* "Please tell me," she begs.

"The food was phenomenal, and those cupcakes were to die for," I say as I pat my stomach.

She laughs. "You're ridiculous."

Pouting, I whine, "You said you wouldn't laugh at me."

Janica shakes her head, still laughing. "I never said that."

"Fine. I assumed you wouldn't. But it doesn't matter because I'm not changing my answer. If it had been my big day, the menu would be the same." She goes silent next to me and stares out the window. *Should I not have said that?* From her hunched shoulders and lowered head, I assume I shouldn't have. *But why? Shit, I don't know.* What I know is that I've done it again. I made an ass of myself in front of the woman who has my heart. Hello, foot. Meet mouth. The rest of our drive is silent as I try to figure out how to break the tension hovering between us.

During the first official month of summer, I continue with my biweekly physical therapy appointments. Robert has me on skates almost every session, to work on improving my strength and speed. Coach Tristan has also been talking with Robert and Matthew about whether I can come to practice and take part in a low-intensity workout with the team. According to Coach, the guys miss me as much as I miss them, and it'll do us all good to be back together. Normally I'd head home to visit my family, but with being away from the guys so much, I decided to stay in town.

On the Fourth of July, I bring Janica with me to Samantha and Lucas's house for the annual barbecue. We have a great time with friends. Ever since kids have been added to the mix, the party starts earlier and is less chaotic. Rocco and I, of course, are up to our crazy antics, although because of my leg, I have to be more careful than in years past.

While climbing in the hot tub, I catch Janica's eyes on me. "Fuck, that feels good," I say. She smiles, likely assuming I mean the hot bubbly water, but it's having her gaze on me that lights me on fire. When I came over, I told myself I was getting in for rehab, but honestly, it's because I want to be near her.

Earlier, I'd about swallowed my tongue when she removed her gauzy cover-up. The flimsy, transparent fabric had given me a taste of her in a bikini, but my imagination was nowhere near accurate. When it was finally removed, she transformed into a goddess. And since then, I've been fighting with boner placement.

Being the joker I am, I flex my muscles and pose like I'm competing for Mr. Universe. Although she laughs, I don't miss the hungry look she gives me. When her gaze reaches my side, her eyes widen as her stare intensifies.

"What?" I ask, curious about her reaction.

Pointing to my side, she asks, "What is that?"

"My tattoo?" I clarify.

She nods. "I've noticed it before but was too shy to ask about it."

Smiling, I trace my fingertips over it, remembering its significance. "It's the serenity prayer. Have you heard of it?"

Again, she nods. Her mouth opens, drawing my gaze to her pink lips, and she goes to say something but stops herself. Giving her a moment, I wait to see if she's going to say anything. "Um, Ace, are you in recovery? Oh, wait. If that's too personal, you don't have to answer. I'm sorry." She flails her hands around, as if they're reacting to the anxiety she's experiencing.

Reaching out, I grab a hand and lace my fingers with hers. She stops moving and her eyes focus on me.

"It's okay. I don't mind answering. No, I'm not in recovery. I got it as a tribute to my siblings," I explain. Not understanding, she cocks her head sideways.

"For your siblings?"

"Two of my siblings, Melissa and Graham, are adopted. Their birth mother abused both alcohol and drugs. Their father left shortly after Graham was born, and things for their mom grew dire. They were removed from the home and came to us. Within mere moments, our family loved them and they became part of us.

"My parents adopted them as soon as the courts said they could. And my tattoo is a tribute to them. They didn't have the best start to life, but I will do whatever it takes to make sure they succeed in whatever they want to do. We take the prayer literally. *To accept the things you cannot change and the courage to change the things you can.*"

Janica moves closer on the bench, kneeling and

sitting on her heels. "It's beautiful," she whispers. I see her hand flex.

"Do you want to touch it?"

She nods and, without hesitation, jumps at me. When her fingertips come in contact with my skin, it's as if a lightning rod poked me. Goose bumps cover my skin, and a shiver shoots up my spine. And as her touch moves over me, heat follows. I wish I could pull her up and move her between my legs. I would ravage her with kisses until we're both dizzy. And it would be impossible to tell if it was from the kissing or the heat of the hot tub.

Looking into my eyes, she says, "That's an incredible tribute."

I smile because I don't know what to say. My siblings are the greatest.

Later in the day, Monica and Christian invite everyone out to her family farm in a few weeks for some event her family is hosting. They're lacking on the details, but I'm guessing if it's farm related, it's probably a barn dance. Of course, I'd never miss an opportunity to break out my boots and cowboy hat, so I tell them I'll be there. Janica has plans with Veronica and is staying home. *Bummer.* If it is a barn dance, what I wouldn't give to hold her in my arms for hours with no one asking too many questions.

On the day of the event at Monica's family's farm, Rocco and I insist we travel together, and we drag our moody asshole captain along. Josh didn't want any part of it, but we figure a little time outside the city and away from Kenzie will probably do him some good.

Rocco drives us to the Fields family dairy farm. Her dad runs it with the help of her three older brothers. I've met Josiah, the youngest of Monica's brothers, as he's hung out with the group a few times. He's a great guy. Mike and Will, her oldest brothers, I will meet today for the first time. I assume anyone related to Monica has to be great. She's one of the kindest people I've ever met.

Rocco turns to me. "Are you ready for this?"

"For what?" I ask as I readjust my Stetson. Just heading out to a farm had me gyrating with excitement; it feels a little like going home. My country boy charm is ready to break out. Friends have said if you spend more than five minutes with me, it's obvious I'm country through and through. I'm sure my drawl, manners, and y'all are dead giveaways too.

We stay in town at the local Super 8. My teammates and I meet there before we all caravan out to the farm. We don't want to overwhelm them, especially if they're busy getting ready for an event. I know first-hand how hectic those can be, so I'm ready to pitch in wherever, if need be. While final preparations are being made around the farm, we're given a tour, including meeting the calves.

"They're adorable," the Steel ladies gush as we're shown the few-days-old calves.

"Can we touch them?" Sam, Shiloh's oldest, asks while Lian, her youngest, edges closer to the Great-Dane-sized Holstein calf. Josiah steps closer to help them do just that.

I move closer to Rocco. "Isn't this cool?"

"Sure, man," he agrees. "Remind you of home?"

Sweating, I lift my hat and wipe my brow. "Yeah, it does. We didn't have milk cows, but my mom always wanted a Longhorn, so for their fifteenth wedding anniversary, Dad got her one."

He laughs. "Wow. He was keeping the romance alive."

I laugh too. "They're still married today, and in love, so it worked for them."

Once we've gotten our fill, they seat us outdoors in a nicely decorated venue. Looking around, I wonder what's happening. This doesn't look like any barn dance I've been to.

Leaning forward, I see Samantha and Shiloh lower their heads and start whispering. They're pointing to something too. Completely clueless, I continue looking around for a sign or something that would hint at what's going on. Then one of Monica's sisters-in-law strolls toward us and hands me a piece of paper.

Picking my jaw off the grass, I can hardly believe my eyes.

Thirty minutes later, we've moved to an elaborately decorated barn. We all stand around waiting for our chance to congratulate the bride and groom, Monica and Christian. Whoops, hollers, and whistles fill the air when they finally appear, and all I can say is *it's about damn time*.

A while after the most amazing dinner, I wander up to Rocco, sweaty and red-faced. Panting, with a huge smile on my face, I say, "Rocco, they're about to cut the cake."

Taking in my happy, yet exhausted appearance, he asks, "Why do you look like you just skated drills for Coach?"

"Because I just taught everyone how to do the Cha Cha Slide. Didn't you see?" I answer as I slump into the chair next to him.

"I didn't. I must have been lost in thought," he tells me while tugging his hand through his hair. He looks like he's working on an impossible-to-solve mental task.

But maybe not. As the resident Steel joker, I can't help myself in teasing him. My best friend looks miserable, and I want to break the tension, so I grin at him and say, "Thoughts of what... or *who*?" My waggling eyebrows are the cherry on top.

Immune to my antics, he just shakes his head at me. "It's nothing. You said something about cake?"

"It's next," I answer while rubbing my belly. He

smirks, making me one happy bastard. I distracted him for at least a moment or two.

After the toast, Rocco and I each devour a piece of the decadent-looking chocolate cake. "Mmmm. Damn, this is good," I say right before shoving another bite into my mouth. I'm not kidding. This is the best cake I've ever eaten. I'm not surprised when I hear that Kenzie at CakeStop made it. Samantha met her a few years ago and has been hiring her ever since for any Steel party she hosts.

We celebrate into the night, and the next morning we meet at the farm for brunch with Monica's family before we head back to Chicago. Thankfully, the ride is pleasant, as Josh is no longer pouting like a giant toddler. Instead, he shares the epiphany he had last night. He's confident it will get Kenzie back. Both Rocco and I volunteer to help him, especially if it keeps him from continuing to be a miserable asshole. He instructs us to wear work clothes when we show up at his house the following weekend. I'm not sure what we'll be doing, but I know Josh appreciates it and would do the same for me. Helping my teammates is a no-brainer.

Chapter 32

Janica

It's hard to believe that Ace and I have been roommates for six months. Even though I've offered, he hasn't asked for rent, to help with utilities, or for my intended date to leave, and I feel guilty. Tonight, I'm leaving work early so I can stop by the store on my way home to grab everything I need to make one of his favorite meals: chicken pot pie. He says his ma makes the best. I've never had one, so she sent me the recipe.

His family is the greatest. I haven't met them face-to-face, but I've talked to them on FaceTime. What I've learned is the Walker family is tight-knit. They talk at least once a week. Usually, during this time, I try to stay out of the way. I don't want to intrude on their time. But there have been times when I've been caught in the crossfire because I'm seated on the couch next to

Ace when they've called. It was during one of these times that I learned how much Ace loves chicken pot pie.

Shortly after I get to work, Veronica hands me a stack of papers. "Can you hang these up on the job board? They just came through."

"No problem," I say, while scanning through them. I don't know if Nicole is still looking for something, but I promised I'd keep an eye open. Flipping to the last paper, I spot something promising. The flyer announces that a new advertising company has just opened and they're hiring for most positions. Before I hang it up, I copy it and put it in my pocket to give to Ace.

———

The house is quiet when I get home that evening. After changing into a comfy pair of shorts and a tank top, I get to work on dinner. I wasn't sure what to serve with it, so while at the store, I grabbed some cut-up melon from the salad bar.

Sliding the concoction into the oven, I whisper, "Please be delicious."

The moment of reckoning comes twenty minutes later when Ace arrives home. He hurries into the kitchen, a confused look on his ruggedly handsome face. He hasn't shaved in a few days and his scruff is doing weird things to my insides. Remaining quiet, he moves from room to room, looking for something.

Watching him from the bar stool, I holler, "What are you doing?"

After I'm sure he's searched the entire house, he comes back to the kitchen. Walking right past me, he marches over to the stove, turns on the inside light, and bends over. My stomach drops. *Does it not smell right?* "What is that?" he asks in a squeaky voice that unnerves me. I want to laugh because it's funny sounding, but my anxiety is through the roof and I want to know if I did something wrong.

Hesitantly, I answer, "Dinner."

He puts his hands on his hips and says, "I figured that, but what is it?"

"It's chicken pot pie. Is that okay?"

He looks around, like he's expecting to see someone. "Who are you looking for?" I ask.

"My ma. That smells just like her chicken pot pie, and I'm wondering where she is."

"She isn't here. I asked for her recipe and she shared it," I confess.

Without another word, he strides over to me and wraps his arms around me. "You made me chicken pot pie," he mutters into my hair.

"I did. She said it was one of your favorites, and I wanted to say thank you for letting me stay here."

He hugs me even tighter. "Thank you, Janica." I don't know how long we stay like that. I love being in his arms. When the oven timer finally goes off, we detangle from each other.

Pulling the pie from the oven, I see the crust is perfectly golden. I am so grateful she told me not to try with a homemade crust.

Waiting for it to cool enough to cut is torture because it smells so good.

Even before I serve it, Ace is in his chair, armed with his fork. His eyes are lit up like a tree on Christmas morning. And his smile... that could charm the panties off of the most devout virgin. He reminds me of a Norman Rockwell painting. It's by far one of the cutest things I've ever seen.

I swear the world freezes after he takes his first bite. He closes his mouth and chews ever so slowly. Waiting for his review almost does me in. My stool is rocking from my nervous leg bouncing, and I'm tightly squeezing my hands together so I won't twist my hair.

Ace finishes his bite, licks his lips, then goes in for another. Needing an answer, I reach forward and block the bite from reaching his mouth and he ends up with my hand in his mouth. "Janbnmca," he says.

Once I've removed my hand from his mouth and given him a napkin, I say, "Sorry. I just have to know. Is it good?"

He laughs. "It's delicious. Try some," he says while

he feeds me the bite already on his fork. As soon as the flavors hit my tongue, I moan. "See?"

I lick my lips. The flakey crust and the creamy sauce cover the chicken and vegetables perfectly. Initially, I didn't understand when the recipe called for shredded cheese and dried Italian seasoning, but I can tell the dish is perfect.

"Oh my gosh. I didn't know something so easy could taste this incredible."

Before long, we've eaten almost the entire pie.

"Thank you, Janica. Other than my ma, no one has ever done anything this kind for me. You're the best roommate and friend anyone could have." *That's it? Just a friend?* My heart squeezes. What did I expect? It's not like he's going to confess his undying love for me.

His talk of friendship reminds me of the paper I copied.

"Hold on. I have something to give you," I tell him before I shuffle off to find my dirty clothes. I grab the flyer from my pants and head back to the kitchen.

"This is for Nicole," I say before I pick up our plates.

He unfolds the paper and scans it. "This is great. I'm sure I'll see her soon."

After the dishes are cleaned up, I turn to him. "What do you have planned for the rest of the night?"

"Nothing." He hesitates. "Why do you ask?"

I smile at him and ask, "When was the last time you've been to Navy Pier?"

He huffs a laugh. "It's been a while. What are you thinking?"

"Maybe you'd be interested in riding some carnival rides? Or we could walk the pier and look at all the stores and grab dessert since we already ate dinner."

Heading down the hallway and away from me, he hollers over his shoulder, "I'm going to grab a sweatshirt, in case it gets cold by the water."

"Great idea, I'll grab one too." When he walks back into the living room, he doesn't look the same. I laugh, tap the ball cap he's wearing, and ask, "What's with the disguise?"

"That's just it. I don't want to ruin the evening if someone recognizes me. I just want to enjoy a night out with you." *That is so sweet.* Be still my heart.

Thirty minutes later, because of light traffic, we park in the parking garage and walk to the pier. Our first stop is the Centennial Wheel. Even though I've been to the pier before, I'd never been brave enough to ride it.

"This is amazing," I gush as we enjoy the three-hundred-sixty-degree view of Lake Michigan and Chicago.

Ace laughs. "Being this high up, everyone below looks so tiny. How high are we?"

I loop my arm through his and lean against him as

we climb higher. "I think it rises to almost two hundred feet."

"You aren't scared of heights, are you?" he teases.

"No, it's more of a fear of falling."

"So you're trying to tell me you wouldn't be interested in doing the drop tower with me?"

"That would be a giant no, thank you." I smirk, and his responding smile makes my knees weak. Good thing I'm still leaning on him for support.

When we finish the ride, we debate whether to get dessert or explore the shops first. "I bet we can't bring desserts into the shops, so why don't we shop first and grab dessert second?"

Patting his stomach, he replies, "I can get on board with that plan. I'm still full from dinner."

As we browse through the shops, we try on sunglasses, point out our favorite candies, and look through all the magnets and keychains for our names, only to realize they're too uncommon. When we walk past the caricature artist, I convince Ace to sit for a picture together. He obliges but refuses to take off his hat because he's sure he'll be recognized. When the artist is all done, he presents us with a masterpiece. "It's great," I say, holding back a laugh.

Ace nudges me as we step away. "What?"

"Anything in the picture that seems that it isn't drawn to scale?" I ask. He shakes his head. "Your ears, maybe?" I mumble with a laugh.

Ace tilts his head. "Now that you mention it, it reminds me of those old Mad Magazine comics."

I snap my fingers. "Exactly." We both share a laugh and a joke about how I'll never be able to sneak up on him because with ears like that, he'll hear me from a mile away.

We grab ice cream for dessert and go sit on the pier with our backs to Lake Michigan. While the lake laps behind us, we take in the lights of the city. It's a picture-perfect moment that I never want to forget.

Chapter 33

Ace

The new season arrives, and I'm more nervous than I've ever been. Robert and Matthew have had me participate in some of the team's practices. They've had me dress out for preseason, but the amount of play time I've had is laughable. But tonight is my first official game back, and I'm hella nervous. Even more so than when I asked Janica to come watch my first game back from the family suite. She easily accepted, knowing the Steel Ladies would be in attendance and she would have some familiar faces to hang out with.

I arrive at the arena plenty early. Janica is coming later, closer to the start of the game. Before I left this afternoon, she hugged me and wished me good luck. She agreed to meet me in the tunnel after the game since I wanted a moment of silence to focus before everything got loud and energized.

I'm across the locker room when I hear Coach push into the locker room. I see him step up to Rocco and say, "Heard Jasmine is here" *What? Why didn't Rocco tell me?* I'd known he'd been making frequent trips back to New York, but he never mentioned her visiting. I totally would have given him crap for that. The fucker smiles and answers with a giant smile and a "yep."

I move over to him and ask. "She's here? Why didn't you tell us? Are we all going out after the game?"

He laughs. *My questions weren't funny.* And I scowl at him. "Whoa, buddy. She's flying home tomorrow. It's just a quick trip. She's not even seeing her parents."

I keep scowling at him, and he elbows me and then confesses, "It's all part of my plan." *What the hell is that supposed to mean?*

Confused, I ask, "What plan?"

Rocco gives me a cocky grin and admits, "I plan to make her mine and bring her home for good."

I raise my eyebrows. "Did you already make her yours?" The fucker just nods.

In disbelief, I shout, "What?" The entire locker room goes silent. I look at my best friend, who's frowning at me. He doesn't like the added attention.

Josh saunters up to us. "What are you guys talking about?" As the jokesters of the team, it's not the first time we've been the center of attention, but this is a more delicate situation. I don't want to throw Rocco under the bus, so I remain mum.

"Does this have anything to do with Jasmine's surprise visit to tonight's game?" Josh presses. Everyone continues to stare, and I start to sweat. Rocco saves us when he clears his throat.

"Jasmine is in town for the first game of the season to cheer us all on." Maybe that's all he'll need to say?

"Is that the only reason?" Josh continues his inquisition. *Shit. Sorry, buddy. That's my bad.* Rocco shifts nervously next to me. *What's he going to say?*

"She's here visiting me because we're together," Rocco admits.

My mouth drops open. I didn't know that. I figured they finally had sex. Looking around, I see I'm not the only one shocked. But that doesn't last long because Lucas lets out a whoop, and everyone goes crazy like we just won the Stanley Cup. *Rocco has to be hating this.* But no. One look at my best friend, and the enormous grin he's wearing tells me he's happy.

I stand up and whistle, getting everyone's attention before I call out, "About damn time." Pretty soon, our teammates join in, chanting, drumming, and whooping. Basically, our team has lost its damn mind.

After Coach's rousing speech and the news of Rocco and Jasmine, we're amped up and ready for the first game of the series. Josh whistles, and we all quiet down before heading out to the ice.

Being my first game back, Matthew and Coach

limit my time on the ice. There aren't words to describe how it feels to finally be back. It's all fresh and new, almost like I'm experiencing it for the first time. And when the third period ends, we've won 3-1.

I rush through my shower so I can get to Janica. I'm also desperate to see Rocco and Jasmine now that their secret is out. When I get into the tunnel, I see Janica talking with Monica and Shiloh. *She fits in with the WAGs perfectly.* With her back to me, she doesn't see me approach. Shiloh leans in, saying something, right before Janica turns around. Her eyes light up when she sees me, and the high I feel from the game is nothing compared to what she does to me. She takes a step toward me, and it's like time freezes. Our moment doesn't last long, as the air crackles with excitement.

I turn to see Rocco stride out of the locker room. His eyes are dark, filled with intensity. Following his gaze, I see he's focused on Jasmine. I smile as he stalks toward her, a heat moving with him. Rocco's a man on a mission and, for the first time in my life, I understand. Pulling Janica to me, we watch them. When he drops his bag, he pulls Jasmine to him, and kisses her like his life depends on it. The entire tunnel breaks out in deafening cheering. Unfamiliar with the tension swirling around Rocco and Jasmine for years, Janica gasps next to me. Concerned, I tug her closer. But the lovesick smile on her face is unmistakable. She loves love, and that is so fucking attractive.

After that epic kiss, Janica is full of questions.

Ushering her to my car, I do my best to temper them until we're alone.

Before I can even buckle myself in, a question is falling from her lips. "What is the deal with those two? That kiss was fire. It was like I was watching a romance book in live action." She turns toward me, intently waiting for an answer.

She's so delectable. I want to lean over and kiss her. "Rocco and Jasmine?" I ask, knowing exactly what she means. Instead of replying, she raises a brow at me. I laugh, holding my hands up in defense.

"They've been friends since they were kids. They've been circling each other for years, and we all wondered when they'd finally collide. But nothing ever happened. When Jasmine moved to New York almost a year ago, Rocco finally figured out he has feelings for her. And ever since, he's been hoping to convince her to move back to Chicago."

Still sitting in the parking lot, she moves closer, almost hovering over the center console. Her body radiates with excitement and her sinfully brown eyes are wide with intrigue and she breathes out, "Really?"

Because I won't let myself kiss her, I reach out and tuck her hair behind her ear. Letting my fingers linger, I run them down her smooth cheek and to her chin, tipping it to me. When our eyes meet, I smile and she shivers. Her breathing hitches and her eyes go wide. *Gorgeous.*

"Ready to go home?" I ask.

Moving her into my house was the best decision I ever made. I'm hopeful she'll never move out and someday she'll be open to making us more than friends.

Janica is quiet on the ride home. She seems lost in thought. Reaching over the console, I gently touch her arm. Her gaze flicks to me, and I ask, "Are you okay? You've been quiet since we left the arena."

She smiles. "I'm good. Just thinking about Rocco and Jasmine and how horrible it would be to have feelings for someone, wondering if they feel the same, but being too shy to ask."

"Yeah, horrible," I say, knowing exactly how that feels.

Returning my hand to the steering wheel, I feel my hands slip from sweat as I turn down our street. I want to tell her how I feel so badly, but the fear that she'll reject me weighs heavily on my heart, causing me to pause. *Can't she give me a definitive sign?*

S ince I was a kid, my hockey schedule has dictated my life. Breaking my leg put a halt on that and then all I seemed to have was time. It was the main reason I started taking college classes. In the almost year I've been off the ice, I forgot how monopolizing my travel schedule is. The first month I'm back on the active roster, I think I'm gone more than I'm home. Thankfully, Janica handles it like a champ. Her only complaint is how lonely the house and bed seem while I'm away. *Is that her way of telling me she misses sleeping next to me?* If so, I totally agree. Having her next to me puts me in the right frame of mind to have a good, restful sleep. I need to feel her body heat and smell her scent in the sheets in order for my mind to wind down. When I'm finally home for more than a few days, I'll figure that out.

"Are you going to lie in bed all day?" Janica asks after her third trip into the bedroom since getting up. I'm currently laid out in the middle of my—*our*—king-sized bed with all my limbs spread wide. "Ace, you look like a starfish, and is that my pillow you have in a death hold?" *What?* From her tone, I know she's baffled. I don't see what the problem is. She got out of bed, so I'm securing what she abandoned. It's as simple as that. *And her pillow?* Yes, I have it in my arms. It's the only way I can immerse myself in her scent without looking like a creeper. Because I know she wouldn't be impressed if I followed her around, sniffing her every few seconds. *Or I don't think she'd like it.*

"I've just missed my bed," I say, defending my odd behavior.

She puts her hands on her hips, and I note the definition of the curve in her waist. Wanting to touch her, I just tug her pillow tighter to my chest and inhale her fragrance. *Damn, she smells good.*

"Don't they put you in nice hotels with comfortable beds?" she asks.

"Hmph." I make a grunting sound in the back of my throat that makes her laugh.

"Tell me," she murmurs.

Propping myself up, I look at her. "It's not the same. The beds aren't bad, they're just missing something."

Confused, she peers at me. "I don't understand. What are they missing?"

Can I answer her question without admitting she's my greatest weakness?

"It's easy. All those beds are missing two things: you and your scent." Her hand flies to her chest. I caught her off guard. This could be good or bad.

"Oh." Dread fills my gut, so I stay silent, afraid to say anything else.

"You're saying you need me in order to sleep?" A pleased smile appears on her face. The dread dissipates like butterflies taking flight.

I chance a smile of my own and give her a half-answer. "Yeah, I guess I am."

She sits on the edge of the bed. "I miss you too when you're gone. The bed, the house... they feel so empty."

An idea takes form in my mind. I crawl over behind her and wrap my arms around her. "How about we FaceTime at night so it's not so lonely for either of us?"

She does her best to hug me back, which is difficult considering the way we're seated. "You'd do that?"

"Of course I would. I miss you too while I'm gone. I've thought about calling, but I didn't know if... after all this time, you might need a break from me." I add an awkward laugh to my confession, hoping she won't look too deeply for my meaning.

Turning her body, she shifts in my arms until we're face-to-face, my arms no longer wrapped around her. "Ace, you are the only person I've never needed a break from." What does that mean? I want to dig deeper, but I'm unsure what to say. Her words have left me speechless.

She reaches up and runs her fingers down my jawline. Ever since I did it that night weeks ago, it's become our thing. I admit, it's odd. It's a secret non-verbal admission that only we share. And because of that, it's invaluable. I can't assume it's the same for her, but every time she does it, I feel like she's trying to tell me something.

She lets out a weighted breath. "Can I ask a favor?"

"Anything," I say, catching her eye.

Fidgeting with her hands is her telltale sign she's nervous. I place my hand over hers. "What is it?"

"What are your plans for tonight?" she inquires.

I shrug. "I hadn't given it much thought. Although staying home sounds awful I want to go out. Do you want to do that?"

Her deep brown eyes sparkle. Fuck, she's beautiful. "That sounds great. We could eat at a new restaurant and then head into the city.'

I love her suggestion. I squeeze her hands, which still rest below mine, and say, "What do you think about axe throwing?"

"Is that a thing?"

Laughing, I answer, "Of course it is. Do you want to try it?" She hesitates for a moment and I say, "There is nothing to fear. You've got this."

She nods her head, adding, "You promise not to laugh?" I nod, and her pink lips part, releasing a heart-warming smile so bright it almost blinds me.

Wishing I had some plaid to wear, I change into a soft black Henley and my favorite pair of worn jeans. Janica blows my mind when she joins me wearing the perfect axe-throwing outfit. Her tight jeans hug her curves in all the best ways. Covering her white tank top is a plaid button-up that is artfully tied below her cleavage. As my eyes trace her body, my thoughts derail.

"Ace," Janica says, "are you ready to go?"

I nod, clear my throat, and say, "I really, really like your outfit. You look very country." Her cheeks turn pink as she thanks me.

We get through the first few practice throws without injury—Janica was incredibly worried she'd throw it backward—but after we've been instructed on proper stance and throwing, we're left to our own devices.

"I feel like I'm holding the axe wrong. Will you help me?" Janica asks. Stepping up behind her, I tuck myself against her. I place my hands on her hips and square them with mine. *Damn, this feels amazing.* Knowing I can stay like this forever, I lean my head forward over her shoulder.

"Pull your arms up." I drag my hands up her sides, past her ribs, and up to her hands. Her breathing hitches, making my pulse throb. I wrap my hands around hers, holding the axe to practice the correct throwing stance.

"That's right," I encourage in her ear. She shivers in my hold, causing her ass to rub against my groin. I pull back so my erection doesn't dig into her. I don't want to make her uncomfortable, but I can't help the reaction I'm having with her body tucked tightly against mine. We practice a few more times before I say, "How about you try again?"

Looking up through her lashes at me, she agrees. I step away and she throws the axe. "Wahoo!" I holler. "That's your best throw tonight. Way to go."

She steps closer, and my body hums with the anticipation of her touch. When it finally happens, and her hand curls around my arm, I feel like I've been shocked. My skin tingles and my body is hot and reactive. "We only have a few minutes in our lane. Do you want to get in a few more throws so that next time we come, you'll be a pro?"

She laughs, and my chest warms, knowing I've made her happy. "Next time we come, we should invite your teammates and their significant others."

"That's a great idea. How about we finish up here and then go to dinner? I'm starving."

Following the fun at axe throwing, we head to a country-themed roadhouse for dinner. We share a deep-fried onion appetizer that is incredible. We practically fight over the zesty dipping sauce. We both select a petite sirloin, baked potato, and broccoli for our main course. Following dinner we head home because she has work in the morning and I have the weight room and physical therapy.

I go to bed thinking tonight was the best date I've ever been on. Then I remember Janica and I were just friends.

Chapter 34

Janica

A week later, after I get home from work, Ace and I are in the kitchen assembling dinner and dancing around to Country's Top 40. I'm having the time of my life. We're working together to prepare Ace's ma's chicken pot pie. Being so close to him, it doesn't take long for my mind to spin. He's been whirling me around in some choreographed dance moves, telling me it's called a two-step. He has my body twisting and contorting in unfamiliar ways. If it weren't for him and his quickstep, I would for sure be nursing a broken hoo-ha. The man has moves on the ice *and* the dance floor, and that makes me wonder if those skills transfer to the bedroom. Feeling the sway of his hips and the thickness of his thigh as he rubs it between mine... Lord have mercy, is it getting hot in here? Until now, I'd never known country line dancing could be so sexual. Honestly, it's always seemed like a lot of stomping, kicking, clapping, and hollering.

The oven signals it's preheated just as he dips me. When he pulls me back up, I see we haven't finished the pie. "Ace, the oven's warm, and dinner's not ready."

A deep groan of displeasure rumbles from his chest while he pulls me close. Within seconds, my body melts into his. Pressed tightly together, our bodies move as one. He lowers his hold on me, pushing his hips into mine, and I'm shocked. There's no denying something below the belt is responding to our nearness. As far as I can recall, this is the first time I've been aware of Ace's attraction to me. *But is that what this is?* I can't deny his cock is rock hard right now and pushed against my center, but I question if it's because of me or because I'm a woman and we're dirty dancing.

Feeling overwhelmed and parched, I rasp out, "Ace."

He pulls back, a goofy, happy grin on his face, and I can't help but beam up at him. He's adorable.

"I need to finish dinner," I tell him. His expression drops, and I quickly add, "But thank you for the dance." I blush. "It was my first two-step, and I really enjoyed it."

Like he can't resist touching me, he pulls me into a hug. "Now that my leg is healed, we'll have to find a country bar that has dancing so we can two-step and line dance."

Imagining myself trying to line dance makes me

laugh. "Okay, but you'd have to promise you wouldn't laugh at me." Putting my hands on my hips, I'm not convinced when his "okay" comes out as more of a cackle.

The rest of our evening is perfect. We snuggle together on the couch, eating sour worms and laughing through a comedy special we found on Netflix. We head to bed after since I have work and he has practice in the morning. Disappearing to our separate bathrooms, which is probably what makes this living arrangement work, we change and brush our teeth. Ace is already in bed when I come into the room. He is, of course, shirtless, because he tells me that's the only way he can sleep. His left arm is tucked behind his head, propping him up, and he side-eyes me when I move to my side of the bed. Before I slip beneath the covers, I grab my strawberry pound cake scented lotion next to the bed and put it all over my legs.

A low, sexy rumble comes from Ace, making me squeeze my thighs together. "It's a good thing I know that's lotion, because it smells incredible. If it weren't, I'd be tempted to lick it off you." *Huh?* Did he just say what I think he did? Shit. Now I'm thinking about how badly I want him to lick me all over. My cheeks grow hot as I fantasize about that. It's a good thing I'm turned away from him, otherwise he'd see how incredibly turned on I am. I squeeze my thighs together again, hoping to dull the ache growing there, as I take measured deep breaths to calm myself down.

"What are you doing over there? It sounds like you're practicing breath holds for deep water work. Are you planning a spearfishing expedition for some time soon?"

Funny guy. I snort laugh at the thought of that. Embarrassed, I hide my face behind my hands. Ace snickers as he appears behind me, trying to see my face. When he finally gets my hands away, he smirks at me, asking. "What was that noise?"

Mortified, I explain. "I once tried to snorkel, and it was an epic fail. Throughout the two-hour activity, I probably drank about a gallon of water. Activities that have me going under the water for any length of time are a hard pass for me. I learned that day that if I want to see underwater creatures, I'm safer going to the aquarium."

Ace's grin melts away all my insecurities. When he returns to his side of the bed, he relaxes back with his arm behind his head again, staring at me. I've never had a man look at me the way he does. He always gives me one hundred percent of his attention. It feels like he sees directly into my soul and accepts all that I am. It's both unnerving and flattering at the same time. I'm shaken to my core. Feeling vulnerable, I crawl beneath the covers. Then I turn onto my side so I'm facing him. He smiles and rolls to his side so he's facing me. Saying nothing, he reaches out and bops my nose. Staring into his deep brown eyes, I realize I've fallen completely for this man. He's been the best friend I've ever had. *But could it be more?* Other than dancing in the kitchen this evening, he's given no sign he wants more. And what would that more be? I know I wouldn't be able to handle a friends-with-benefits situation.

My mind fills with questions as I ponder how to start that conversation. I turn to my back, needing space to consider everything. I'm fearful if I say anything and he doesn't reciprocate my feelings, it will cause tension between us, and our friendship will pay the price. But if I say nothing and then have to stand by and watch him date, it'll kill me. My heart twists. *I hate this.*

Lost in my head, I don't realize Ace has moved closer. Reaching out, he turns my head to look at him. He's frowning. His eyes are stern as he asks, "What's on your mind?"

I blink back tears but am not fast enough to catch them all. Ace wipes a stray tear away. "Please talk to me, Janica. Did I hurt you?" His deep voice wobbles.

I shake my head and rasp, "I've just got a lot going on in my head, and I'm trying to untangle it before I share it."

His eyes soften. "Promise?" I nod, silently agreeing. He pulls his hand out, thrusting his pinkie at me. "Melissa always had me pinky promise, and because those are ironclad, I think we should do it.

Laughing because I can't tell if he's serious, I lift my pinkie to his and seal the deal. I go to pull my hand back, and he doesn't let me. Instead, he threads our fingers together. It isn't the first time we've held hands, but this, right now, feels different. It doesn't tell me what I need to know, but it settles my heart enough.

Yawning, I turn back toward Ace. "Thank you for always being there for me." With our hands joined, lying only inches apart, we both fall asleep.

Chapter 35

Ace

I wake early this morning and watch Janica slumber. She looks ethereal. The sun shines through the window, highlighting her soft hair. I stretch my fingers, wanting to leisurely drag them across her skin. Lying there with my arm behind my head, my heart pumps like I've just finished a workout. Being this close to her always leaves me wanting more. I don't want to be just friends anymore, and I'm tired of waiting.

When she stirs and lifts her gaze to meet mine, I say, "Good morning, my queen."

"Your queen?" she asks sleepily.

Smiling widely, I answer, "Yes. Aren't you Queen Amidala?"

Pushing up and severing our contact, she smirks. "Isn't she a queen in *Star Wars*?" I nod. She looks thoroughly confused. "I don't get it. Why would you call me that?"

Reaching out, I tug on the ends of her hair. "With that crazy foam thing in your hair, you remind me of her."

"Didn't she always have those outlandish head-dresses?" Again, I nod. Janica laughs. She pretends to fluff her hair and asks, "So you think I look ridiculous with my foam curlers in?" *No. You're fucking adorable.* Still laughing, she pretends to scoff and informs me they'll save her at least a half an hour in the bathroom. She tosses back the covers and gets out of bed. "I better go take these out before you decide on another name to tease me with." Then she sticks her tongue out.

Darting out of my hand, I grab her wrist. "I was only kidding. I think you're adorable."

"Adorable?" She scrunches her nose. "That's just what every woman wants to hear. Now, please let me go so I can go make myself more presentable."

Refusing to let go of her wrist, I shake my head no.

"No? What's that supposed to mean?" she argues while trying to pull away.

"It means exactly that, Janica. I'm not letting you pull away from me anymore. You are fucking adorable and it's time you know I think that," I state, then I pull her to me and kissed her like I've been wanting to for over a year. And from the first touch of our lips, I know she'll be the last person I'll ever kiss.

The kiss starts out hesitant, but then it turns

passionate. Waiting so long gave me ample time to consider what I want. I drop her wrist and cup my hands around her face, moving her exactly where I want, and push things further. In no time, our tongues work in sync, and a sweet moan escapes from her.

I want this moment to last forever, but I need to slow things down before I have her stripped naked on the bed with my head between her thighs. There is no way I'm rushing this. If she's agreeable, we'll take our time learning and discovering together, but I have to be sure she wants this as much as I do.

Pulling myself from her, I mutter, "fuck," as I rest my forehead on hers. We both remain silent as we try to control our breathing. Once I feel my heart isn't beating out of my chest and I can talk without sounding like I'm out of breath, I look into her gorgeous eyes. "That was incredible. And we need to talk, but you have to get to work and I have practice. How about I pick you up from the library later? We can grab takeout from Mateo's and have a long overdue talk."

Janica smiles at me. "Sounds great." Then she affects a fake haughty expression, and says, "Now the queen has to go get ready for work." I pull her into a hug before she slides off the bed and leaves the room. When she's gone, I collapse on the bed, relieved I finally made my move.

After practice, while sitting in an ice bath, I replay the night before in my mind, and muse about the possibility of taking my relationship with Janica to the next level. The flames of our mutual attraction have been building for some time and were bound to combust. Until last night, when we danced in the kitchen, I'd never had the pleasure of holding her in my arms for more than a few seconds when we hugged. Even now, I'll never forget the way her body melted against mine. In those moments, having her curves pressed against me, I permitted myself to imagine if we weren't wearing any clothes. Normally, my fantasies of Janica occur when I'm home alone in my shower. Out of respect for her and our friendship, I try my best to tamp my lust down when we're together. But with each day that passed, that feat became harder and harder, just like my dick when we two-stepped.

As the night continued, the sexual tension between us hung heavy in the air. It reached an all-time high for me when she came to bed and was putting lotion on her legs. Even though she turned away from me, my imagination filled with what my eyes couldn't see. Lying in bed, I pictured it as she rubbed up and down her sexy legs with her strawberry pound cake-scented lotion. My mouth had watered, and I'd licked my lips. It's like I've developed a Pavlovian response to her.

Closing my eyes, I transport myself back to that moment. The lotion smelled edible, and I wanted to lick it off her. I even told her that. She'd sounded surprised about what I'd said, but she hadn't been mad. *Damn.* Despite the ice bath and the extremely harsh environment I'd willingly put myself in, my cock grows painfully hard. Looks like I'll be taking a moment before I get out of this frigid water.

"Ace, you almost done?" Josh hollers out across the training room.

Swallowing hard, my teeth chatter as I force out my answer. "Just a few more minutes."

I mentally jog through every boner-killing image I can drum up as he comes closer. Swapping our towels, he kicks off his slides and waits for me to finish up.

With my boner finally deflated enough, I turn to him and raise a questioning brow. "What's got you in such a rush?"

"I want to get to the bakery before Kenzie closes," he replies.

Shaking my head as I step out of the ice bath, I understand where he's coming from. Every night I'm not on the road, I anxiously await Janica's return home. Those evenings are my favorite. We fix dinner together, snuggle on the couch in front of the TV, then go to bed, holding hands. It's been months of this, and during that time, our sleeping positions have changed. No longer are we sleeping as far away from each other as possible. Now we're right next to each other. Sometimes, I'll even wake up to our legs entwined and her head on my chest. On those rare occasions, I lie as still as I can, soaking up the uninterrupted few minutes I have before her alarm goes off. It's on these mornings that she's her most adorable. Her cheeks are always flushed when she finally lifts her head off my naked chest to make eye contact.

Still covered in goose bumps from the frigid soaking I just had, I head to the showers with the memory of this morning on repeat. *Finally, things are changing.*

Chapter 36

Janica

As I float—I mean walk—down the hallway to the spare room to get ready, I pat my hair. There are now two reasons I'm grateful I put my foam roller in my hair last night before bed. The first is I believe it encouraged Ace to kiss me. The second is that I know when I remove it, I will have effortless curls that require little work to make presentable.

When I get to the library, I'm still buzzing from the feel of his lips on mine. Ace's kiss had blown me away. When he pulled away and explained he wanted to slow everything down, I wanted to scream *no*. It's been a year since he moved me into his apartment, and with each new day, my attraction to him grew.

On a normal day, I can't wait to get home and see him, so, of course today is dragging by painfully slow.

"Is this day over yet?" I ask Veronica as I lean against our shared desk.

Her responding laughter answers me perfectly. *Nope.*

"You look different today. You're glowing. Why?" she asks.

Ignoring her, I say, "I'm done filing back books. Do you have anything that will either distract me or increase the speed at which this day is traveling?"

I should have known that after that kiss, my brain would be scrambled all day.

Leaning forward on the high counter of our desk, she lifts her eyebrows inquisitively. "Why are you so eager for the day to get over? Do you have somewhere you'd rather be?"

I remain mum. Then Veronica flashes her brilliant white smile at me, and alarm bells go off in my head. *Back away now.* "I... um... Ace and I sort of kissed."

Her eyes widen and her smile grows larger.

"You did? Finally. I swear you two took forever." My mouth hangs open. *What is she talking about?* "Good thing I didn't place any bets on when I thought that would happen, because I would have lost." She laughs.

"What?"

"Oh, come on, Janica. Anyone who spends over five minutes around you can tell you have a connection with him and something was going to happen. I just didn't expect it to take this long. I'm happy for you. Ace is an amazing guy and you're lucky to have him."

I nod, processing her claim that everyone knew there was an attraction between us and was waiting for us to get together. "So," Veronica hedges. "How was the kiss? Did it go any further?"

I sigh. "No, we just kissed. But it was perfect, and that's why I need a distraction. Because I swear time is going backward today."

"A distraction, you say. I'm glad you asked. The pre-kinder group is here for books and art in ten, and you know helping me will both distract you and pass the time."

I drop my forehead to the desk and mumble, "I hope this isn't like last time. We'd been working on gluing things in a book we were making about animals, and I ended up with glue in my hair."

"If I recall, it wasn't that bad. After a few extra washes, you were good as new. Plus, I run the group every week and I'm still alive. And they're cute for little people." They are cute, I can't disagree with that. A humorless laugh gets stuck in my throat. *Here we go.*

She leads me into a room where a handful of kids are already seated and waiting. Veronica starts explaining the story she read to them last week, as well as the craft we'll be constructing together. Everything sounds doable until she gets to the last step. She and I are supposed to help the kids put glitter on their projects. *God help me.*

By the time we're done, I resemble a human-sized disco ball. Slipping off to the bathroom after the parents have claimed their children, I try to scrub the craft supply from hell from my face and hands. It shakes out of my hair easily, but I suspect it will be like sand, appearing on my pillow days later. But Veronica was right. My day is already half over.

As I fill my cart with all the books I need to re-shelve, my thoughts drift to this morning. Every time I think about the conversation Ace mentioned having, butterflies take flight in my stomach. I'm hopeful he'll admit he has feelings for me and that he wants to date. That's the direction I want things to go, but without his confirmation, there is no way I'm going to make the first move. *Was he telling me without words that he wants more than friendship?*

By the time I shelve the last book, I'm dying to see Ace. Weaving my way through the far stacks on my way back to my desk, I'm not paying attention when a pair of hands cover my eyes from behind. "Guess who," the mystery man says against my ear. His breath tickles me, sending goose bumps all over my body. *Focus, Janica. Who is it?* Even though I'm effectively blind and he's tried to disguise his voice by dropping it, I know it's him. His amber scent winds around me, and my body instantly relaxes, leaning back into him.

"Ace, what are you doing here?"

His laughter fills the quiet space, and he answers, "I missed you."

"I missed you too," I tell him. He moves in front of me, pulls me to a stand, and hugs me tightly. He nuzzles his face into my neck. I close my eyes, relishing having him so close.

"There you go," he says while gently setting me down.

"What are you doing here?" I ask again, beaming at him.

He puts his hands on his hips. *He is so sexy.* "Did you forget our plans?"

I shake my head and look at my watch. "I must have been in the zone. I wanted to get every book shelved before you got here.'

Looking at the empty cart, he smirks. "Now you're free to go?"

"I am."

He grabs the cart and starts pushing it to my desk for me. I walk beside him sure I'm grinning like an idiot.

After a quick bye to Veronica, we head out. While walking out of the library, Ace grabs my hand, interlocking our fingers. My heart flutters. His innocent touch lights my body on fire. When we get to his car, he opens my door like the gentleman he is.

"I already called in our order at Mateo's, and it should be ready by the time we get there," he tells me.

Our stop is quick, and as the heavenly aromas of our dinner fill the car, my stomach growls and I laugh.

Ace laughs too. "Better get you home so we can feed you. I don't want you turning hangry."

"I don't get hangry. I just get a little annoyed when I'm overly hungry," I defend.

Ace laughs again. "Isn't that the exact definition of hangry?" I'm tempted to stick my tongue out at him, but I don't. Instead, I wave him off.

Giving him a smirk, I answer, "I don't know. But let's not test it."

"Yes, ma'am" he says while getting on the highway. All the way home, the smells of garlic, butter, roasted tomatoes, basil, and oregano invade my nose. Finally, we pull into the driveway. I throw open my door before Ace, and hop out of the car, my arms loaded with hot to-go containers.

"Last one in is a rotten egg," I shout over my shoulder as I jet into the opening garage. I hear Ace's door shut as I reach the stairs. Kicking off my shoes, I try to shuffle the containers so I can get a hand free for the doorknob. But luck isn't on my side because I soon discover that for me to accomplish this, all the to-go containers would tip out of my arms. My shoulders slump. Admitting defeat, I holler Ace's name.

"Do you need something, my dear?"

I grit my teeth together and swallow down my ego. Trying my best to shift so I can see him, I spot the smirk he's wearing. *Turd.* In a sickeningly sweet voice, I ask, "Darling, would you please help with the door?"

"Since you asked so nicely." He leans around me and pushes the door open. "There you go, my lady."

Turning to him, I frown and ask, "Why do you have to be so cute while you're being a butt?"

He scoffs. "I don't know what you're talking about. I'm being a complete gentleman." I roll my eyes and walk inside. He follows behind, laughing. I set the to-go boxes on the counter while he goes for plates, silverware, and napkins.

"What do you want to drink?" I ask while reaching for cups.

"Water, please."

Sitting at the island with our dinner, we share how our days went. At one point, Ace reaches over and tugs on a lock of my hair. "Why do you have glitter in your hair?"

"I unintentionally became a disco ball for the pre-K reading group."

Setting a hand on my thigh, he laughs hysterically. "I would have paid good money to see that. Please tell me Veronica took a picture.'

I laugh too, because it was funny. "No. I didn't let Veronica take a picture. It was her fault anyway."

Scratching his head, he asks, "How? Did you read a book about the seventies and it mentioned a disco?" He continues laughing.

"Har, har. You are so funny. If you must know, the star of the book was a very sad iguana named Eleanor. She had lost her sparkle. So, our art project was to give some sparkle to our paper iguanas, just like her friends did in the book."

"But how did it end up all over you? Wait. Did Veronica get covered too?"

Scowling, I shake my head. "No, she chose to help with the front of the craft and left the end to me. And I can reliably say kids aren't always the best with their dexterity and following instructions. After about ten kids, both the iguanas and I sparkled so much, the astronauts on the ISS would have been able to see us from space."

Ace turns toward me and then spins my stool around. He puts his hands on my thighs, and I suck in a breath. Heat radiates from the point of contact and into the rest of my body. Need puddles in my center as I wonder if he'll go higher.

"You are adorable," he says. But because all my focus is on how good it feels to have him touching me, I don't catch it.

"W-what did you say?"

"You are adorable," he repeats.

My head drops. *Ugh. Really?*

"What?" he asks while tipping my chin up.

"I want you to think I'm sexy, not adorable. Sexy is someone you desire above all things, someone you want and crave. Adorable is a new puppy, cute at the moment."

He is too gorgeous for his own good, and here he is

calling me adorable, like I'm some toddler. "It's nothing. It's fine," I say, wanting to disappear.

His eyes darken as a frown appears on his face. "I know what *it's fine* means. I have a ma and sister, remember?" he grumbles.

"Oh yeah, all-knowing man? What does *fine* mean?" I challenge. I don't mean to be arguing with him, but he said I was adorable, and that was after the kiss that rocked my world. I'm not sure what's coming next, and I'm psyching myself out.

Sitting up straighter, with his hands still on my thighs, he snarls, "*Fine* in women's lingo means anything but."

Crossing my arms over my chest, I counter, "If you're so smart, what was I reacting to?"

He lifts his hands and says, "You got me. Why don't you just tell me and save us both some time?"

Sitting there for a moment, I consider his argument. I guess it would save time, but I don't want to make this too easy. Making him wait another few minutes brings me enjoyment. "It was because you said I was adorable."

"But you are," he counters.

"Despite that, following the kiss this morning, no woman would want her crush calling her that."

His eyes light up. "Did you just say crush?"

Yes, I did. I hadn't meant to disclose that information until the conversation we were supposed to have tonight.

I dip my head and slowly nod. Chancing a glance at him, I see he's wearing a gigantic smile across his handsome face. *Guess we're starting that conversation now.*

"Janica." He squeezes my thighs. "I have a crush on you too. Well, at this point, it's more than a crush, but the point is, I really like you. And I think you are adorable, sexy, smart, funny, and kind."

Blown away, I stare at his mouth. I watched him say all those words, but I'm struggling to believe this moment is real. I pinch myself. "Ouch," I mutter.

"Why'd you do that?" he asks, worried.

I give a humorless laugh. "Just making sure I'm not dreaming and that this is really happening."

He leans in and places his lips against mine and growls, "It's very real." Then he moves his mouth against mine, kissing me. His hands leave my thighs and curl around my hips. His tongue wrestles with mine, and I lean farther into him, trying to get closer. He releases a deep moan and pulls me onto his lap to straddle him. Our centers kiss and he shifts my hips, rubbing me over his hard cock. My clit tingles from the extra friction, and I whimper. I pull my lips from his. "More, please" I beg.

Closing my eyes, I tilt my face to the ceiling as my body chases a high. He licks up my neck and then blows on the same path his hot tongue took. Shivers race down my back and I grind my hips, adding more pressure against his throbbing cock. His large hands move from my hips to my ass and he cups me. He gives each cheek a squeeze before he rocks me into him. The movement changes the point of friction, and after a few swipes, an orgasm rips through me. "Ace," I moan.

When I come down from my high, my head sags, putting us face-to-face. He leans in and places sweet kisses on my lips. I can feel he is still harder than steel below me. My mind is mush as I try to form a plan so I can take care of him. But even before I can move an inch, Ace asks, "Ready for that conversation, babe?"

"Yeah, but maybe we could move to the couch?" I suggest, knowing I'll need a few inches between us if I'm planning on paying any attention to what words come out of his beautiful mouth.

Ace helps me off his lap, and I grab our dishes to clean them off before we talk. He joins me in the kitchen as I wash dishes. Coming up behind me, he nudges his cock against my butt and wraps his arms around my waist, pulling me closer. Placing a kiss below my ear never seemed sensual until he did it. I melt against him.

Chapter 37

Ace

Excusing myself to the bathroom while Janica finishes our dishes seems like the right move. When I'm behind closed doors, I can berate myself privately. *What was I thinking?* Problem was, I wasn't. Having her close to me had scrambled my brain. It had been a long time coming. So, when the opportunity was presented to me, I selfishly gave in and took it.

Tonight, when I'd ordered dinner, I hadn't ordered a side of orgasm. But that didn't stop me from savoring it. When she told me she had a crush on me, I lost it. And fuck me, it was worth it. Watching her come was the most beautiful thing I've ever seen. From her labored breathing to the pink that spread from her neck up to her cheeks, it was magical. And right away, I needed more. The only problem is that we haven't had our conversation yet. You know, the one I'd insisted on this morning after the world's best kiss. "Ugh. Why did I insist on that?" I ask myself as I stare into the mirror. My brown eyes look wild and almost black. I splash some cold water on my face. "Get it together," I mumble as I run my hands through my hair, trying to remember what I want to say to her. The bullet points I'd outlined earlier today are incredibly difficult to recall with a throbbing cock in my pants. "Holy fuck." *This woman.* Without even trying, she has me twisted up tightly, and I need to focus if we're going to have a conversation about us. Hope bubbles up in my chest at the thought of that. *Me and Janica.*

After I've gotten my shit together and forced my cock into submission, I go looking for Janica. She's seated on the couch, sipping a hot beverage. "Is that coffee? You know that will keep you up late," I remind her as I near the couch.

"And if I want to be up late?" she asks, her eyebrow raised in question. The air crackles between us, the tension we've been avoiding for months, supercharged.

I smirk. "Any reason you want to be up late?"

A sexy smile follows the nonchalant shrug of her shoulders. Taking a sip of her coffee, she whispers, "Maybe I'll discover a worthwhile reason for depriving myself of sleep." My cock jumps to life, offering to entertain her. *Down, boy. Talk first.* I adjust myself, and her eyes widen. Sitting down next to her, I hear her swallow. *Yeah, baby. He wants to get to know you better too.*

"Since you called this meeting, Ace, what did you want to talk about?" she asks, then takes another sip. The French vanilla creamer wafts past my nose, and I salivate. I want to taste it off her lips and tongue.

Trying to stay focused, I turn to her. "I don't know how to say this eloquently, so I'm just going to blurt it out. Okay?" She nods, a beautiful smile on her face. *Man, I love that smile.* Suddenly nervous, I take a deep breath, pushing it out of my nose. She sets her mug on the coffee table and takes my hands in hers. Her thumbs rubbing circles on my palms calms me. "Janica, I have liked you for months, and I can't hold it in anymore. You are the most incredible woman I have ever met. You are my best friend, confidante, cheerleader, and roommate. But I want more. I know I should have told you all that before I kissed you this morning, but when I'm around you, my brain turns to mush, and I just reacted. It was the best kiss of my life, and I hope I didn't make things awkward between us."

Janica scoffs and shakes her head. "We're good, Ace."

"Good, I'm glad. I hope I'm not being too forward in saying this, but I want to date you, take you out, hold your hand, snuggle with you, kiss you, laugh with you, make love to you, do all the things."

Her hands squeeze mine. "Really?"

I nod like a fool, and she smiles, then crawls in my lap. "I have feelings for you too, Ace, and everything you said sounds amazing and I want to do it all. I think this thing between us has been brewing for a long time, and I, for one, am glad that we're finally talking about it." Then she leans in and kisses me. I lick her lips and they taste like vanilla. Leaning back on the sofa, I tug her with me so she stays close. The feel of her body against mine is everything. Even though we're clothed, the heat being exchanged could start a three-alarm fire. She moans against my lips, opening her mouth to me, and I sweep my tongue inside. More vanilla. *She tastes divine.*

Janica moves her hands up and cups the sides of my face, pulling me closer. When she's got me where she wants me, her hands move up to my ears and she plays with my earlobes. *That's new, but I like it.* When the kissing turns more intense, nipping and biting, she tugs at my earlobes, delivering a lick of pain. My cock loves it and grows harder She seems to notice and grinds down onto my lap. I place my hands on her hips, moving her right on top of my hard cock, and pull her tighter against me. The friction is insane, and even though I'm afraid I'll blow in my pants, I won't take her release from her.

She arches her back, pressing her breasts into me. *Hell yeah.* I thrust my hips up, making them jiggle. *Ride me, cowgirl.* I can't wait until she's on my cock. Picturing that, I thrust even harder, and she pulls her mouth from me. "Ace, right there," she pants. I lift my arm, pull one breast free from her shirt, and lower my mouth to one hardened, rosy-pink nipple. I nibble it before I suck it into my mouth, and she grinds harder against me. Looking up, I see her cheeks are flushed and her eyes are closed. *She is gorgeous.* Needing more, I let go of her nipple. The pop it makes causes Janica to open her eyes and look at me.

"Do you need more baby?" I ask, and she whimpers. Pushing up from the couch, I secure her legs around me and head for the bedroom.

Laying her gently down on the comforter, I remind myself to take my time. Hovering above her, in a gravelly voice, I ask, "Are you okay with this?" She nods. "Words, babe. I need words," I say, giving her full control of the situation.

She reaches up with one hand and makes sure I'm looking at her before she says, "I want you, Ace. I've wanted you for so long."

My heart doubles in size and thumps rapidly in my chest. "Okay," I rasp before I lick my lips and get started worshipping my woman.

Chapter 38

Janica

It's finally happening. Ace grabs the cotton shorts I put on after I'd done the dishes. Wanting to be comfortable during our talk, I went with cute and casual instead of my boring work clothes. Shimmying my hips, he drags the shorts off me, leaving me in a lacy pair of red panties. He sits back on his heels.

"What are you doing?" I ask, nervous because this is the first time he's seen me almost nude. Maybe he doesn't like what he sees? *Shut up, brain.* Thinking back, he'd seen me in a bikini before at Lucas and Samantha's months ago, and he didn't look repulsed. Instead, he looked hungry. Kind of like he does now. His brown eyes darken and he licks his lips. *Please lick me.*

"I'm admiring the view," he explains. "But something's missing." He reaches out and pulls my tank top off over my head, revealing my matching red lacy bra.

"There, that's better." He smirks, then adds, "Almost." He untucks the breasts still being held captive by my bra. "Now you're perfection."

"Sure," I say under my breath. I know I'm probably not his usual type. I'm not a statuesque model; I'm curvier and softer. I'm happy with myself, but I'm struggling to understand his attraction to me. I mean, he is a perfect specimen. He has muscles in all the right places, probably zero percent body fat, and from the outline in his athletic shorts, a quite substantial cock. Besides that, he's drop-dead gorgeous, polite, caring, responsible, smart, and funny. It doesn't get better than him.

He lowers his head to my soft belly and runs his tongue from my panty line up to my bra. Cupping each breast in his hands, he nuzzles, kisses, and nibbles them before reaching behind me to unhook my bra. He slowly drags it off me and throws it over his shoulder. Craving his touch, I arch my back. He takes a finger and runs it from my throat, over my sternum, and down to my belly button. He traces it, then walks his fingers down to my panties. Lowering my body, I chase his touch. Hooking a finger in each side of the lace, he pulls them down my legs, scooting off the bed as he goes. Raising them to his nose, he gives them a sniff before a sexy smirk covers his mouth.

Ace removes his t-shirt with one hand. *Could that be any sexier?* I lift my legs so I can press my thighs together and ease the growing ache I feel. Watching my every move, I see his eyes light up. He steps forward and forces my legs apart. "Open these so I can see you." His deep voice makes me wetter. I've never been with anyone so demanding, but I like it. I slowly open my legs to him as my body buzzes with anticipation of what he'll do next. He drops his shorts and boxer briefs to the floor, and his firm cock stands proudly. He grabs it in his large hand and gives himself a few strokes as he stares at my dripping sex. He licks his lips and growls, "beautiful," before he steps forward and drops to his knees. He wraps his hands around my calves and tugs me toward the end of the bed. Uncertain, I close my eyes the closer I get to his face. I'm a mix of emotions, vulnerable being the most prominent. The feel of his hands releasing my calves, then running up my thighs toward my center, has me opening my eyes. Overwhelmed with desire and unease, I blink, trying to focus on his face. A devastating smile meets me, and I melt deeper into the bed.

"Can I taste you, Janica?" he asks, waiting patiently for my reply.

"Yes," I whisper.

Leaning down, he blows cool air against my sex, and my body tenses. *Relax.* I haven't had a man pleasure me in so long, I barely remember what it feels like. "Ahhh," I moan. This is the most intense sexual moment of my life. Nothing else I've experienced compares. Looking between my parted legs, I'm confident it has everything to do with the man pleasuring me.

"Do you want more?" he asks with his mouth against my clit.

"Please," I beg in a throaty tone.

He sucks my clit into his mouth, and my butt comes off the bed. He reaches up with one hand and splays it over my abdomen while saying "be still." I breathe out and do as he says while he drags his tongue through my folds from back to front. Each time he does it, he flicks my clit before sucking on it. It doesn't take long to feel my insides tighten. An orgasm builds and my toes curl. As it gains strength, my sex gushes and my hips flex. Ace laps at my center, moaning his approval. Once I'm clean, he takes his other hand and inserts a finger into me. The friction feels so good. Then he adds another finger and pulls them both into a curl. He rubs the tips of his fingers against my G-spot, and it feels like I've touched a live wire. A jolt of pleasure shoots up my spine and a moan falls from my lips. He wraps his mouth around my clit and sucks hard as my orgasm rockets through me. My hips pump and flex, and my stomach contracts just as my internal passage does. "So tight. I can't wait until you squeeze my cock like that." My cheeks grow hotter. I like this dirty-talking, rough cowboy. And I can't wait to share all the things with him.

Opening my eyes after succumbing to the most intense orgasm, I stare at Ace, who is still kneeling at the end of the bed. I scoot back and say, "Come here." He climbs onto the mattress, his cock bobbing between his legs. Wanting to touch it, I reach out and wrap my palm around his smooth, hard shaft. He tips his head back, revealing his body from the sexy arch of his neck all the way down to his treasure trail. The groan that falls from his pleasure-soaked lips rattles my bones. I run my thumb over the mushroom-shaped head, collect the drop of pre-cum, and smear it down his shaft.

"Shit, I need to grab a condom," he mutters before he reaches over me and into his nightstand. "I can't believe I forgot that."

Reaching up, I touch his chest. "It was a good catch. I hadn't thought about it either. Just so you know, I've been tested since breaking up with Trevor. Even though we always used condoms, I felt it was important to be checked out after I learned he'd been cheating. I'm clean." Ace leans down and softly kisses my lips.

"I was tested a few months ago when I had to have lab work done for the team. I'm clean too." When he's fully sheathed, he presses against me. Moving his hand, I drag his cock through my wet lips. We both moan. I line him up and he takes my lead, slowly inching himself into me. The deeper he goes, the more my body stretches to accommodate him. Pressing my legs back, he opens me wider. Then he pushes himself the rest of the way in.

"Ace," I whimper.

He freezes and looks down at me. "Are you okay?"

"So full," I mumble.

His face contorts with worry. "Too much?"

"No. Can you just start moving slowly?" I ask, my voice strained.

As he hovers above me in a push-up position, I watch his arms flex while he fights to maintain control. His face is tight with concentration as he slides in and out of me. After a few passes, I feel much more comfortable and I wrap my legs around his hips, pulling him in close.

"Better?" he asks.

I lay a hand on his cheek. "Much, thank you," I tell him just before he lowers to kiss me. As our tongues tangle, I use my heels to pull him into me. He takes the hint and pumps his hips. He slips a hand between us, finding my clit plump and wanton. His fingers rub aggressive circles on it, beckoning another orgasm from me. I feel my muscles tighten and he releases a low, throaty groan. I release my leg hold on him and pull my legs up. His thrusts go deeper, and I whimper into his mouth. He pulls back to check on me, and I moan, "Please, Ace." He knows what I'm begging for, and he pistons his hips, pushing my body to its limits.

He turns us on our sides and slides me up and down his cock. When he grabs my breast and suckles it, my insides squeeze him tight. "Fuck," he grunts, and he slams his body into mine. I shift my hips so my clit rubs against him every time he bottoms out.

"Right there. Almost. So close," I pant out while he continues thrusting into me. He explodes within me and I follow right behind. Our hips continue to move on their own. I slip my hand down to my clit and rub it, prolonging my orgasm. My head flops forward, hitting his chest. And his chest vibrates as he lets go of a deep chuckle.

He wraps his arms around me and holds me tight, kisses my lips, and says, "That was a thousand times better than I imagined it." All I can do in response is sigh. *This man.* I'm sure he's won my heart completely.

Chapter 39

Ace

Going on the road two days after we first slept together is physically painful. My chest is tight as I drive to the arena. When I board the team bus, my stomach begins turning. *What is going on?* I question while waiting for my teammates to finish loading. I pull a spearmint Lifesaver from my travel bag and suck on it, hoping it will settle the uneasiness I'm feeling.

"Ace," Rocco hollers out down the aisle, as if it's been months since he last saw me.

It's been a day. We had practice yesterday. "Hey, man," I answer, sticking out my fist for him to bump.

He does, then slides into the seat next to me. "How are you feeling about going to Vegas?"

Shrugging, I say, "It'll probably be a pretty even game."

"Yeah, I agree." He pulls out his headphones and drops them around his neck. "Hey," he says.

I look at him. "Huh?"

"Why do you look so miserable? Are you feeling okay?"

I drop my shoulders. "I'm fine. I just wish we were at home longer this time."

"You can say that again. It was tough forcing myself out of bed this morning. But it's just a few days and then we'll be home again."

Forcing a smile, I reply, "Yeah, and these are important games. We want to seal our spot in the playoffs."

"Damn straight," he says. I smile.

Not long after we get into town, we're bussed to the arena for a practice skate. It goes well. Coach reviews the film from earlier in the season when we'd played the Stars in Chicago. We'd won that game, but it hadn't been easy. He reminds us to keep our focus, especially around Deacon Smith. Smith is one of the best centers in the league. With his top-notch skills in skating and stick handling, he's a force to be reckoned with.

Following practice, we return to our hotel for dinner. After that, I head to my room, with plans to call Janica.

Me: *Do you have time to talk?*

Janica: *Of course.*

"Ace," she answers, her voice breathy.

Sitting on the edge of my hotel bed, I ask, "Did I interrupt you?"

Her sweet laugh fills the line. "Not at all. I was remaking your monstrous bed. I was putting on the fitted sheet when the phone rang, and I had to detangle myself before I could answer it."

She's so adorable. I laugh, imagining what she described.

"After all the recent activity they've seen, I figured they might be dirty and need a good washing," she adds.

I bark out a laugh. She isn't wrong. "You know I would have helped you."

"It's no biggie. I got some cardio in. Other than my current workouts with you, it's the most I've exercised in forever, and it's reminded me how out of shape I am."

I let out a growl. "Babe, you are perfect the way you are. Your body is gorgeous. And now that I've had you, I can't get enough."

She laughs.

"Are you rolling your eyes?" I ask, picturing her beautiful face.

She laughs again. "Yep. 'Cause that was truly sweet but corny. I think I just thought of a nickname for you."

"Oh yeah?"

"You will now be known as 'Ace, my sweet corn dog.'"

"Really? Can't we shorten it?" A groan rumbles from my chest. "Maybe call me sweetheart or, better yet, horn dog?"

Janica's snort fills the line as she says, "Horn dog." And I can't help but smile. She makes me so happy. In the few days we've been official, I've allowed myself to feel and imagine more with her. I'm not naïve. I understand it's new, but this thing between us is special, and I'm going to do whatever I can to protect it.

"If it makes you happy, you can call me your sweet corn dog." I know relationships are give and take, and you have to sacrifice for those you care for. So if this is one of those things, I'll stand aside, fully supporting her.

"Oh, Ace. I was only kidding. I just named you that to get a reaction. And I think it worked," she teases. I laugh.

Fluffing my pillows, I lean back in bed. *I wish she were here, or we were in our bed.* "Hey, that has me thinking. Did you have any nicknames growing up?"

She hums to herself for a moment before she finally answers. "Nothing good. People called me Jan, which I hated. How about you?"

"Well, Jethro wasn't a very common name growing up, so most of the time it was people's unique pronunciations of it. In grade school, everyone started calling me Ace, and that stuck. Most people don't know my birth name."

"What was the weirdest pronunciation?" she asks.

I laugh because it's still funny. "Probably the ones that stick out the most are Jet-a-row, Jet-hero, or Jet-throw. I'm not a boat, plane, or blanket."

She sighs. "That's sad. It's not a hard name. Do you miss it?"

"Honestly, no. The only person who still calls me Jethro is Ma, and I like that. It's something special we share. She's one of my best friends."

"That is so sweet. From the stories you've told me and talking with them several times, I already adore your family."

"I know they adore you too." I shift my legs in the empty bed. "I don't like when you aren't in bed next to me."

"I was just thinking the same thing. In fact, I may have taken one of your sweatshirts and pulled it over your pillow so I could snuggle with it while you're gone."

I groan. "That's a great idea. I'd do that too, but whoever I end up rooming with would give me constant shit."

She laughs. "Maybe we'll have to brainstorm another less obvious thing for you."

Yawning, I tell her we'll work on that when I'm home in a few days. "It's getting late. I need to get to bed so I'm not dragging for the game tomorrow."

"Good night, Ace. I miss you. I hope you sleep well. I can't wait until you're home."

Home. That's what it's become since Janica moved in. I don't think of it as my house anymore; it's our home. Because I want her there permanently.

"Good night, sweetheart. I miss you too. I'll talk to you tomorrow."

Ace

With each week that passes, I find myself on the road more than at home, and it's killing me to be away from Janica. I was spoiled during the last half of my rehab in having her live with me and getting to spend so much time with her.

We're in Pittsburg tonight, taking on the Pirates. It's the last game of the regular season. The buildup to the Cup has been intense. Since we haven't won it in three years, my teammates are going with drastic options. And I'm not sure how I was roped into their bizarre superstitions. Two weeks before the playoffs began, Josh and Lucas convinced the trainers to rework our diets and maximize protein intake. Then they started organizing team activities like steam room Saturdays and meditation Mondays. It doesn't matter if we're traveling or not.

One morning a week ago, during our flight to Houston for a game against the Riggers, tempers heated as Lucas led us in a mini yoga routine—on the plane.

"Yoga," *Jersey spits. His tone is acidic as he pouts while remaining seated with his arms crossed against his chest.*

Looking at Rocco, I whisper, "What's that about? Usually, Jersey is a team player." Rocco shrugs and we both turn to watch what's going to happen next.

"Jers, come on, it's just a few stretches," Lucas drawls.

Jersey just sneers and shakes his head no.

Lucas moves closer, dropping his voice. "Man, I know you hate yoga, but as our goalie, the stretching won't kill you."

Grumbling, Jersey stands up and moves out to the aisle. "Happy?" he growls.

Lucas winces and then forces a smile. "Thanks, man." As we move into the first pose, out of the corner of my eye, I watch Jersey. He's stretching, but it's definitely not yoga. Shrugging, I return to my stretch.

When these team activities started, I questioned their value. Lucas explained the purpose and thinking behind each one, and while some seemed farfetched, his reasoning was sound. Hell, if it would help get us the W, I'd give it a shot.

Right before the playoffs begin, we're summoned to

Lucas and Samantha's house for the team's newly adopted final activity.

Rocco and I decide to ride over together. After he picks me up and we're on the road, he asks, "What do you think we're doing tonight?"

Laughing at the memories of all we'd endured the previous weeks, I say, "I hope we aren't bleaching our hair. Do you know how awful that would be?"

Rocco groans. "We can't do that. Jaz would kill me if I showed up at our wedding with orange hair."

I laugh. "But can you just imagine?"

When we arrive twenty minutes later, we're shown into their kitchen, where they've set up an assembly line for whatever they plan to do.

"Is everyone here?" Lucas asks while he carries Chloe, his almost eighteen-month-old daughter.

Mika steps forward. "How long is this going to take? Aurora was up a lot of the night and I need to get home and help Shiloh get dinner and bedtime routines done."

Samantha points to a chair. "Sit there and take your socks off." *Huh?*

Without question, Mika does as he's asked, dropping into a dining room chair. After having him point out which side is his dominant one, Samantha gets to work painting his toenails. Blue for dominant and gold on the other. In a little over an hour, the work is done and we all have freshly painted toes. Surprisingly, there is very little grumbling. I can't wait to show Janica.

A nd damn if by the time we head into the championship bracket against New York, we all agree that our painted toenails are the reason we've gotten so far.

Seated in the locker room, fully dressed in my gear, I listen to Coach talk about the challenges we're going to be facing. He drives home the importance of speed, smart puck handling, well-executed passes, and maintaining possession.

Since the first games are in New York, and we're all in desperate need of toenail touchups, we decide to book pedicures in our hotel's spa. When we ask Coach to make it happen, he rolls his eyes at us and mutters something under his breath. So, the day before the first game, our larger-than-life team files into the spa and has mini pedicures. With freshly painted toes, we again feel invincible and untouchable.

But the luck doesn't last. The Chargers win both games. The first is an overtime win, and the second comes down to the last minute. With only seconds left, Mika is called for roughing. During their power play, Damien Smith, the Charger's rookie center, has an amazing wraparound goal. While trying to defend his net, Jersey's injured. It looks like he gets twisted up with another Chargers player who was camped out in his crease. Jersey collapsing to the ice slows time, and my heart beats rapidly as I wonder if he's okay. We learn later that night that Jersey suffered a groin pull. He spends the next few days working with trainers to make sure he's ready before New York visits Chicago for the next two games.

Mika and Josh step up and do an amazing job of keeping the Chargers away from Jersey in the next two games. Because of their diligence, we secure two wins, making the series split down the middle.

You can feel the nervous energy on our flight back to New York. Even with everyone on our team in tip-top shape, New York has one of the loudest crowds in the NHL community, and that can rattle even the most focused player. Jersey stays strong, keeping the puck out of the net for the first game, and we secure the win, leading the series 3-2.

Unfortunately, tonight is another story. Throughout the playoffs, it's been apparent that the Steel and Chargers are the best of the league and they should be the teams battling it out for the Cup. Both teams are stacked with skill and determination.

When I pull off a hat trick tonight, I feel fairly confident we're going to win the game and the Cup. But that's not what happens. With one period left, our locker room is chaos as we try to keep everyone pumped up and on their game. When we get back onto the ice, the Chargers are already there, and you can tell the air has shifted. A shiver runs down my back, immediately putting me on the defensive.

Running through the mental list of holes I see on our team, my eyes flick to Jersey. He's still nursing a groin injury. I can't help but wonder how long he can withstand the pain. Skating past him, I see he's focused on shaving down his crease. I hear him mutter something, but it's indiscernible. Wondering if he's talking to me, I turn but notice his head's lowered. *Not talking to you*. Watching him, I see as he mumbles something else while tapping on the posts. *Goalies are weird.* Knowing I need to get refocused on the game, I move to the bench to see if Coach has any last words for us.

"You got this," he says to our huddle.

As soon as the puck is dropped, you can feel that things are different. The Chargers players are skating faster than they have the entire series. It's like they are all hopped up on energy drinks. They hand our asses to us, scoring time and time again. When the buzzer goes off, signaling the end of the game, the score is 5-4. We managed to close the gap between us, but it wasn't enough.

The last game will be back home, and I couldn't be happier. Just like the other home games, I got Janica a ticket in the family box. She just doesn't know it yet.

We take a mid-morning flight back to Chicago, and after a short drive home I practically skip into the house. "Hey, babe, I'm home," I call out, wondering how she'll respond.

A squeal comes from the bedroom, followed by several concerning thuds. My heart thumps in my chest. *Is she okay?* Tossing my bag down, I jog over to where I heard the noise coming from. "Janica, are you okay?" I ask as I rush into our bedroom. Stopping in my tracks, I blink to verify I'm seeing correctly. My girlfriend looks like an earthworm who's stuck on a driveway on a hot day. Her arms and legs work in tandem as she tries to free herself from whatever she has wrapped around her body. "Babe, are you okay?"

She grunts, wiggles again, and says, "I've almost got it."

Confused, I scratch my head. "Almost got what?"

"Your surprise," she groans. Again with the wiggling. But in the few moments I've watched her gyrate her body, I don't think she's made any progress with whatever she's trying to accomplish. Angry, she picks up her feet and slams them down on the bed. *That was adorable.* I can't say that, though, or I'm sure my balls will be severed from my body.

"I'm stuck." She whimpers.

"It's okay, babe. I'll help you get out of whatever this is." I run my hands over the material, which feels either like rubber or latex.

"But this was supposed to be a surprise for you," she whines, sticking her lower lip out in a pout.

I smile at her. "I appreciate you doing this for me, even if it didn't turn out the way you imagined. Now, let's get it off of you." I'd rather trace my hand over her silky, soft skin than a latex suit any day.

Finally, when she's free, she wraps her arms around my neck, seals her lips to mine, and presses her breasts against me. The heat coming off her is insane, warming me to the core. I want nothing more than to pull her into bed and show her how much I missed her, but it's dinnertime. If I want to keep her up all night worshipping her, we both need the sustenance.

Pulling my lips from her is sweet torture. I give her tender kisses while I tell her, "Babe, we need to eat dinner and then we can resume this."

"Okay," she says as she settles against my chest. I run my fingers up and down her naked back, each stroke dipping lower and lower.

"What do you want to eat?" I ask as I trail the fingertips of one hand around her waist, tickling her. Her hips shift, rubbing against my hard cock. "B-babe," I groan out, pulling her tight against me so she stops moving. "Food, then fun," I remind us both.

She runs her hand up my chest. "Are you still sticking to your diet?"

I tip her chin up, forcing her eyes to mine. "Depends on what you're willing to bargain with," I croon.

She lowers to her knees, then unbuttons and unzips my pants. Her hand slips inside the opened pants and palms me. Peering up through her thick lashes, she says in a sultry voice, "I can have a before-dinner snack." I say nothing, stunned by her boldness. She's never given me a blowjob before and her kneeling in front of me is causing my neurons to misfire.

When she pulls my hard cock out of my underwear, she kisses the tip before letting it go. Bobbing before her, it waves like a red flag to a bull. She rises off her heels, dips her head, and runs her tongue up the underside of my shaft. A low growl travels up from my chest. When she seals her lips around my cock and sucks me into her throat, a throaty moan falls from my lips. "Babe, that feels so fucking good." Janica swirls her tongue around my shaft, and I push my hand into her hair, tugging her closer. She moans around me, and the vibration makes my heart rate skyrocket. Her nails trace up my thigh, heading to my balls. She cups them, gently rolling them within her warm palm.

With my eyes closed and my head tipped back, I bark "fuck" as she tugs on my balls. When she reaches farther back and rubs against my taint, my hips involuntarily thrust forward. The sound of her gagging makes my eyelids spring open. Her beautiful eyes water, and immediately I feel guilty. "Did I hurt you?" I ask while I run my hand down her chin. Slowly, she slides off my rock-hard shaft, swirling her hot tongue around the head of my cock.

"No, I'm fine," she pants. She squeezes my throbbing shaft in her fist, making me lightheaded. Leaning forward, my eyes focus on her as she licks the tip of my cock before sucking it back into her mouth.

"Babe, your mouth is fucking heaven, and I want it on me again, but if you don't want to swallow the fruits of your labor, then I'd suggest you stop sucking on me like I'm your favorite lollipop." My voice is full of gravel.

She smirks around my shaft and continues sucking while pumping my lower shaft with her hand. When she pulls on my balls again my orgasm explodes into her mouth, spilling across her tongue. My hips pump, and she reaches farther back and taps my taint, extending my orgasm.

She slowly slides off me, catching every drop of my release. When she's done, I tug her up to her feet and slam my lips to hers. Tasting my orgasm on her tongue is a first for me. And a feeling of possessiveness rushes through my body, lighting it on fire. In the past, blowjobs have only been about satisfying a need. This right here is so much more. Almost religious.

"About dinner. What did you want? Consider my diet null and void," I say.

The radiant smile spread across her gorgeous face takes my breath away, and right now I'll give her anything she wants. "I've been craving deep-dish pizza."

"Malnati's?" I offer. She nods as she wraps her arms around me, hugging me tight.

Forty-five minutes later we're fresh from the

shower, where I took her against the tiled wall after she'd teased me with a sudsy show. I'm not a saint. Watching her run her hands over her hot, soapy body was something I couldn't resist.

We lounge on our bed while we share the city's best deep-dish pizza. Once we've both had our fill, we resume the activities Janica had started this afternoon when she'd unfortunately gotten stuck in her lingerie. At the time, I'd wanted to laugh because, damn, it was funny. But when I saw the sadness and disappointment on her face, I knew I would do whatever I could to make her feel better. Though, I'm still struggling to understand how the outfit was supposed to look. Maybe I'll have to google it.

Chapter 41

Janica

Having Ace in town for the last game of the Stanley Cup playoffs is a dream come true. Before him, I never paid attention to any sports, but it's different now. To see all the work that he and his teammates have put in, and being able to watch the games they've played during the playoffs, it's fun to feel like I'm a part of history. Granted, if the Steel win, my name won't be on the trophy, but I'll be celebrating big with one of the champions.

It's been a few years since the Steel won the Cup, and I know they're ravenous for it. When we were lying in bed last night, our bodies completely sated, I asked Ace how he was feeling.

After a deep breath, he tells me, *"I've never felt more driven. It feels like I'm finally one hundred percent again after my leg. The team is cohesive and desperate for the win."*

Ace fluctuates between confidence and nerves this morning before he leaves the house. He keeps repeating, "Tonight decides everything." He's right. With each team having three wins under their belt in the series, this game will determine the next Stanley Cup champion.

I try my hardest to appear confident for him, but as soon as the door closes, my ball of tension unravels. Plagued with fear for the team, what-if scenarios fly through my mind at warp speed. I'm making myself a nervous wreck.

Hoping to calm myself, I practice some mindfulness exercises. With my eyes closed and my breathing regulated, I can focus on calming myself and ridding my body of all the negativity I'm carrying. It takes longer than I thought it would, so when I finally order a ride, I know I'm going to be late for the game, but I want to be my best for Ace.

Getting to the game takes less time than I figured, probably because the game has already started. Arriving at the family box, the always laid-back, positive energy of it wraps me in a warm hug.

"Janica!" the ladies shout when I step inside. Their welcome is the best. Stepping closer, I glance at the scoreboard. It's still scoreless. Breathing a sigh of relief, I'm glad I didn't miss anything while I was trying to get my shit together.

"How are they playing?" I ask Nicole as I hug her.

Ever since I met her, we've shared a special connection that's only deepened since she recognized me in Dragon's Lair that night I caught Trevor cheating. If they hadn't gotten ahold of Ace, I don't know where I'd be. I shudder. A shiver runs down my back at the thought.

"This is going to be a tough game," she answers. I look at her and nod my agreement. "Oh, there goes Ace," she exclaims, and my attention flies back to the ice, looking for my speedy number eighteen.

"Go, Ace!" I yell as I scoot forward in my chair. There goes the man who's stolen my heart. My heart soars with him as he collects the puck and races down the ice. Only a single defenseman stands in the way of him having a one-on-one versus the goalie. He lines up and takes a shot at the space above the goalie's shoulder. The Charger's goalie lifts his pad just in time to knock it away. When the puck drops to his side, he grabs it with his stick and he's able to pass it to one of his teammates before Ace can intercept it. The entire family box groans while the Chargers make their next drive down the ice.

Hanging his head, Ace returns to the bench, his shift over. Coach Tristan says something to him, and he nods before taking a seat. Leaning forward, he grabs a water bottle and squirts water into his mouth. *Sexy.* I squeeze my thighs together. Why is watching a thirsty man drink making me hot? I'm so distracted I miss Lucas's goal, giving the Steel the lead.

Ace plays another few shifts before the period is over. During the intermission, I grab some food now that my stomach has mostly settled. While trying to select the perfect amount of finger foods, the leader of the Steel ladies approaches. *What do you know, I'm a Steel lady now.* I smile to myself, knowing my relationship with Ace is still so new. Right now, we're keeping it to ourselves.

"What's that smile about?" Samantha asks while she holds Chloe on her hip.

"I'm just happy," I rush out, hoping to appease her and the rest of the ladies who have joined us. "And nervous. Terribly nervous," I ramble.

Chloe fusses, and Samantha bounces on her toes. I join her, and realize I find the movement oddly cathartic. Jasmine approaches, giving me a puzzled look. I glance down at my outfit. *Did I spill on myself? No. I pat my head. Is my hair messy? No.*

"Jasmine, what's wrong?" I ask.

Still looking confused, she smiles and says, "I understand why Samantha is bouncing, but why are you?"

I shrug. "I don't know."

"Well, that's better than whipping out your boob all the time. That isn't something you would do, right?" she jokes.

Before I can answer, Samantha says, "Breast-feeding is normal and better for the baby." Shiloh nods in agreement.

Unsure if that's truth or opinion, I don't reply. Thinking about having a family makes me think of Ace. We're not ready for babies yet, and we don't have to decide on breastfeeding until we're talking about having babies or I'm pregnant.

Trey hollers across the box, "Game's back on."

We turn to him, and I can't help but be excited for my friend Nicole, who he has tucked into his side. His hand is possessively curled around her hip as she uses her fingertips to draw on his chest while staring up at him. They are hopelessly in love, and it's beautiful to see. Ace and I aren't quite at the point yet, but the thought of being able to show him affection without worry of what people might do is thrilling. It's also scary. People can be downright mean. What if some people don't think I'm good enough for him and say something? Although I don't think Ace would care what people say, I realize he lives his life in front of the cameras, and being with him is something I'll have to adjust to. But for him, it's worth it. Giving up some privacy to publicly call him mine is well worth the cost.

I make my way back to the seat I'd been using and focus back on the game.

Within minutes of getting back on the ice, the Chargers get a lucky goal, tying things up. It isn't long after that for a penalty to be called on them. During the power play, Ace takes advantage of the Chargers being a man down and makes some impressive plays, resulting in a brilliant goal. The score is 2-1 in favor of the Steel. With barely enough time to celebrate, they are already switching lines to get fresh legs on the ice to handle the Chargers being at full strength again.

As the last minutes of the period wind down, Coach Tristans barks orders to the guys on the ice. Mika takes heed of Coach's words and wins the puck in our corner. He passes to Lucas, who's at the center line. He cradles the puck with his blade before taking off toward the goal. The Charger's best defenseman, Rod Thomas, challenges him, but Lucas steps up. Using stellar stick-handling skills and precision skating, he puts on a show. Lining up, he lifts onto one skate and fires a slapshot to the exposed section right above the goalie. It hits the back of the net and lights the lamp even before the goalie has time to react. His smile is infectious as he bumps fists with his teammates. His goal gives the Steel a bigger advantage as they head into the third period.

When the guys return to the ice for the final period, you know things are different. Both teams are more determined than before. Within the first few minutes, several penalties have been called on both teams.

From the bench, Coach Tristan yells and waves his arms. Before the puck drops on one of our power plays, he leans over, animatedly talking to Josh and Mika. The guys remain on the ice, skating a longer shift. They look exhausted when they return to the bench.

The game is so charged, time flies. With five minutes left, Chargers' Damien Smith secures a breakaway during their shift change. We are completely vulnerable, and all we can do is watch. As if it were in slow motion, I see him line up with Jersey, and a gasp leaves my mouth. Mika bolts off of the bench, racing for Damien, hoping to intercept him before he gets a shot off. Too late. Damien fakes Jersey's right and shoots left. The puck flies right over his lowered shoulder. With their goal, we now only have a one-point lead.

Jersey is slow to get up. The game stops and we watch as the training staff rush onto the ice to check him. Leaning forward in my chair, my hands clasped in a praying pose, I hope he's not too injured. Intently focused on them, I see he brushes them off. You can see them hesitate, but when Jersey rises to his skates and readies himself for the next play, they have no choice. Jersey taps both posts with his stick and drops into a squat. *Let's go, Steel!*

As the last seconds of the game tick down, the anticipation in the arena grows to unbearable levels. Ace looks up into the crowd, finding me glued to the window in the family suite. My heart is thumping in my chest and I have my hands clasped together in hope. From the pull on my cheeks, I can tell I'm wearing an enormous smile. I lift my hand and give him a wave, and he winks at me. *Swoon.*

He skates back to what will be the final puck drop of this year's Stanley Cup and everything goes silent. The clock counts down agonizingly slow. 3... 2... 1. When the buzzer sounds, the suite erupts with cheering. My throat is hoarse from yelling. The guys held off the Chargers, leaving them the new Stanley Cup champions. The bench and the crowd go wild. It's insane. The family box is loud too. It's filled with whoops, hollers, and hugs as we celebrate the team's accomplishment. From up high, we laugh, watching the spectacle of the team trying to fit championship t-shirts over their bulky hockey gear. At some point, they all abandoned their helmets for championship hats. They're boisterously celebrating, hugging, and congratulating each other. Like true competitors, they stop celebrating to shake hands with the Chargers players. It could've gone either way, and both teams know that.

Once the Chargers have left the ice, the presentation of the Cup begins and Josh is called to the carpet to receive the trophy. Instead of watching him shake hands with the commissioner, I find Ace. His smile has never been bigger. *This is huge.* I know it isn't his first Cup, but it's the first after breaking his leg. What could have been a career-ending injury became part of his victory story. He worked his ass off to get back onto that ice, and he didn't let his boys down. I am so happy for him.

Once they finish with the speeches and pictures, Josh receives the trophy, which he hoists high above his head. My heart soars. I've never experienced anything like this. The energy inside the arena is unbelievable. Smiling wide, my eyes flick back to Ace. I'm so proud of him. And I cannot wait to celebrate with my champion.

Epilogue

Ace

When you're the Stanley Cup champions, the festivities and celebrations last for months. Whether it's visits to the White House, appearances on television, or interviews for publication, it's steady.

Life has changed for me, and only for the better. Janica and I've only been official for a few months, but this last week I finally convinced her to move her belongings out of the spare room and into mine. Armed with her happy yellow bins, her stuff has now taken up residence in my walk-in closet, and my heart feels like it's going to burst with happiness.

With all the chaos surrounding the Cup, and my classes being done for the semester, we decided to keep our relationship quiet until the hype died down. But with the new season approaching in a few months, we're finally ready to tell our friends and my family about us.

The day after our three-month anniversary, we bite the bullet and start small with our parents. Or at least I assumed we would call both sets of parents.

"Do you want to call your parents or my family first?" I ask while joining her on the couch with my iPad.

Sitting next to me, she fidgets with her hand. Placing my larger hand over hers, I say, "Listen, babe, if you aren't ready, we don't have to say anything yet."

"It isn't that I don't want to tell your parents and siblings. I just don't want to tell mine." She forces a smile. Confused, I ask why.

She grimaces. "Because they will only pretend to be happy for us. It'll look good for them—their daughter dating a professional athlete. And I don't want them using our relationship to help them climb their social ladder."

I frown. Anger tears through my chest every time I think about how they've devalued her throughout her life. She is precious and valuable. Each time we talked about them, Janica would sense my anger, and rub out the scowl creases in my brow line. "It's their loss," she states. And she's right.

"Okay, we won't call your parents, but can we call mine? Ma is going to be over the moon." My folks and siblings have been on multiple FaceTime calls with

Janica and me, so us calling at dinner time when I know everyone will be at the house isn't a surprise.

"Jethro. Janica," Ma croons into the phone.

"Hi. Ma," I say before asking, "Is everyone there?"

Ma changes the screen to show the rest of my family, who are waving and talking over each other. From the way they're behaving, you might think I never call home, but I try to call at least every week. Janica is good about keeping me on schedule.

Seeing everyone, I whistle to get their attention. Janica covers her ears, and grumbles, "Warn a girl before you do that right next to her head." I laugh.

"Sorry. I'm used to only doing that outside. I forgot how loud it is." Then I tease her with my sexy smile.

She flutters her eyelashes, then pats my chest and mumbles, "Stop it."

"Jethro, why did you whistle? Was there something you wanted to say?" Ma asks.

I nod and then look at Janica. Her radiant smile is just what I want to see. "Janica and I wanted to tell you we're dating." A chorus of whoops and my ma's "hallelujah" fills the line.

After everyone settles down, my siblings want to know when she'll be visiting the farm. We haven't discussed it yet, but I know she's dying to get there, meet my family, and, of course, see Harold. Ever since I mentioned him, Janica always asks my family for a Harold update. They now call it Harold Watch. She even talked my sister Melissa into going to the barn and showing him live on a FaceTime call.

I couldn't be happier with my family's reaction to our news. I knew they'd love her as much as I do. *Love? Is that what this feeling is? I know I'm crazy about her and she's always on my mind. She is everything to me. But is it love? Is it too soon?* I should ask Rocco. Maybe he'll be able to help me decipher all the things I'm feeling and thinking.

A week later, our team is celebrating an exciting event. Right before it's time to go, Janica steps out of the spare room and sucks all the air from my lungs. My eyes don't know where to focus first. *She's a goddess.* "You look breathtaking," I pant out. From the dip of her plunging neckline to the flirty tie at her waist, I'm completely blown away. Her cheeks flush and her eyes sparkle. I step closer, noticing the shimmery thread that's woven into the satin material matches the emotion in her eyes. "Babe, turn for me, please?"

On her black high-heeled sandals, she spins, and a flirty ruffle dances at her knees. When she stops, the dress lands against her perfectly smooth, sun-kissed skin, revealing a sexy tease. My fingers twitch, wanting to trace up her leg and investigate what's hiding underneath.

All I can say is her name before I pull her close, putting my lips on hers. She melts into me, reinforcing the thought that we fit perfectly and are meant to be. *You need to tell her.*

Pulling back, I watch as her eyes flutter open. A sultry smile appears across her mauve-painted lips. I'm a needy man with an addiction to this woman. I'm beyond tempted to dive back in for another taste. But I stop myself, knowing what I need to do.

"Babe, there's something I need to tell you."

Janica freezes, confusion marring her face. "O-okay?" she says, and her gaze flicks to the floor.

Reaching for her hands, I cradle them in mine. "Can you look at me, please?"

Slowly, she lifts her head. Nerves fly through my body at warp speed. *Tell her.*

"I don't know how best to say this, so I'm just going to rip off the Band-Aid."

Her eyes grow big in question.

"Janica, over the past few months, we have grown closer and become more than just roommates and friends. Not only are you my best friend and cheer-leader, you have become my lover." Her eyes shine as she stares up at me. "But you are more than that. You are also the woman I love."

"What?" she breathes out. I drop her hands and pull her closer.

"I love you, Janica."

Lifting on her toes, she places her lips to mine and whispers, "I love you too."

I kiss her hard, pulling her body flush with mine. This is the first time I've spoken those words to a woman, and I'm so glad I waited for her. I can't even form the words to explain how it feels to hear her say the same. Hugging her tightly, I finally pull my lips from hers, reminding us both, "We have a wedding to get to." Her shoulders slump and I laugh. Placing a kiss on her nose, I promise, "Tonight is ours." A lipstick-smudged smile appears on her face.

"I just need to check my makeup after that kiss and then we can go."

***

This is the first time I've seen most of my teammates since all the media hubbub surrounding winning the Cup. Even though some of them may have suspected Janica and I are together, I still haven't officially told them.

The wedding is just how I'd expected it to be: perfect. Jasmine looks beautiful, and Rocco cleans up well. They make a handsome couple. Because they opted for a small wedding, the couple only have one attendant each. Jasmine picked Nicole and Rocco chose Trey. Although he's one of my best friends, whom I'd stand up for any day, it was Trey who got the pressure of being Rocco's best man. I could sit in the crowd, holding Janica's hand, while we listen to the vows our friends make to each other. I may or may not imagine doing the same with the woman beside me.

"That was beautiful," she says as she wipes a tear away after the ceremony concludes.

I nod my agreement, thinking my teammates have found incredible partners, and I'm grateful for that. We've all become incredibly close, and Janica fits into the group perfectly.

When the DJ announces Rocco and Jasmine as they enter the reception tent, my teammates and I obnoxiously catcall the couple. Instead of being annoyed, Rocco and Jasmine just laugh. Dinner comes next. Prepared by Rocco's ma and nonna, it's amazing, as usual. Over the years, I've had the pleasure of being invited to the Romano family dinner many times. Janica has not yet.

"That was the best Italian food I've ever had," she gushes.

Looking at her, I feign shock. "Better than Mateo's?" She just smiles.

When it's time for the first dance, I pull Janica into my side. "Are you going to dance with me?"

She laughs. "I can slow dance, but anything else... it's probably better if I stay off the dance floor."

"You can't be that bad," I tease, and she frowns at me.

"I assure you, I can. And I'm not about to embarrass myself in front of my new friends to win an argument. Even if it would prove you wrong."

After our slow dance, Janica moves back to our chairs while I do everything from the Y.M.C.A. to the funky chicken. We're having a great time, I only wish

Janica were out here with me. She'll like the next part, though, I'm sure of it.

We have a surprise just for Jasmine. Rocco asked me a month after they got engaged to help him with it. My teammates clear the dance floor while I escort Jasmine over to a chair I've grabbed from a nearby table. Seated near the edge of the floor, she looks around nervously, wondering what's happening.

Then the music begins, and the DJ makes an announcement, calling us guys to the dance floor. We all find our spots and begin the first of the choreographed dances I've assembled. Looking up as I bop, shuffle, and move, I see Jasmine is grinning, and she is surrounded by all the other Steel ladies, including mine. My heart thumps in my chest as I see Janica's eyes widen when I thrust my hips. *Yeah, baby, you recognize that move, don't you?* She licks her lips, and I have to shift my focus so I can finish the dance.

Toasts and cake cutting come next, and Janica sighs. "That is the prettiest cake I've ever seen. Do you think Kenzie made it?"

"I bet she did." I laugh.

"Good, then it will taste as amazing as it looks."

Because there aren't many singles at the wedding, I snag the garter when it flies off Rocco's hand. Everyone laughs when I declare, "It's mine." I look at Janica, and a blush covers her face, making her even more beautiful. Not wanting to waste another minute, I walk over to her, pull her into my arms, and place my lips on hers.

Catcalls surround us, and we pull apart. We're the center of everyone's attention.

Jasmine walks up and hands her toss bouquet to Janica. The photographer insists on a picture of the four of us. After capturing it, he slips away.

Rocco moves to my side, shakes my hand, pulls me into a bro hug, and whispers in my ear, "I'm glad you finally made your move."

Thank you for reading Tripped By You, the seventh book in the Chicago Steel series. If you want to read an extended epilogue of Ace and Janica, click here to start reading: https://dl.bookfunnel.com/jfn8a9f618

If you'd like another peek into the Chicago Steel world, visit my website at https://907publishing.wixsite.com/my-site and sign up for my newsletter. While there, don't forget to snag the extended epilogue for Tripped By You and any extras for the rest of the series. Keep reading to check out the World of Chicago Steel.

World of Chicago Steel

Have you read Hooked By You, the first book of the Chicago Steel Series with Lucas and Samantha? If not, you can click on the link to start reading. The entire series is available with your Kindle Unlimited subscription. Here's a small taste of each to whet your palate.

Hooked By You–Chicago Steel Series Book One

Lucas

She's a goddess in heels. Absolute perfection. Well, almost. Samantha Fox is the heiress of Fox Sporting, my new management team. As one of the best wings in the NHL, I have never shied away from a challenge, and she is definitely a challenge. But if her company representing me doesn't stop me from wanting her, the fact she's engaged should, right? But the noticeably absent sparkle from her left ring finger makes me question. I vow to myself that I'll find out what that's all about. And if she's single, I plan to make her mine. Or at least, mine for the night. I just need one taste of the divine.

Samantha

Off-limits. That's what he is. Lucas Bouchard is the prestigious new client acquired by my family's company. From what I know, not only is he an amazing hockey player, he's a humble and generous philanthropist too. Also, he's a walking aphrodisiac. It doesn't matter that I've just broken off my engagement to a cheating, using loser. Every time our eyes lock, I find myself captivated. But he's not for me. No matter how many times I remind myself of this, though, it doesn't compute. Plain and simple, I want him. And keeping my distance might prove impossible.

Checked By You–Chicago Steel Series Book Two

Mika

She's the uber-sexy, single mother living next door. Everyone tells me to keep my distance. But there's something about her. Specifically, her eyes. They speak to me. Drawing me in like a siren. I want to know her, but she's more guarded than Buckingham Palace. However, after one afternoon in her presence, I find myself addicted and wanting more. Willing to do whatever I have to just to make it past her defenses.

Shiloh

My next-door neighbor is an insanely hot, single professional hockey player. As if that isn't bad enough, he's a nice guy too. After spending an afternoon where he showed my son how to skate and took us out to ice cream, I want to let him in. My past cautions me to put on the brakes, but I find myself going full steam ahead, ignoring all the red flags waving at me.

Clipped By You—Chicago Steel Series Book Three

Monica

She's his. Or she has been since her freshman year of college. According to Monica Fields, no man will ever hold a candle to Christian Fox. Too bad he's completely unaware. Or is he?

Christian

Since meeting her, a sweet dairy farm girl has captivated Christian entirely. But he's a guy. And he's the one who isn't quite ready to be done sowing his wild oats. Will he ever be? In this game called love, sometimes chasing after a woman is just the wake-up call you need. But what if chasing her to her family's farm and following her through a field scattered with cow patties in limited-edition white Nike Air Force 1s is the only way to catch her? And, when you finally do catch her, will she want you? Forever?

Speared By You-Chicago Steel Series Book Four

Tristan

Since he was little, Tristan's dream has been to play in the NHL. Then he falls in love with his soul mate in high school. A few years after being drafted, an injury cuts his professional career short. Devastated, he questions what is next for him. Instead of seeking solace from the woman who's remained faithfully by his side, he pushes her away.

Stephanie

Since high school, Stephanie's known she is going to do two things: marry Tristan Murphy and get a degree in business. Her plan is to work for a non-profit that focuses on breast cancer. Several years later, though, she finds herself recently divorced and in a new city with a new job. And she's learned a couple of major life lessons. 1. Life can be tricky. 2. We don't always get what we want.

What happens when their paths cross again?

Slashed By You-Chicago Steel Series Book Five

Josh

As the captain of the Steel, Josh is always in control and confident as hell. In relationships, not so much, especially after being majorly burned. Then a gorgeous baker enters his life and changes everything. Her confections are pure magic, and now she's all he craves.

Kenzie

Kenzie's always dreamed of owning her own bakery. With a heart of gold, everything she does is filled with love. Busy running her shop, she doesn't have time for relationships. However, priorities shift when she catches the eye of a kind and sexy professional hockey player who has developed a major sweet tooth.

Delayed By You-Chicago Steel Series Book Six

She's always been his. He's always been hers. Best friends since they were kids, everyone always assumed they'd end up together. But Rocco and Jasmine forge their own life paths. Despite remaining close, she discovers she needs a break from the life she's been living in Chicago. When she moves to New York, things change for him. And he panics, thinking he's lost her forever.

Rocco

Since the day she moved in across the street when we were kids, Jasmine has held my attention with her sparkling green eyes and spunky spirit. She's independent and headstrong, and I've always admired that about her. Hiding behind my bachelor status, no one is the wiser about the secret feelings I harbor for her.

Jasmine

Rocco has always been by my side. Whether it's making me laugh, teaching me something new, or sharing confidences, he's been steadfast. When he morphs into a man seemingly overnight, I find it tough to temper my attraction to him. But he doesn't see me as anything more than a friend.

Happy Ho, Ho, Holidays-Chicago Steel Novella

Trey

As soon as I see her, I'm bewitched by the bohemian beauty. One look from her and I'm done. Too bad after spending most of the evening together, I forget to get her number or her last name. As the owner of the Chicago Steel, the city's professional hockey team, you'd think nothing is out of reach for me, but finding her has proved challenging. Months pass, and as my hope of ever finding her fades, she walks through my office door, hired to be my temporary PA.

Nicole

He can't be real. The summer heat must be getting to me, because everything about this man seems too good to be true. We spend most of the night together, talking and laughing. And guess what... he is the complete package. The one worthy of a trip home to meet the parents. If you ever visited home and hadn't written it off years ago. But as soon as he appears, he's gone without a way to contact him. Do I write it off as bad luck, or do I storm their headquarters demanding to be seen? But what if it's all one-sided and he isn't longing for me like I do him?

Acknowledgments

I am so grateful for all the fantastic people who are supporting me as I chase after this dream of mine. I never imagined what it would entail. It's been more challenging than I ever could have imagined. But then I read a review, and the kind and thoughtful words that many of you leave for me encourage me to keep pressing on.

It is undeniable that I couldn't pursue this career without the full support of my husband. Darren, you may not read my books, 'cause let's face it, they aren't your jam, but you cheer me on just the same.

To my editors, Shauna and Nicole. You are invaluable. Your insight, suggestions, and knowledge of this world have shaped me into the author I am becoming. I look forward to what the future holds. Thank you for being a part of this experience.

To my book cover designer, Karen, you are so much more than that. I treasure you and the valuable advice you've given me. I know I never would have made it this far without you. Hold on... get ready for the ride. It'll no doubt be bumpy, but I promise fun along the way. Thanks for being part of this path we call life.

To my friends, family, and readers, you keep me going. I love that so many of you have fallen for the Steel men. As the end of the series is slowly approaching, my mind is busy with what's next. I hope you stick around to see. Thank you for believing in me and giving me your time.

Happy Reading!

Also by Jessica Buss

Chicago Steel Series

Chicago Steel Series

Hooked By You (Lucas & Samantha)

Checked By You (Mika & Shiloh)

Clipped By You (Christian & Monica)

Speared By You (Tristan & Stephanie)

Slashed By You (Josh & Kenzie)

Delayed By You (Rocco & Jasmine)

Tripped By You (Ace & Janica)

Coming Soon

Blocked By You

Owned By You

Stick By You

Chicago Steel Series Novella

Happy Ho, Ho, Holidays (Trey & Nicole)

About the Author

Jessica Buss was born and raised in Anchorage, Alaska. She is married to her high school sweetheart and has two sons. Although she has both her bachelor's and master's degrees in Psychology, she stepped away from that field to be a stay-at-home mom. Now that her kids are growing up and she's getting more time to herself, she's giving this writing thing a chance.

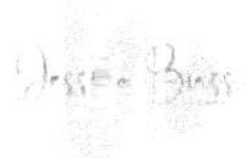

907publishing.wixsite.com/my-site